TEA TIME

A DEADLY BLEND OF MYSTERY & SUSPENSE

Barbara K. Luff

HISTORICAL PAGES COMPANY
188 Main Street, Poultney Vermont 05764

Published by the Historical Pages Company
188 Main Street, Poultney, Vermont 05764
Website at www.historicalpages.com

First Edition
Text copyright © 2008 Barbara Luff
Book Design and Production: Imagesetdesign
Cover Design: Bill Loring, Bromley Brook Design
Cover Art: Daniel Hobbs

ISBN 978-0-9818668-1-9

PRINTED IN USA

June 2008

For my children: Alexandra, Richard, and Antonia

Acknowledgements:

A good deal of the fun I had in writing Tea Time was doing the research. I wish to thank Ginger and Michael Cook of Green Mountain Specialties, Inc. in Bellows Falls, Vermont, and Dennis J. Chafee, General Manager, Putney Paper Co. in Putney, Vermont. I am most grateful for the time they spent with me, and their careful explanations about paper mills and the process of making paper.

Thanks to Roger Riccio and Michael Reynolds I was able to transfer the charm of River Mist, their Bed & Breakfast in Bellows Falls, to my Burt Street Inn, in Tea Time.

And last, but far from the least, thanks to Historical Pages Company and Peter Campbell-Copp for your interest and encouragement.

Bellows Falls, Vermont – October, 1955

ONE

Jenette Furneau was standing at the curb. Holding a small baby close to her chest, her teeth chattered and strands of dark, thick hair kept slipping out of the ponytail and blowing around her delicate face. At eighteen years of age, she looked much younger. Her rich brown eyes were bright with the anticipation of seeing Hal. She watched his Plymouth station wagon as it turned down Canal Street into the village of Bellows Falls, Vermont. When he stopped opposite her building at the corner of Depot and Canal Streets, Jenette ran to his car.

Hal Walker reached across the front seat and pushed the car door open as Jenette struggled to get in while holding the baby securely in one arm.

"Hurry up and shut the door," said Hal.

"Okay, okay, why are you so late?"

Hal shrugged, shifted into first and continued down Canal Street, toward Route 5 and out of town.

"He looks like you, Hal." She smiled and removed the blanket from the baby's head. "My mother says he's

1

the spittin' image of you. 'Just like lil' Hal,' she says."

" How does *she* know how I looked as a baby?" Hal tightened his grip on the steering wheel. "Why do you want to call him Hal?"

Jenette was slow to respond. "I...wasn't going to. I was thinking of calling him Paul, after my father."

"Oh," said Hal.

"Do you like it?"

"Yeah."

In spite of the cool weather, Hal felt hot. He pulled at the crew neck of his Shetland wool sweater. Then, with both hands back on the steering wheel, he made an abrupt turn off Route 5 onto a dirt road. He cut the engine, and looked at Jenette. She leaned toward him, expecting a kiss, but Hal didn't move.

Jenette giggled. "Don't worry, Paulie won't mind."

Hal looked at the steering wheel. "Listen, um...I'm not sure, I mean – um..." He turned toward her. "Jenette, jus' 'cause we fooled around a little doesn't mean..."

Jenette stiffened. "Huh...? What are you saying?"

Hal pulled at his sweater again

Jenette felt her throat tighten. "*Fooled around...* Hal – what's going on?"

"Nothing," said Hal. "That's just it."

"I – I don't understand. When I got pregnant you talked about getting married – after you graduated." Tears rolled down her cheeks. "We were going to tell your folks, 'n then – "

"No! I mean, how do I know he's really mine…? My parents don't even know we were dating, forget about – "

"Hal! You saw me in June – before you went to England…"

He cleared his throat. "Yeah, to say goodbye."

"But you sent me a postcard…from London."

The baby made a little squawk. Hal glanced at him, then quickly looked out the window. He tapped his fingers impatiently on the steering wheel. "I'll be moving to New York," he said, "and…well, it just won't work."

Jenette could barely speak. All of her dreams, the plans… "Look. Look at this baby's face! Can't you see…? What am I supposed to do…?"

"I dunno. What about your mom…the church? Don't they help people?"

"What are you talking about?" said Jenette.

Hal sighed, squeezing his forehead between his thumb and index finger; something he always did when troubled. "I'm sorry. I don't know. And I don't have any money." He threw his arms up in the air. "I'm still in college."

"You're horrible. College is an excuse? I told my mom you were different." She grabbed the door handle to get out of the car. "You really are horrible!" she shouted.

Hal tried to grab her arm. "Don't. Let me take you home."

Holding the baby tightly against her chest, Jenette rocked back and forth in the seat. "I jus' don't understand..." She wiped her tears with the baby's blanket. "All those things you said..."

Clenching his jaw, Hal jammed the gear stick into first, turned around in the middle of the dirt road and drove back to town. .

"Shh – it's okay; we'll be okay," she said reassuringly to Paulie.

Hal slowed down as he approached Canal Street.

Jenette stiffened. "Keep going." She hugged the baby. "Pull up to the door."

Hal drove to the front of the four-story tenement building. He started to get out of the car to help Jenette with the baby.

"Forget it." Jenette slammed the car door.

"I'm sorry."

Jenette said nothing. At the steps of her building, she stopped and turned to see Hal's car round the corner. Tears welled in her eyes. She couldn't find the keys in her pocketbook.

Hal parked his car in the gravel driveway next to his parents' rambling Greek Revival house on Atkinson Street. This was the only house he'd ever known. With no siblings and doting parents, he was given every advantage, particularly when it came to sports. Now, at six feet two inches, he had a lean athlete's build.

Throughout high school he'd played a variety of sports and was continuing the same interests in college, but never with the competitive edge his father had expected. Indeed, Hal's choice of soccer at Dartmouth, instead of varsity football, was a huge disappointment for Harold Walker, a former Dartmouth quarterback. He viewed his son's soccer playing as a lack of ambition. In spite of his father's grumbling, Hal liked coming home. The privacy of his large third floor room and an abundance of good food made it a comfortable retreat from college. But now, with Jenette's words on his mind, everything had changed. He hurried past the manicured gardens, neatly mulched with evergreen boughs, and up the steps of the wrap-around porch facing the street. All but two of the wicker chairs had been put away for the winter. He bumped into one and angrily pushed it aside. The large, solid oak front door was festooned with unruly vines of bittersweet berries. They almost covered the brass door handle. Irritably, Hal brushed them aside as he opened the door and walked into a large oak-paneled foyer.

"Arrgh – they're everywhere," said Hal, looking at branches of bittersweet arranged on the mahogany table in the front hallway. He heard his parents talking in the library and was about to call out when the door opened.

"You're early," said Trudy Walker, giving Hal a peck on the cheek. Then she patted his shoulder. "Goodness, you're all tense. Mid-terms? Too much studying...?"

"Um – no – that's not 'til January," said Hal,

distracted as he watched his father put a 45 record on the hi-fi. "Why don't you get a 33? You'll get a lot more Strauss."

"Your mother and I like this recording of the 'Skater's Waltz,'" said Harold, carefully placing the needle on the edge of the small record.

"It's what your father likes to hear during tea," said Trudy.

"What's the matter with Dartmouth? I thought they had a good football team, or have they gone the way of your frog-frenchy soccer players?" said Harold.

Ignoring the sarcasm, Hal picked up a vanilla cookie from a Lowestoft plate on the tea tray, and sat in a wing chair next to the fireplace. "They *have* a good team; they've only lost two games – in spite of the quarterback's bum knee."

"Tell him to put lots of ice on it," said Trudy.

"Um...yeah, right..." said Hal. "Uhh – actually I might see him tonight..."

"Oh! Is he coming for dinner? I'll tell Marie to set..."

"No, Mom. I've gotta go back up to Hanover. Things have changed." Hal's hands felt clammy. The thought of seeing Marie made him feel sick.

"Surely not before dinner," said Trudy. "I've invited the Aldriches. Your father wants you to meet them."

"Damn right," said Harold. "Sam Aldrich is big in banking; knows people – people *you* will need to know."

Hal swallowed the whole cookie. "I can see him at

your December 'pulp' party."

"That's enough sarcasm," said Harold. "You know how hard I've worked to keep the mill operating."

"Yes, Dad, I know: 'Walker Paper Mill keeps this town on the map,'" he said, repeating his father's pet comment "I promise; I'll meet your banker at the Christmas party."

"All right, that's settled," said Trudy. "Have some tea and tell us what you've been up to." She headed for the kitchen. "I'll ask Marie for another cup."

"No," said Hal. "I mean, don't bother her."

Marie was the Walkers' maid, and Jenette's mother. For years – since Hal was a small boy – she'd been coming in daily to clean and serve at occasional parties. And now, since Trudy had initiated the ritual of afternoon tea, Marie frequently stayed later to serve it. Trudy's reasoning for "tea time" was more to stall "cocktail time" than to emulate the English custom. Lately, Harold had been leaving the paper mill by mid-afternoon and closeting himself in the library with bourbon and his favorite records.

Hal admired his mother's efforts. Today, however, he really didn't want to sit around with a cup of tea. He stood up. "I've really gotta go…"

"Sit down," said Harold." It won't kill ya to say hello to Marie."

"At least have some tea," said Trudy. "Marie's a new grandmother; she might even have a snapshot to show us."

"Yup," said Harold, "another mill baby to feed. They breed like rabbits. God knows who the father is."

Hal got up.

Working in the kitchen, Marie heard Harold's booming voice and his "mill baby" comment. It was all she could do to keep from throwing the teakettle across the room. Earlier she'd watched Hal get out of his car. When he didn't come in through the kitchen door, as he usually did, her heart sank. She knew that he was not going to tell his parents about little Paulie.

Trudy breezed into the kitchen. "Hal's home, not for long, but I know he'd love to see you. We'll need another cup and more of those yummy – "

Marie put the kettle down. She handed a teacup and saucer to Trudy. "I have to leave." She pointed to a cookie jar. "You'll find more in there."

Startled, Trudy stood in the middle of the kitchen floor watching Marie put on her coat. "Is everything all right?"

"Mrs. Pierson needs me," said Marie. "I'll be back tomorrow – usual time." Marie was out the kitchen door and running down the back steps before Trudy could say another word.

Indeed, Trudy knew better than to question Marie. For the ten years she'd been working there, Marie had revealed very little about herself, other than the fact that she came from Canada. It was Harold who told her Marie's husband had died last year, and Marie was the sole provider for her daughter, Jenette.

Still puzzled, Trudy went back into the library. "Well, no baby pictures today. Marie's gone. Something to do with Margarite Pierson." She put the teacup down. "Does make one wonder…"

"No mystery, my dear," said Harold. "It's just the locals, doing what they damn well please. If the mill didn't need warm bodies, I'd fire every one of 'em."

"Oh Harold, be quiet – you know perfectly well Marie's not like that. I was *wondering* about Margarite's health; she never says a thing."

Ignoring his parents' ongoing bickering, Hal put another log on the fire and stood staring at the weak flames. He was relieved that he didn't have to see Marie, but… what if the baby really *did* resemble him, and in a few years…? He gave the log a swift kick. Flames shot up.

"Easy, easy," said Harold, "let's not burn the place down."

Trudy nodded in quick agreement. "Yes, have some tea, and tell us what you've been up to. Any girlfriends in the picture?"

"Nope. Too busy studying," said Hal.

"Oh, come now." Trudy looked carefully at her son

"Leave him alone," said Harold. "Let the boy graduate and get a job before you start planning a wedding."

Hal finished the lukewarm tea in one gulp. "I've

gotta go. Thanks for the tea."

Harold and Trudy watched Hal leave.

"If you ask me, our son *has* a girlfriend," said Trudy.

Harold started the "Skater's Waltz" again. "He ain't tellin' us, and it's time for a waltz."

"Well, *something's* bothering him," said Trudy.

Marie marched past the imposing Federal and Greek Revival mansions on Atkinson Street, many of them half-hidden behind privet hedges and fading hydrangea bushes. She was angry that she had encouraged her daughter to ever meet with Hal.

She thought back to the beginning, when Hal first invited Jenette to the movies. Marie's husband, Paul, was upset about it; repeating constantly in his thick French-Canadian accent, "Ees not vor oou – 'ne va pas.'" Finally he relented, after Marie convinced him that Hal was a nice boy. For ten years, she'd watched him grow into a polite young man. Now, miserable with guilt, she wished only that the clock could be turned back. She didn't hear Hal's car pulling up alongside of her.

"Marie…"

She jumped.

"Oops, didn't mean to startle you."

Marie glowered at him.

"Look, I'm sorry, but I can't – "

Marie looked directly at him. "No, Hal, you *won't*!"

"Marie – you don't understand," said Hal.

"Hal Walker," she said, in barely a whisper, "don't you talk to me about understanding. I *understand* your family better 'n anyone. I remember you as a little boy; you were decent. I had hope for you – what happened?" She shook her head in despair and walked away.

Hal didn't follow her.

Marie walked on at such a furious pace she almost forgot that she *really had* promised to visit Margarite in the afternoon. She turned around to go back a block to Margarite's street.

Gavin Hanley, the Aldriches' handyman, called out from behind the top of the privet hedge he was trimming. "Well, sumpin's got you on fire; pret' near see the steam comin' off your head."

Marie stopped short. "Oh, Gavin, I didn't see you."

"No, I guess you didn't…"

"I've got a lot on my mind – walked right past Burt Street."

"Yes, you did," observed Gavin.

Marie pointed to the top of the privet hedge. "You missed a spot." Then she smiled and kept walking.

But Gavin got the last word, "Remembah – you gotta *cross* the street for Margarite's house."

Marie chuckled, feeling a little better for having seen Gavin. Their friendship went back twenty years, when Marie and Paul had arrived in town fresh from St. Jovite, Canada.

TWO

In spite of her worries, Marie smiled when she saw Margarite Pierson tending her flower garden: a veritable jungle of overgrown shrubs and flowers, accessible only by narrow brick pathways, vanishing beneath leggy chrysanthemums clinging on to the last of fall. Margarite heard the little garden gate open. Pushing strands of gray hair back into a loose bun, she straightened up enough to see Marie.

"Hello there, I didn't expect to see you so soon. How nice!"

"Yes, I left the Walkers' early," said Marie. "If it's ready, I'll take your laundry now. I want to get back to Jenette.

Margarite was sitting on a gardening stool. Due to arthritis, she could no longer get down on her knees. "There's not that much today." She pointed to her skirt. "See? The same one I wore yesterday, and the day before. You can wash lots tomorrow." Sensing Marie's anxiety, she reached for a cane to support her arthritic joints and started walking toward the porch. "Let's have a cup of tea."

"No, not today, thanks. Tea wouldn't set well."

Margarite pointed to some chairs on the porch. "At least sit for a minute."

With a weak smile, Marie followed Margarite to the porch. She paused at a grape arbor next to the house. "Frost hasn't killed them yet?"

"Oh goodness, no; just sweetens 'em. Take a bunch."

Marie reached for a clump of shiny black berries on a vine, next to the Concord grapes.

"No, no," laughed Margarite. "You don't want those; that's deadly nightshade – atropa belladonna. The leaves are highly toxic; deadly, in some cases. I reckon the berries are none too healthy either."

Marie jumped away. "Well, why…"

"Why do I keep the vine?" Margarite laughed again. "Keeps other critters away from my grapes."

When they were both seated on the porch, Margarite came right to the point. "The Walkers don't know, do they?"

"No, and Hal's not about to tell."

"No, of course not," said Margarite.

"But I thought he loved Jenette," said Marie, sadly shaking her head. "It's all my fault. I never should have let her go out with him."

"You couldn't have stopped them," said Margarite. "And you can't change what is: Hal is not going to disappoint his parents. He's their only child."

Marie slammed her foot down on the porch. "I see.

My Jenette doesn't count. My only child doesn't matter!"

"I don't mean that…" said Margarite.

"Yes, you do. It's as plain as the nose on your face – and that's growing longer!" Marie stood up. "My Paul was right: you all lie as it suits you."

Margarite sighed. "Please…sit down. I'm not lying…" She struggled for the right words. "I'm just telling you the way it is. What's done is done. *Now* I'd like to help; you and Jenette, and your little grandson."

Exhausted by the emotional upheaval of the day and moved by Margarite's simple words Marie wiped away a tear, but remained standing. "Thank you. I understand, but now I have to go home."

Margarite clapped her hands together suddenly. "I just remembered!" She motioned to the front door. "My present for Paulie – it's in there. Open the door."

Dutifully, Marie opened the door. "A baby carriage…?"

"Yes, indeed," said Margarite proudly. "I retrieved it from my neighbor's garage. She had no use for it. Now it's yours…" She laughed. "Or more precisely, Paulie's."

"I don't know…" said Marie, "I can't accept…"

"Yes, you can," commanded Margarite. "Take it and give it to Jenette."

Marie was too tired to argue. "All right, I will." She pulled the carriage onto the porch and down the steps to the sidewalk. "Thank you. Goodbye."

"Goodbye," said Margarite. "Bring that baby by

sometime," she said, looking at Marie's slumped shoulders as she walked away.

~~~~~~~~

The fraternity house was packed and noisy. Post-football parties were starting. Hal walked past the crowded living room and up the wide stairway, two at a time.

His roommate shouted up to him, "Hey, Hal, the beer's down here!"

Hal waved over his shoulder, "Yeah, I know," and continued upstairs. In his room, he grabbed a bottle of bourbon from the bookshelf, poured some in a glass and took several swigs.

"What a mess…" In a pointless, almost unconscious gesture, Hal opened his wallet. A twenty-dollar bill and the face of President Jackson stared at him. "You're a big help – this'll go a long way for the kid." He leaned back in his chair and shut his eyes, squeezing his temples as hard as he could. "Think – think of something!" There was a pad of paper on his desk. He tore off a page and stared at it.

A few minutes later his roommate, Jeremy, burst in the room. "Hey, Karen…what's-her-name – Rhine-ham-hone…?"

"Rhinelander," corrected Hal.

"Well, she's downstairs asking for you." Jeremy shook his head. "Boy, some guys get all the luck."

Hal took another swig of bourbon. "I'm not in the

mood; tell her I'm sick."

"With what?"

"Does it matter? Tell her I have the clap."

"What – that townie in Bellows Falls – did she…?"

Hal slammed his glass on the desk. "No! That's a joke, you idiot. And Jenette's not a *townie*!"

Jeremy shrugged and started to back out the door. "Um…you wouldn't mind then, ahh… if I made a move on Karen?"

"Be my guest," said Hal, waving his arm.

Jeremy beamed a big, goofy smile and fled.

"Hey, shut the door!" Hal pushed himself away from his desk and gave the door a firm kick. One of the casters came off his chair. He replaced it, and then he started writing.

Dear Jenette,

I know it's hard for you to understand, but as long as I can remember my dad has wanted me to be…"

Angrily Hal crumpled the paper, then ripped it to shreds. "You're full o' crap, Walker!"

He began again.

Dear Jenette…

Sometime after midnight Hal finished the letter. Downstairs the party was in full swing. Not wanting to be seen, he went outside via the fire escape. No one saw him drive away.

~~~~~~~~

Pushing the baby carriage from Margarite's house to

Canal Street had helped Marie simmer down. After opening the outside door of number twelve, her first concern was squeezing the carriage and herself into the tiny vestibule of the tenement building. Marie plopped her pocketbook in the carriage and walked up the long, narrow stairway backwards, pulling the carriage along. At the top, she parked the carriage on a small, unadorned landing. Years ago, when she and Paul first moved in, Marie had tried decorating the little hallway with a small table and flowers, but they just got in the way: boots, boxes, and tools took over. Even though this was company housing, owned by the paper mill, Paul always made small repairs; fixing windows, a broken step, and every winter he kept the front walk shoveled. When Paul died, the paper mill people in charge of housing let Marie stay on, paying minimal rent. Of course, Marie knew that Harold Walker, or most likely Trudy, had arranged that. Reaching for her keys, Marie paused and took a deep breath before unlocking the door.

"Jenette...? I'm home – come see what I've got." Marie heard muffled sobs coming from Jenette's bedroom. She put her pocketbook on the worn, overstuffed couch. Next to it, on a Mission-style oak table, was her wedding photograph, framed in silver filigree: she and Paul in front of All Saints Church in St. Jovite, Canada. Marie straightened the lace doily beneath it, then touched the picture of Jenette in her First Communion dress. "Oh dear..."

Jenette was lying face-down on her bed with an arm around the sleeping baby. Marie sat on the edge of the bed and smoothed her daughter's hair. "I'm sorry. I never should have let you talk to him."

Jenette turned onto her side, careful not to disturb the baby. "I had to; he's the father…"

"Yes, but that's no matter now," replied Marie calmly. "You're the mama; little Paulie's yours to love and raise."

"But how…? I don't have any money…" said Jenette.

The baby began to stir. Marie picked him up, wanting a distraction before presenting her plan. She, too, had been worried about money, and while walking back from Margarite's, she could think of only one solution. Gently rocking the baby in her arms, she steadied her voice. "Most days I'm home by three. You can work on the mill's night shift."

Jenette shot up from her bed; tears streamed down her cheeks as panic overwhelmed her. "I won't – I can't!" she shouted. She felt cornered, completely defeated. Growing up, all she'd ever heard from her parents, and in school, was 'self improvement – learn a skill – get beyond the mill.'

"What happens when you're *not* home at three; when you have to stay at their house?"

"Paulie goes with you," said Marie, with a conviction she didn't feel. Privately, she hoped that on the rare night when Jenette might have to take Paulie with her, the mill foreman would look the other way. Right now she was too tired to think of anything else. Forcing a smile, she reached over and brushed the hair from Jenette's eyes. "Here, hold Paulie for a minute. I have a surprise – for both of you." She hurried into the living room before Jenette could say anything.

Jenette looked in the mirror above the pink and white dresser covered with cheerleader pompoms and high school memorabilia. In the corner of the mirror were two small snapshots: one of Hal, and a smaller one of both of them. They were taken last summer in a carnival photo booth. Holding Paulie over her shoulder, Jenette quietly tucked them away in a drawer. At the same time she noticed a rubbing of an Indian petroglyph that Hal had done when they were having one of their many picnics on the "island," a spit of land in the Connecticut River accessible by bridges from the Vermont and New Hampshire sides of the river. When Hal told her about the many hours he had spent looking at the carvings, they decided to make it their "secret" place. On warm summer evenings, Jenette would make a picnic supper and join Hal at the petroglyphs. Together, they theorized about the carvings: Did the anthropomorphic heads with eyes, mouths, and horns depict celebrations? Battles? Sometimes, Hal spoke of wanting to study archeology. But no, his dad expected him to be a banker and that was that. Then Jenette would laugh and say: "You can do both – study *old* currency."

On top of the piece of paper with the rubbing Hal

had written: "Two heads are better than one. Love always, your thick-headed Hal."

"I just don't understand…" Jenette hugged Paulie and kissed the top of his head. "*You* can be an archeologist!" She stuffed the paper in the back of the drawer and slammed it shut. Then, shutting her eyes tightly, she tried to push the memories away. Paulie, and the paper mill, would be her future. She started combing her hair and called out to her mother.

"Will *they* have to know I'm working *there?*" She didn't want to say the word 'mill,' even to herself.

Marie was pulling the carriage in from the hallway. "Don't worry 'bout that. From what I hear, Mr. Walker never goes on the floor." She adjusted the carriage blanket and stood back to admire it. "And there's plenty o' days he never even goes *to the mill.*" She wheeled the carriage into Jenette's room. "Here we are!"

Jenette was overcome with emotion. She stood there, rocking Paulie in her arms. "Oh, Mama…"

"Well, let's try it out," said Marie, taking Paulie and placing him in the carriage.

The baby wiggled and smiled. "Oh, Mama, look! He likes it!"

"Sure he does," laughed Marie, "he knows a good thing." She went into the kitchen. "Let's get us a little supper, before he wants his."

Jenette pushed the carriage a few turns around the small living room, and then parked it in the kitchen. Out of habit she sat at the round table in the middle of the room and watched her mother prepare a meal.

Marie opened the door of the small gas refrigerator. "How 'bout some hot dogs 'n beans?"

"Sure," said Jenette wistfully, as she traced the daisy pattern on the thick plastic cloth covering the kitchen table. "Do you think he'll ever…"

Knowing that the 'he' Jenette referred to was Hal, Marie cut her off. "No, I don't know – and you can't dwell on it." She opened the can of beans and dumped them in a saucepan. The hot dogs were boiling; Marie poked them with a fork. She was as upset as her daughter was – more so. She had *let* this happen to Jenette – her own daughter; she had approved of Hal Walker! Now she wondered how to mend her daughter's broken heart. "These are done; would you get the plates?"

Obediently Jenette took two plates from the kitchen cabinet above the linoleum counter top. They were part of Marie's wedding china: white, with pink and yellow roses, usually saved for special occasions, but Marie had enjoyed using them as "everyday" plates. They brightened her modest kitchen.

"I guess I won't be selecting china patterns anytime soon," said Jenette softly.

"No, not right now; but like I said: don't think about what *isn't*." Marie started dishing out the beans, and put the hot dogs in some rolls. "Milk or apple juice?"

"Milk, please," said Jenette flatly.

Marie sat down and began to eat. "You have a wonderful little boy; life is filled with possibilities."

"That's right," replied Jenette sarcastically. "Slaving away in a paper mill; just what I've dreamed about. And how can you keep working for *them* – in that house?" Jenette knew why: her mother needed the money.

"Stop it – right now! I don't hold with self-pity. There's always something ahead. In time..." Marie was trying to think of something.

"Name one," said Jenette.

Marie concentrated on her hot dog, applying mustard carefully, ignoring her daughter's bitterness. She was trying to remember where she saw an ad for a correspondence course. "Yes, the paper!" She jumped up and flipped through a stack of newspapers in a corner of the kitchen. "Here, look. You can take a secretarial course by mail. You already know how to type."

Jenette wasn't convinced. "I did that in high school; all they did was teach us how to write a business letter." She took a mouthful of beans and washed them down with some milk. "A lot o' good that'll do – besides, we don't have a typewriter."

"Yes we do, – a second-hand one. Your father stored it in the basement a few years ago." Marie left out the fact that it had belonged to the Walkers. She was simply pleased with the idea. "You see, the future *can* be yours."

"Oh, Mom, first you say I've gotta work in the mill, now you're talkin' about..."

"…Possibilities for the future." Marie completed the sentence.

"Hmmm – whatever you say," said Jenette, forcing a smile. "God knows I don't want to stay in that mill; I'll end up like Dad." Jenette looked down – ashamed – she didn't mean to make that reference to her father.

Before she could apologize Marie cut her off. "Leave your father out of this."

Paulie gave a little squawk. Happy to change the subject, Marie finished her hot dog and started clearing the table. "You take care of him, I'll wash up."

After feeding Paulie, Jenette turned on their small television and sat with him on the couch. Television reception had recently come to Bellows Falls, and most people were able to get two or three channels. Milton Berle on Saturday nights was one they liked. "Mom, c'mon – it's your favorite: Uncle Milty."

Marie dried her hands on the dishtowel and went into the living room. Jenette was rocking Paulie in her arms. For a moment she was taken aback by the baby's resemblance to Hal. She shut her eyes and shook her head, as if to change the image, hoping that Jenette wasn't aware of the similarity.

Later that night, long after Jenette had gone to sleep, Marie was still on the couch, sitting in semi-darkness. *The Milton Berle Show* was over; the only light came from the flickering screen. She squinted at her wristwatch: 1:00 a.m. – she must have fallen asleep. She was tired, and knew that she should go to bed, but thoughts and worries kept her mind spinning. Jenette was right: how could she keep working for the Walkers? But she had to; like her daughter, she had no choice: they needed the money. And, of course, she thought bitterly, it's all the same: Harold Walker's house – Harold Walker's mill, what difference did it make. She sighed heavily and got up from the couch. A creaking noise on the landing outside the door caught her attention. Marie stood still, listening to footsteps receding down the stairs. Then, slowly, she moved to the door, listening again before opening it. At her feet, stuck under a corner of the toolbox, was a large white envelope. On it was Jenette's name. As Marie leaned over to pick it up, she heard the street door shut. She took the letter back into the living room and opened it.

Dear Jenette,

Last winter, when we were in Montreal, I really did start thinking about us together – as a couple. I liked the feeling I had when we walked along the streets, and ate in the restaurant. Everything seemed to fall in place. After graduation I WAS going to tell my parents that we wanted to get married. But then, Jenette, the baby changed everything. I was (and still am) frightened. I don't know how to be a father; I don't even have a job. I don't know how we'd live. My parents expect me to go to New York and work in a bank. I'm not sure I could do that with you and a baby along. I mean, I don't know if I would even get the job – under those circumstances. This doesn't sound nice, and it isn't; I feel like a bum. I hurt your feelings this afternoon. I do not expect you or your mother to forgive me, but please know that I will send you money when I have a job. I will never stop thinking about you and the baby.

Love always, Hal

Slowly, folding it carefully, Marie put the letter back in the envelope and placed it in the bottom drawer of her small desk.

THREE

Jenette was making another batch of baby formula to put in the refrigerator. Soon her mother would be home to take care of Paulie, while she worked the three-to-eleven shift at the mill. She'd been working in the paper mill for two months. Her days were as regimented as her nights. Routine tasks: cleaning, washing, feeding the baby, all were done within an exact schedule. She didn't want to think of her work at the mill; it was just a numbing continuance of the day. Her one chance for a change in this routine was gone. That morning she had received a reply from the secretarial school. The correspondence courses had been discontinued; classes would be held weekday mornings – in Springfield, a thirty-minute bus ride away. Mornings were Paulie's wide-awake, bouncy time; she could never take him to a class, and she wouldn't allow her mother to take Paulie anywhere near the Walkers' house. Jenette was about ready to throw the letter away when Marie came home and saw it on the kitchen table.

"Oh, they've answered, so soon..." said Marie.

"I can't do it," said Jenette, without any explanation.

Marie looked at her daughter closely. "I thought you wanted…"

"The only classes are mornings – in Springfield." Jenette picked Paulie up with one swoop of her arm. "I've gotta change him."

Marie stayed in the kitchen for a few minutes reading the letter. "I see," she said, walking into Jenette's room, "and of course you don't want me taking him to the Walkers'."

"That's right." Jenette turned to her mother. "Forget it, Mom. I know what my life is."

"For Pete's sake, will you listen for a minute? They're going to be away for the whole month of January. Florida, I think." Marie smiled at a squirming Paulie. "Hi, little one." She handed the letter to Jenette. "Write them, see if you can double up the classes – get it done in a month."

Jenette threw the letter on her bed. "I said forget about it. For the last time: I know what I have to do!"

Marie put her arm around her daughter's shoulder. "You didn't hear a word I said, did you?" Slowly she repeated herself: "The Walkers are going to be away for the whole month of January; I can take care of Paulie – all day – every day."

"That means I can…" said Jenette, slowly understanding.

Marie picked up the letter from the bed and handed

it to Jenette. She waved her daughter's apology aside. "It's time to look *forward*; that's our motto." She started walking back to kitchen. "I almost forgot: the Walkers' Christmas party is this Friday. You'll have to take little Paulie to work with you that night."

Paulie gave a happy gurgle. Jenette laughed. "He likes that idea. He can flirt with Shirley."

Just before leaving for the mill, Jenette went back into her room to get the letter from the secretarial school. "Shirley might be interested in this; mornings wouldn't be a problem. Her kids are in school."

Marie smiled in agreement. "That'd be nice; you could ride the bus together."

~~~~~~~~

The whistle was blowing for the end of the daytime shift. Weary workers came filing out of the brick building. Jenette was waiting at the bottom of the stairs for a few stragglers to come down from the second floor. The wooden stairway was narrow and steep; single file was the only way. Shirley ran up behind her, breathless.

"Whew! I made it." She caught her breath. "Those crazy kids of mine: I tell 'em to come right home after school, *before* goin' out to play so I can show 'em what to eat, and talk to 'em for a minute – sumpin' their father *never* does – but no, they jus' gotta be contrary." Shirley and Jenette started up the stairwell. "You're lucky your Paulie stays in one place. Ha, I can't even remember back that far – when kids stayed put." She looked closely at Jenette. "Hm – you're looking happy – what's up?"

Jenette handed her the letter. "I'm going to enroll. Take a look, maybe you can too."

Shirley glanced at the heading: Springfield Secretarial School. "Ha! Like pigs'll fly – but what the heck – I'll look at it…" Shirley pointed to the lady at the end of the paper machine. "Better wait for our break; Tammy's waiting for us."

Both women worked at a paper machine. It was their job to guide the heavy sheets onto a platform, which dropped gradually as it filled with paper. When the number of sheets reached a ream – 480, a bell went off, and Shirley and Jenette placed "tickets" on top of the pile before the next sheet came down. The reams fell onto skids for easy handling by the men. The skin on Shirley's hands was inured to paper cuts. Jenette, however, was still putting Band-aids on her fingers. Standing in one spot all night was hard, and her arms ached from the constant motion, but Jenette was glad not to be in the noisy, dirty pulp house. The pulping process in the Walker mill was mechanical, yielding fewer tons of pulp per day than the chemical process now used by many paper mills; but Chester Walker, Harold's grandfather, liked machinery and would have it no other way. He stipulated in his will that the mill could never change to a chemical process. Harold Walker had no affinity for machines, and blamed the plant's woes on his grandfather.

Just before the six o'clock break the roller slowed down, almost to a grinding halt, then went back up to speed. The overhead lights flickered for a few minutes.

"What's that all about?" asked Jenette.

"Same old stuff – been goin' on for months," said Shirley. "Le Bec's been…"

"Who…" asked Jenette.

"Ray – the foreman," said Shirley, "Ray Le Bec. He used to assist the other guy – Gavin – before he got canned."

"Oh yeah, Ray. Sorry, what's he…"

"He's been trying to figure it out." Shirley snapped her chewing gum. "Me? I could care less; I could do this with my eyes shut, though…" she patted the machine, "… ole Bessie here has to keep rollin'."

Jenette didn't really care either. She wanted to go downstairs, have some coffee and show the brochure to Shirley. "It's six; let's go."

Shirley sipped her coffee, and tried not to put a damper on Jenette's enthusiasm about the secretarial course. "This looks real good. You could get a nice job after learnin' all this."

"So could you," said Jenette.

Shirley smiled. "No, 'fraid not. Not now; my kids still like to eat, and Joe – he ain't too reliable. Some days he works…and some days he don't." She sighed. "This job's good 'n steady; I can't be leavin' it." She gave the brochure back to Jenette. "Thanks for thinkin' of me."

"Sure," said Jenette. "But maybe someday, in a few years...?"

A loud buzzer sounded, signaling the end of their break. "Hmpf, no problem with that thing," laughed Shirley.

~~~~~~~~

Hal was trying to organize his notes for a paper due on Monday. He couldn't concentrate. He knew his parents were expecting him at their annual Christmas party. *Expecting* – humph, he thought, more like a command performance. He gave up and stuffed the cards in his desk.

His roommate was asking about ties. Jeremy held up three for Hal's approval.

"The Regimental – the one with the stripes," said Hal. Then he reached for a bag on the shelf in his closet. It dropped, and a teddy bear fell out.

"Whoa...what's that?" laughed Jeremy. "A teddy for a Colby lass?"

Hal grabbed the bear. "No, none o' your business. It's for one of my cousins – at my parents' party."

"Tonight?" said Jeremy. "You're supposed to be goin' to Colby – big night – lots o' girls. Without dates."

"Can't. Gotta be in Bellows Falls," said Hal.

Jeremy threw a pillow at Hal. "C'mon – you need some fun; you've been acting like a jerk lately."

Hal put on his tweed jacket and started out the door with the teddy bear under his arm. "Sorry, I promised my folks."

Jeremy shrugged. "Okay – your loss…"

~~~~~~~~

Jenette was bundling Paulie in a wool baby bunting for the walk to the mill. "You're comin' with me tonight. You can show Shirley how big you are." She tugged on the bunting. "You've almost outgrown this – you big boy!"

Marie hovered around them with last-minute instructions. "Call me if Paulie gets too fussy; I'll come get him."

Jenette gave her mother a withering look. "If you think I'm calling the Walkers' house…"

"I'll be answering the phone…" said Marie.

"That's not the point." Jenette picked up Paulie and prepared to leave.

"I'll be back here by nine," said Marie, still trying to be helpful. "Their Christmas party always ends at eight."

Jenette was out the door. "We'll be fine."

"Call me here…if you need anything," said Marie softly.

Jenette walked carefully down the snowy sidewalk. Three inches of snow had fallen, and shoveling had been sporadic in front of stores and the occasional house. Single strands of Christmas lights framed a few doorways along Canal Street, and in some windows a miniature nativity scene was displayed. Jenette hugged Paulie extra hard. She was glad to have him with her tonight; it helped block out the memories of last year at this time, when she and Hal were together. Instead of going to his parents' Christmas party, Hal had picked her up and they drove to Montreal – all day. They ate in a French restaurant and stayed in a nice hotel. She remembered feeling all tingly, thinking that it was just like being married. The next day it was snowing – almost a blizzard, but Hal drove them home safely.

Jenette kissed Paulie and brushed a tear away. "Just like Mama said, we're on our own – you an' me...an' your gramma."

As people assembled for the three o'clock shift, talk revolved around Christmas festivities: parties, church concerts, and shopping. Jenette had Paulie bundled up so much that he was hardly noticed until they were upstairs.

Shirley was the first to speak up. "Hi there, handsome, where'd ya get them bright blue peepers?" She looked squarely at Jenette's rich brown eyes and laughed. "Not from you, that's for sure."

Jenette tried to sound neutral. "No, his dad has blue eyes."

Shirley knew better than to go any further, and kept it light. "Ha – works every time: blue-eyed papa – blue-eyed boy!"

Changing the subject, Jenette looked around the floor. "Where's the best place to put my lil' fella?" Jenette had brought a collapsible basket and put that on the floor, layering it with an extra blanket. "How 'bout if I put him here, under the window?"

Shirley took one of the large sheets of paper off the roller. "I'll fold this; it'll make a good mattress."

Jenette watched as Shirley created a perfect nest for Paulie. When she put him in it, both of them were treated with big smile. "He likes it!"

"Sure. He's warm and he's high enough to keep an eye on you. Babies just like to watch their mamas."

About an hour into their work, Shirley and Jenette noticed another slowdown of the rollers on the paper machine, similar to the one a few weeks ago. Shirley touched the on/off switch. "Ouch! That's hot." The overhead light flickered several times and went out. "What the?"

Jenette looked at the other machines on the floor. They were slowing down. Two more overhead lights went out. She tried to turn on a wall switch, but jumped back after touching it. "That's wicked hot." She walked over to Shirley and spoke softly, not wanting to be an alarmist. "Shouldn't we call Ray?"

"Lot o' good it would do; he's at ole man Walker's Christmas party – probably tanked; be nice if we all got invited." Laughing, she glanced at Jenette. "Don't ya think?"

Jenette looked down at the floor, saying nothing.

Ut-oh, thought Shirley, *Walker has a son*. She wanted to kick herself. The lights went back on; the rollers got up to speed. "Whadda ya know? The Ghost of Christmas," said Shirley, trying to be funny. "Okay, everybody, I guess we can keep working. Goody-goody."

Jenette noticed that the wall light was flickering. "How'd that happen? A minute ago it…"

"It does that," said Shirley. "I remember Ray saying how all these machines – running like they do, twenty-four hours a day – suck the juice outta everything." Shirley saw a spark come out of the ceiling light. "Whoah – there it goes again!"

Jenette saw that Paulie was sleeping soundly. "Guess it doesn't bother him, but before all the lights go crazy, I'll run down to the bathroom. Would you keep an eye on him?"

"Sure thing. Take your time," said Shirley.

Jenette was pleasantly surprised to find the ladies room warm for a change; usually all the heat went right up the stairs, never touching the first floor bathrooms.

FOUR

Trudy Walker was a stickler when it came to her parties. She felt that her Christmas party set the standard for the rest of the holiday season. Like all the other houses on Atkinson Street the front door was decorated with a large balsam wreath. But Trudy wanted something extra. She had a Blue Spruce placed on the porch, just to the right of the door. On the day of the party, it was Harold's job to string it with lights.

"Not too many," instructed Trudy, "we're not Italian."

Harold was standing on a stepladder, clipping the lights onto the top branches. "I thought you said Hal was going to be here at two."

"Just a little to the right, dear, uh-huh – that's it," said Trudy. "Now, if you could get the fire going in the living room…"

Harold stepped down and brushed the spruce needles off his sweater. "It's three o'clock. I believe you said that your son would be here at two."

"I did, but he's not here, is he? And I can't worry

37

about it. Marie was late getting here, and I've got a million things to do."

"*Marie* will not be discussing business with Sam Aldrich. Our son, however, is *expected* to be on time and show an interest."

"Don't worry, he will." Trudy was looking at her list and rearranging the poinsettia plants on the hall table. "I want to review the food with Marie. Why don't you change now?" She gave Harold a quick, mechanical smile. "You know how the Howards always arrive early. It would be quite awkward if..."

Harold checked his watch. "There's plenty of time for me to change. Ray Le Bec called me this morning; I've gotta go to the mill."

"That's ridiculous. Just call him back. Anyway, he's coming to the party." Trudy glanced in the library on her way to the kitchen. "And look – you haven't even put out the liquor." She pointed to a long table covered with a white linen tablecloth. "It goes there – next to the glasses and the ice bucket – which Marie will fill at four o'clock. I don't want the bartender in the kitchen. He gets in the way."

"I'll take care of that," said Harold, heading for the liquor cabinet in the library. He put an assortment of liquor bottles on the table: gin, scotch, bourbon, vodka, a small bottle of vermouth, and an old, expensive bottle of sherry, which no one drank but Trudy thought it looked nice. Then, after filling the ice bucket, he put some ice in an old-fashioned glass and filled it up halfway with bourbon.

Trudy had just finished repositioning the liquor bottles. "What are you doing?"

Harold stopped and looked directly at Trudy. "I am going upstairs," he said, "to enjoy my drink. And then, I shall change."

"Hm, all right, but don't touch anything on the bed. My dress is there. I'll be changing myself, as soon as I talk to Marie."

Harold put the drink on a table next to his side of the bed and sat down on the edge, careful to avoid Trudy's dress. He called the mill again, asking the operator for the direct line to Ray Le Bec's office. No answer. Harold leaned against the headboard and stretched his legs out on the bed. "Well, Frenchy, you'll just have to wait 'til Monday, I'm sure as hell not talkin' business with you here in my house." Harold viewed his employees as a necessary evil. He disliked the paper mill and everyone in it. His resentment extended to his grandfather, who built the place, and then to his parents, for dying and leaving him nothing but the paper mill. He never would have stayed in Bellows Falls if they'd left him some real money instead of a dying mill and a bunch o' French canucks yammering for more money. Harold heard Trudy coming up the stairs. He shut his eyes and pretended to be sleeping.

~~~~~~

Hal had not taken his foot off the gas pedal since leaving Hanover, but a police car parked on the side of Route 5 caused him to slow down and concentrate on his driving. For the past thirty minutes he'd been planning just how to leave the teddy bear with Jenette. It seemed easy enough: he'd park his car on Canal Street, walk up a flight of stairs, knock on the door and say, "Merry Christmas! This is for the baby." He wouldn't need to elaborate because his letter had explained things.

But he didn't go directly to Canal Street. He stopped at the Riverview Tavern on Rockingham Street. It was a working-class bar. He looked out of place in his tweed jacket and tie, but after a few stares, people resumed drinking. He sat at the end of the bar and greeted Frank, the bartender. In times past, they usually exchanged a few words about sports, but not tonight. The bartender had the good instinct to leave Hal alone, asking him only if he wanted his usual Budweiser. Hal thanked him with a smile, and Christmas greetings. He poured the beer into a glass and took a long drink.

Ray Le Bec was sitting at a small table in the corner of the tavern, playing solitaire and nursing a whiskey. It bothered him to see Hal there. He wanted to play cards and sort out his problems at the mill before going to the ole man's party. He sure as hell didn't want to talk with the kid. However, after a couple of seconds, he realized that young Hal wasn't in a talkative mood either. That beer of his was goin' down mighty fast.

Four beers later, Hal left the Tavern and drove to Canal Street. This time he stopped and walked directly up the stairs to Jenette's apartment. He knocked on the door, waited, and knocked again. After waiting a minute, he put his ear to the door and listened. No voices. Carefully he took the teddy bear from the bag and placed it on top of Paul Furneau's old toolbox. No gift card, just the bear with a red bow around his neck.

Hal drove around town for a few minutes to clear his head. He ended up on Westminster Terrace overlooking Bellows Falls. Standing in front of his car, he had a good view of the town, the Connecticut River, and his father's paper mill. It was a clear night. Enormous puffs of black smoke from the stacks seemed to dominate the sky. Hal couldn't help thinking how that one paper mill pretty much supported the town. Without it...what else could take its place?

~~~~~~~~

When Jenette returned to the paper machine she was happy to see that Paulie was still sleeping. She smiled at him and went to her place at the rollers. "Still working okay?"

"Yeah, at least for now – don' know what's goin' on with that light," said Shirley, nodding toward the ceiling. She shrugged. "As long as these babies keep rolling..." She patted the side of the large roller, "...I guess we keep workin'."

At seven o'clock the lights started flickering again.

"That does it," declared Shirley, "time for a break, everybody." She turned to Jenette. "I'm goin' downstairs now – while I can still see 'em – ha-ha."

~~~~~~~~~

The Walkers' Christmas party was in full swing. Trudy Walker sparkled in an emerald-green, taffeta cocktail dress, with her silver-blond hair almost as shiny as the diamond necklace and earrings she wore every Christmas season. Moving effortlessly among her guests, she chatted briefly with everyone, all friends and acquaintances from Bellows Falls. A few people from the paper mill had also been invited: Ray Le Bec and his wife Lois, and Martin, the accountant, and his lady friend, Maud. Harold's secretary, Phyllis, always came with her husband, Dan, who taught science at the high school and was constantly asking for tours through the paper mill, all of which were denied on the grounds of safety.

Trudy expressed an interest in their lives, asking about their children and each child's hobby. Intimidated by their surroundings, the women usually answered in monosyllables, and the men were too busy eating and drinking to offer much in the way of conversation. Before any given party, it wasn't unusual for Trudy to brief Harold on the guest list, citing the best topics to bring up. Generally, Harold went along with this and rose to the occasion, laughing heartily over his own jokes – usually anecdotes about native Vermonters. Tonight, however, Harold wasn't as relaxed as he wanted to be.

Several people from the mill had arrived, but not Ray Le Bec. Even though Harold had planned on no more than two minutes of conversation with Ray, it miffed him that an employee would *not* show up on time. And then, for some fool reason, his own son had yet to make an appearance. He overheard Trudy making excuses to Sam Aldrich for Hal's tardiness.

"Yes…what can one do with these college boys?" said Trudy. "They seem to live in a different time zone…" She picked up a silver bowl of candied pecans and passed them to Sam. "You've got to try these. Harold orders them from South Carolina, a nifty little place in Charleston. He calls them his 'picture-perfect pecans.'"

Sam tried one. "Hmm – they are good."

"Did I hear my name mentioned?" said Harold, as he patted Sam on the back and gave Sam's wife Susan a peck on the cheek.

"Yes," said Susan, "we're discussing your pecans…" She reached for the bowl. "Which my husband won't share…"

Sam laughed and relinquished the pecans.

"Trudy tells me that Hal will be along shortly," said Sam. "I'm eager to feel him out about New York. This is a good year for banking." He finished his glass of scotch and soda. "The economy's in good shape, and next year's election is a done deal – Eisenhower'll win in a landslide."

Harold took a handful of pecans from the dish Susan

was holding. "Thank you, Susie." He popped a few in his mouth and spoke between mouthfuls. "Well, Ike better win – though can't say I think much of his pal, Nixon. Where'd he get that hound dog?"

Sam chuckled. "Don't worry about Nixon. He's loyal; he'll do what Ike's boys tell him to do."

"He'd better. Stevenson's a liberal crackpot. His ideas will crush us."

Worried that Harold was headed for one of his political diatribes, Trudy changed the subject. "Well, ha-ha, I think we have a serious crisis right now. *Thirst* – we need a refill." She pointed to Sam's empty glass and jiggled the ice cubes in hers.

"She's right, ole man," laughed Sam. "That scotch goes down real easy – particularly with the pecans." He handed his glass to Harold.

Harold clicked his heels in mock servitude. "At your service, sir! How 'bout you, Miss Susie…?"

Susan looked at her highball glass. "Thanks, I'm okay for now."

Harold wended his way through small clusters of guests toward the bar, smiling and making brief comments. "Nice to see you Ed, how's that quarterback of yours? Bellows Falls is real proud…" And never one to forget the ladies, Harold smiled broadly when he saw the exquisite frame of Priscilla Goodman. She and her husband were a new addition to the Bellows Falls group, from Canada and rumored to have pots of money. Harold was impressed and wanted to learn the source of their wealth. Indeed, he was a little miffed that his friend Sam hadn't told him about the Goodmans. Bankers are *suppose* to keep tabs on people's dough.

"Why, Priscilla – how wonderful to see you – hope you're enjoying our fair city…"

"Oh my, yes," said Priscilla. "We love the slower pace – much more relaxing than Montreal."

"I hope it won't prove to be too slow," said Harold.

"Not at all," said Priscilla. "I've met a lot of nice people, your dear wife among them. I understand you are in the paper business."

"Guilty as charged," chuckled Harold.

Priscilla grinned. "So are we, indirectly, you might say. Lumber's been the family business for so long I'm surprised we don't look like board lumber – or trees."

Trudy, impatient for the drinks, came over to Harold. "You'll have to let me take Priscilla now. I want to introduce her to Sam and Susie." She pointed to the bar. "Now shoo – we're getting thirsty."

~~~~~~~~~~

The ladies room was very warm. When Shirley stood at the sink to wash her hands, the light next to the mirror went out. Through the cracks in the floorboards she could see flames.

" Almighty God– that's a fire!"

The bathroom began filling with smoke. Screaming, Shirley pushed the door open into the hallway. More smoke came billowing up through the floorboards. Her screams were smothered in smoke. She couldn't open her eyes. Patting her hands along the wall, Shirley yanked at the first doorknob she came to. It was the door to the boiler room. Flames and smoke sucked her down the stairwell into the fire below. With the din of machinery, no one could hear her screams. The door to the second floor was closed.

Jenette stood by the sluggish rollers of the Yankee dryer, waiting for the lights to come on again.

Brian Mallory stepped back from one of the beating engines and looked under a vat in which the pulp was mashed. "I smell smoke."

Erwin Jewell was checking the watery pulp as it came out of the vat and drained over a wire screen. The whole process was slowing down. He worried about the Yankee dryer. With just a few ounces of excessive pressure, its large drum – ten feet in diameter and full of hot steam – could explode. Steam for the Yankee dryer came from a boiler in the basement.

Erwin's eyeglasses were covered with bits of pulp. He shouted to Brian and pointed to the Dryer. "Check the pressure – don't want that sucker to blow!"

Brian ran over and checked the gauge. The pressure was actually lower than normal. He shook his head. "Nothin'." He checked a fuse box on the wall. "I tell ya I smell smoke. Where's Le Bec?"

Erwin shrugged. "Geez-um – I dunno."

Jenette could smell the smoke now. She looked at Brian. "Um – Shirley...she said Ray had the night off; maybe you could call the – "

"Yeah – that's it," said Brian, "he's at the ole man's Christmas party." He picked up the phone on the wall. "Your mom works there – what's the number?"

"Six-four-seven-two," mumbled Jenette.

"Six-four what?" shouted Brian.

"Seven-two," repeated Jenette.

Little Paulie began to fuss. She hurried over to comfort him before he cried and attracted Erwin's attention. So far no one seemed to object that she had brought him to work. Shirley must have stepped out for a cigarette, thought Jenette; she's usually back by now. From the window, she could see an orange glow spreading across the parking lot in front of the mill. Jenette thought the moon must be full. It made her think of Hal. She wondered if he was standing on his parents' porch, away from the guests. He used to say he'd do anything to avoid their parties.

~~~~~~~~

Harold Walker was getting drunk, and angry. He thought it was a lousy party. He didn't know whether to blame his son for not showing up, or his wife for inviting too many locals who, as far as he was concerned, came only for the free drinks. He knew they didn't like him any more than he liked them. And now, to compound matters, his own foreman, Ray Le Bec, had the gall not to come. Harold decided to fire him on Monday, and that made him feel better. He mixed another bourbon and smiled at Stanley Footer, owner of Bellows Falls Hardware and a Baptist teetotaler. "So – Stan, how're the ole nuts 'n bolts?" He poked Stanley in the ribs. "Ha-ha!"

Trudy had an uneasy feeling about the party as well. Her husband's poor performance notwithstanding, the heightened level of chatter and laughter that comes after a few drinks and tasty cocktail food was not there. She really wanted to tell Harold to *shut-up* and start behaving like a proper host, but thought it might be too late for that. Instead, she turned up the volume of the Christmas music and then asked the bartender to start uncorking the champagne.

She took a small wreath of brass bells off the mantelpiece and started shaking it. "Okay, everyone – let's all get a glass of champagne and make this the official start of a very Merry Christmas season – it's the only one we'll have for 1955!"

People smiled and rallied around the bar, happy to have some direction. They started talking about Christmas, what a good year it had been, and maybe it would snow on Christmas Eve.

While Marie passed the last tray of deviled eggs to the guests, she heard the telephone ringing in the library. Nobody answered it. Back in the kitchen she heard it ringing again, but not for long. Harold Walker got to the phone in the library just after the last ring. He expected it was his son with some half-baked excuse for being late.

At this point Trudy had the guests singing carols to the beat of her Christmas bells. No one heard the first fire alarm when it started going off across town.

Except Harold. He had just stepped out of the library and stood in the front hallway, unsure of what he heard. He opened the front door a crack and listened: three blasts. He waited; again three blasts. "Oh god, that's the mill." He rushed upstairs to use the phone in the bedroom. There was no answer. He asked the operator to dial it again.

"Mr. Walker, the phone at the mill is out of order," replied the operator.

Harold threw the telephone on the bed, ran out to the upstairs hallway and down the back stairs into the kitchen.

On the landing, next to the coat rack at the back door, he bumped into Marie. She was putting on her coat.

"What – the...what are you doing?" said Harold.

"Going to the mill!" said Marie.

Harold moved in front of the door. "You can't do that."

"Oh yes I can. My daughter's there."

"What are you talking about?"

"I said, my daughter's in your paper mill, and it's on

fire!"

Harold was rigid, glowering at Marie. Then he opened the back door. "Come on, get in my car."

They both ran down the outside steps to the driveway.

"Wait here – I'll back out," said Harold.

Marie followed Harold into the garage and got in the passenger seat of his Buick sedan. She didn't trust him enough to stop the car after he backed it out of the garage.

As Harold turned his car to drive out of the driveway, Hal came barreling in. He had to jam on his brakes to prevent a collision.

Harold rolled down the window and shouted at Hal, "A little late, aren't you. Move!"

Hal pulled over to the left of the driveway so Harold could get by him. He wondered why Marie was in the car with his father.

Marie rolled down her window. "The mill's on fire. Jenette's – " Before she could finish Harold was out of the driveway.

Hal followed, backing out so quickly that a car coming down Atkinson Street had to swerve to miss him. Hal barely noticed. He was terrified and confused. "What the hell? Why is she there?" Of course, he knew why. Money. He pounded the steering wheel.

Hal was suddenly right behind his father's Buick as they continued down Atkinson Street. Black smoke and flames from the mill were visible. Fire engines screamed into the parking lot. Two policemen, parked at the entrance, tried to stop Harold.

"Get outta my way," shouted Harold, "that's *my* mill."

Marie jumped out of the car and ran past the police barricades. Light snow falling on an icy crust made it slippery underfoot. Hal ran after Marie and grabbed her arm, trying to steady her. She was hardly aware of him.

"My babies are up there," she screamed. "Help them!"

Hal froze at the word *babies*. Pointing to the second floor windows, he shouted to Marie, "Is the baby up there, too?"

Marie pulled away from Hal. "Yes!" She cried running toward the burning building.

A fireman grabbed her. "Lady, get back – it's gonna blow!"

"Marie wait here!" Hal yelled. "They'll get them out."

Firemen had put a ladder up to a second floor window. The basement and first floor were in flames. Only those who had seen an open doorway through the smoke, were safely outside. Just as a fireman started up the ladder to help the trapped mill workers, several window frames exploded from the brick building. Glass, wood, and bits of brick flew out, leaving holes where the windows had been. Inside, Jenette, with Paulie completely covered in a blanket, ran to the far end of the second story. Brian and Erwin were struggling to open the last window. They ended up throwing themselves against the glass to break it. A large piece of glass sliced Brian's shoulder, and shards peppered Erwin's neck. They wanted Jenette to hold Paulie and jump. On the ground firemen were holding a net. Marie and Hal could see them at the window.

"What are you waiting for...?" shouted Marie.

"It's the baby," said Hal. "She's afraid to jump with him."

Harold Walker had been standing silently by his car, rigid and resigned to the final collapse of the Walker Paper Mill. Now he just wished that the remaining people inside would get the hell out. He muttered impatiently to himself, "Toss the little bastard out, and then jump, you fool girl."

Moments were precious. Wind off the river was picking up. Fire was devouring the mill, racing through north to south – every minute there was another explosion and bricks came raining down. Jenette, Brian and Erwin could hear the roar of flames approaching. Jenette was panic-stricken – frozen in place. She couldn't scream. Brian saw only one thing to do. He pried her fingers off the baby's blanket while Erwin gently removed Paulie from Jenette's embrace. Holding the baby in his arms, he leaned out of the opening they had made in the window, then, shouting to the firemen

52

below, he dropped Paulie into the waiting net.

Jenette opened her mouth as if to cry out, and stumbled forward. Where was the floor?

As flames burst through the floor boards Brian and Erwin tried to lift her up to the window, but it was too late, the floor gave way. All three of them fell away with the burning timbers as the entire second floor collapsed.

From the ground Marie and Hal saw a wall of fire. Burning timber and bricks were falling from the building.

Choking on her tears, Marie watched Emile Chaqette, a volunteer fireman and long-time friend of her husband Paul, lift baby Paulie from the net. Tearfully, he handed the baby to Marie. Marie couldn't move or speak. Her eyes were riveted to the burning shell of bricks – to the spot where her daughter had been. Emile had to fold her arms around Paulie so he wouldn't slip from her grasp. Gently, he guided Marie toward his car.

With tears streaming down his cheeks, Hal walked back to his car. His father hadn't moved from the side of the Buick. When he started to say something, Hal stopped him. "Tell Mom, I've gone back to Hanover."

"Stop at the house," said Harold.

"No, I'll call later."

It made Harold Walker uncomfortable to see the tears on his son's face. He hoped that no one saw his son crying. "Fine. Go."

Before leaving the burning mill, Harold spoke to the fire chief and asked him to mail a fire report to his house, the probable cause and damage estimate. He assumed the hospital would give him an account of the dead and injured. Then, he wondered how much his insurance would cover.

Within two hours, Harold was back in his house. All of the guests had left. Trudy was in the living room picking up empty glasses.

Harold went to the bar and filled a glass with bourbon. "The mill's gone," he said. "Burned to the ground."

"I saw you leave, with Marie, and Hal following," said Trudy. "You could have said something." She put down a tray of empty glasses and walked over to Harold. "You should have told me! No – you take off and leave me to put two 'n two together."

"I didn't want to alarm our guests," said Harold.

"*Alarm* our guests! *What* are you talking about? They're not deaf. When the singing stopped we all heard the alarm ringing. Three – that's the mill! They went flying out of here, just the way you did – without so much as a thank you. I was left here alone, no car – no nothing. Thanks a lot." Trudy turned her back on him, picked up the tray and headed for the kitchen.

"Marie's daughter died in the fire," said Harold.

Trudy stopped. "No…" She felt her knees buckling. Her whole body started shaking. She put the tray on a side table and sat in a chair near the pantry door. "Where's the baby?"

Harold cleared his throat. "Um-uh, it was tossed clear – out a window." He drank some bourbon. "I saw a fireman lift him from a net and hand him to Marie."

"Oh, dear God," said Trudy very softly. Slowly she got up. Not trusting herself to carry the tray of glasses, or say any more to her husband, she left the room.

FIVE

Three days later a memorial service, arranged by Harold and Trudy Walker, was held at Immanuel Episcopal Church for the twenty-five fire victims and their families. Most of Bellows Falls attended. Marie did not. The Walker family sat in the front pew. Following the service, ushers led the Walkers down the aisle and outside to a waiting car. Trudy was erect and dignified in a tailored black wool crepe suit adorned with a single strand of pearls, a black hat and gloves. Harold Walker, holding her left arm, walked with deliberation, his eyes focused straight ahead. He did not want his wife stopping to express sympathy for families of the victims. The whole thing made him uncomfortable. However, once outside the church, Trudy insisted on it and stood talking with people for several minutes before getting in the car. Hal stood numbly by his parents, with hands folded in front of him and eyes toward the ground. His grief-stricken face was ashen; his shoulders slumped over so far that his chest appeared concave.

Marie had a private service for Jenette in St. Charles

Roman Catholic Church. In the spring she would bury Jenette's ashes in a plot next to her husband Paul. The only emotion she felt was hatred. She didn't sleep at night and during the day only for an hour or two when Paulie was napping. The feelings of love she had felt for the baby were frozen along with her heart; she simply took care of him: dry diapers, warm clothes, and timely feedings. She pulled his crib into the living room and closed the door to Jenette's room. Once a day she would bundle up Paulie and take him with her to the corner market to buy his formula and a few canned goods for herself. Hal Walker had telephoned several times and stopped by twice with the hope of talking to her. Marie rejected all of his efforts. She refused even to open the door. Written notes from him were thrown away unopened. Flowers sent by well-meaning friends were put in the trash. She didn't even read the cards. Their sympathy angered her. How *dare* they remind her that Jenette was gone? How *dare* they try to tell *her* how it felt, and what to think? She hated them all.

With each passing day an overpowering desire for revenge consumed Marie. It was the Walker family who put Jenette in that mill; whether they understood that or not was immaterial. At night, sitting in the kitchen, Marie's mind turned and twisted. She devised one plan after another. Her heart would race as she came close to an idea, then crumble as flaws in the plan became evident.

Christmas passed, and the New Year came. Marie wouldn't have noticed, but for a new calendar on the wall in the corner market. During the second week of January, a cold spell settled down on Bellows Falls. The river was frozen solid. An ice storm had left trees and the few scraggly shrubs on Canal Street crystallized. Marie had not been outside for several days. The wind was fierce and she knew that the sidewalk in front of her building would be a sheet of ice. But when Paulie's formula ran out, she had no choice. She rolled him up in a blanket – like a papoose, and tucked the whole thing under her coat. Then, holding Paulie against her chest, she did her best to navigate a narrow pathway between the icy street and a chain link fence running alongside the river. Someone had spread sand on the path and a few patches remained in spite of the biting wind. She walked slowly, trying to keep Paulie's face protected. Looking ahead for a safe place to cross the street, Marie noticed something shiny and black clinging to the fence. As she approached, a strange smile came over her face. She hadn't smiled in a month.

"Well, I'll be…" she said to Paulie, brushing the snow and ice crystals off the berries. A thin layer of ice had formed a protective shell around the vine.

Paulie started crying. Marie hugged him. "Shh, hold on, Granny wants to look at this." Beneath the ice most of the leaves were intact. Marie was pleased. She smiled at the vine. "I'll be back."

At the market she chatted amiably with the proprietor, Ferris Muncton. "Looks like we're in for real cold spell."

Ferris, having grown accustomed to Marie's downcast, sad demeanor, hardly knew what to say. "Um – ya – they're talkin' twenty below – for the whole week."

Marie looked at her grandson. "That's okay. Paulie doesn't mind as long as he gets his milk." She pointed to the shelf behind Ferris. "I'll take some extra formula today; twelve cans will do."

Ferris put them in Marie's cloth shopping bag. "That's kinda heavy; want some help carrying?"

"No, thanks. That's why I've got two arms: one for the baby an' one for heftin' things." Marie paid and left.

Ferris remained behind the counter. "Careful..." he said, but Marie had already shut the door. Sadly he shook his head. Good thing she's strong, he thought, won't be easy...raising that little kid.

Marie's thoughts raced ahead of her. She was barely up the stairs of her building before the ideas fell into place. She put her shopping bag on the landing and unlocked the door to her apartment. Paulie was crying non-stop. She put him in his crib and rushed to the refrigerator.

"Phew, there's one left." She removed a bottle of formula and put it in a saucepan on the stove. She called to Paulie, "Three minutes – you'll be eating."

Then she walked over to a pile of unopened mail and sifted through it, picking out two items. One, a pale green envelope with hand-painted daisies along the edge. Inside was a note from Margarite Pierson: "...and when you are ready I hope you will bring that baby over for a visit."

"Yes, we will," said Marie, looking at Margarite's flowery signature, "for as long as you'll have us."

The next letter was in a pale blue envelope with an address engraved on the back: Mrs. Harold C. Walker, 10 Atkinson Street, Bellows Falls, Vermont. Marie opened it without emotion. She dismissed the words of sympathy, but paused at the part that interested her. "Tea time isn't the same without you; do call when you feel up to helping me out again." It was signed, "Most sincerely, Trudy Walker."

Paulie's hungry screams strengthened. She put the letter down and took the bottle of formula out of the saucepan. "Okay – Granny's comin'." It was the first time Marie had smiled at Paulie since Jenette's death.

Later that evening when the baby was sleeping, Marie called Trudy Walker and told her that she would be at their house the day after tomorrow, in time to serve tea. Then she telephoned Margarite to ask if she could leave Paulie with her while she was at the Walkers'. Margarite was delighted and said that she had a hair appointment in the afternoon but Clara Fawcett, her helper, would be there to greet her. She would be home about five o'clock.

Just before sunrise Marie checked Paulie to see if he was still sleeping. Assured that he wouldn't wake up for awhile, she put on her coat and hat, dropped her apartment keys in one pocket and an empty jelly jar in another. After one more look at Paulie, she put on her gloves and quietly left the apartment.

The air was so cold, it almost took her breath away. The sidewalk was covered with treacherous "black ice," so named because of its transparency. The pavement looks crystal clear beneath the ice. Only a bad fall teaches a person to avoid it. Marie stepped carefully onto the road where walking was less hazardous. When she reached the corner of Canal and Depot, she stepped up to the curb and grabbed the wrought iron fence for support. After a quick look to confirm that no one else was out at that hour, she proceeded to pick the black berries from the deadly nightshade vine. She checked each one carefully; some were completely encased in ice. She decided to leave them that way, for they appeared to be plump and shiny. When the jelly jar was full, she broke a dozen leaves off the vine and put them in her coat pocket.

Paulie was just beginning to stir when Marie returned to the apartment. She went immediately to the kitchen and put the jar of berries on the counter. Then she put some newspaper down and carefully placed the leaves on it, separating them to thaw evenly. She thought about doing the same thing with the berries but changed her mind, concerned that they might roll off. She stood for a minute, admiring her handiwork. Then, somewhat nervously, she took a deep breath. She had a lot to do.

As if to relieve her anxiety, Paulie chimed in with some early morning squawks. Marie smiled, hung up her coat and went to the business of preparing his breakfast. She changed his diaper while the milk was warming.

"You're getting so big." Marie held his arms up. "Yes – so…big."

At three months, Paulie was almost too heavy for Marie to hold and feed comfortably. When the milk was warm, she propped him up against two pillows on the couch. He guzzled the milk down.

"Hey, you'll get hiccups." She put him over her shoulder for a burp. "You know what? I think you can handle some rice cereal. We've got a busy day ahead of us. First the library and then grocery shopping, before we go visiting on Thursday."

She poured the remaining bit of milk from the bottle into a small dish, then mixed a tiny bit of rice cereal with it and spooned some into Paulie's eager mouth. "Well, look at you, an eager beaver – just like your m…" The word froze in her mouth. Marie's heart twisted. She wiped away a tear and finished feeding Paulie in silence.

The library had just opened. The librarian was

pulling up the venetian blinds on the windows facing east, hoping to let in some early morning sun. She apologized for the cold temperature in the building, speaking to the room at large, as if it were filled with people.

"Most days it takes thirty minutes for the furnace to kick in, but today, with that wicked northwest wind, we probably won't feel any warmth." She seemed to be on a mission, checking each radiator. "For heaven's sake! No one bothers to bleed these properly. My father taught me years ago." She had a screwdriver in one hand and a tin cup in the other. By opening a valve on top of the radiator for a few seconds, pockets of air, along with some water, were released from the system, thus allowing water to circulate freely through the radiator and in turn, radiate more heat. She dutifully went to all five radiators throughout the building.

Marie was pleased on two accounts. She didn't know this librarian and the radiators were keeping her busy. Quietly Marie went to the stack of encyclopedias in the back of the library. Paulie was sleeping soundly. She removed her coat and folded it inside out, making a little bed for him on the table. Then she scanned the bookshelf: "Nightshade...N – N, here we go." Removing a volume of the eleventh edition of the *Encyclopedia Britannica (1911)*, Marie placed it on the table with reverence.

She read: *"NIGHTSHADE, a general term for the*

genus of plants known to botanists as Solanum. She turned the page. *Deadly nightshade, dwale or belladonna: it grows to a height of 4 or 5 feet, having leaves of a dull green colour, with black shining berries. All parts of the plant are poisonous."*

Marie's excitement mounted. Yes, yes, that's the one...

She read on. *"The plant is a native of central and south Europe and can be found in England and parts of North America. Its leaves and roots can be used for medicinal purposes (see Belladonna)."*

Quickly Marie searched for volume three: AUS to BIS.

"Bella-bella." Yes. *"Belladonna: widely used because of the alkaloids, of which atropine is the most important."* Her fingers raced across the page. *"Toxic doses of atropine – and therefore belladonna, raise the temperature..."*

Marie wiped small beads of perspiration from her forehead. She read on: *"A variety of medical conditions can be treated with judicious application of atropine. They are based on the experimental TOXIC, as distinguished from the LETHAL DOSE. A lethal dose of belladonna would result in death from combined cardiac and respiratory failure. Depending on the dose, and if it had been ingested on an empty stomach, paralysis would occur almost instantly, and death within a few hours."*

The librarian finished with the radiators and, pleased with her efficiency, clucked her way toward the research area of the library. Quickly, Marie returned the encyclopedia volumes to their correct spot on the shelf. Paulie began making hunger cries.

The librarian was startled. "My goodness, I didn't know you were here."

"Oh yes," said Marie. "You were busy; I didn't want to bother you." She picked up Paulie and headed for the door.

"Come again," said the librarian to Marie's back, "and next time please announce yourself."

~~~~~~~~

Trudy was trying to knit again, this time a Norwegian ski-jumping hat for Hal. She'd started it two years ago when he made the Nordic ski team at Dartmouth. When it wasn't ready for his October birthday, she tried for Christmas this year. She reached for her cup of tea. Blue and white balls of yarn fell from her lap and rolled across the floor.

"Phooey." Slowly she put down the teacup and sat back in the wing chair. "Harold, would you mind kicking those back in this direction?"

Harold put the record needle down at the beginning of the "Skater's Waltz" and looked at the rolling balls of yarn, then at Trudy. "Is that the famous ski-jumping hat?" He chuckled. "You are aware that it's January, the ski season ends in another month, and our son will graduate in June?"

The family joke about the Nordic ski hat did not

amuse Trudy today. Right now knitting was an excuse for sitting by the fire and not talking, or pretending to listen to Harold as he discussed their future, now that the paper mill was gone.

Harold put a log in the fire and stood at the hearth, feeling pleased with himself. "Had a good talk with the insurance company this morning. It seems the mill was completely covered."

"Pearl two down…shh, I'm thinking," said Trudy.

"Soon as the paperwork is done I want to put this place up for sale," said Harold.

Trudy couldn't ignore that. "What?"

Harold smiled. "We'll sell, move to Boston, do some traveling." He walked toward the kitchen. "Any of those Christmas cookies left?"

"What in blazes are you talking about?" said Trudy.

Harold pushed open the door to the pantry. "Cookies – those Christmas things." He was opening cupboards. "Maybe you'll even get me to Europe."

Trudy stopped all pretenses of knitting and waited for Harold to sit down.

"This is all I could find," said Harold, holding out a plate with four star-shaped sugar cookies on it.

"Harold," said Trudy, "in the first place, I do not want to live in Boston, and secondly, how can you even *think* of moving away so soon after what's happened? My God – people have died!" Trudy looked at her husband with a mixture of anger and bewilderment.

"Died. In your mill."

"Now just a minute here," snapped Harold. "I ran that mill for *them*. They're the ones who wanted to work at night – don't hang that on me!"

"Yes. Work…at something safe…" Trudy hesitated, thinking she'd gone too far.

"Oh, now you're suggesting I ran a faulty mill?"

"I'm not suggesting anything, I…" Trudy searched for the right words. "I feel we should support the families, we have a moral obligation to – "

"To what?" said Harold. "Feed them? Fine – open a soup kitchen."

"No," said Trudy. "I'm just not going to run out of town. I'd like to see how people are getting along. Marie's coming tomorrow. She's been through a lot."

"I suppose that's my fault," said Harold.

"There are some nasty cold germs going around." said Trudy, wanting to change the subject. "Doris at the drugstore said Dr. Barnes had to cancel his appointments for two days."

"Ha, way to go, Doc, close your doors as soon as the sickos show up."

"*He's* the one who's sick," said Trudy. She picked up her teacup and walked toward the front stairs. "I don't feel so great either. I'm going to bed."

"You're not going to finish your tea?"

"I'll take it up with me," said Trudy.

Harold picked up the last sugar cookie from the

plate. "Tell Marie to make some cookies tomorrow."

~~~~~~~~~

Marie gave Paulie a little extra milk for lunch. He gurgled and smiled. Sunbeams bouncing off the ceiling held his attention. Marie pushed the crib toward the window so he could continue enjoying the light show, while she busied herself in the kitchen. She removed a saucepan from the stove. While the "nightshade tea" of berries and leaves was cooling, she cleaned two empty nose-drop bottles. She tested the dropper, filling it with water and squirting it out. Then, satisfied that they worked, she filled each bottle, carefully screwing on the combination top and dropper. She held each bottle up to the light. The liquid was a dark green color. She was pleased. It would blend nicely.

It was rough going, trying to push the carriage on a snowy sidewalk, but Marie knew it would be easier for Clara Fawcett to keep an eye on Paulie if he was contained in the baby carriage. And of course, Margarite gave her the carriage. She had to use it.

Clara opened the door with a burst of enthusiasm. "Come on in! I can't wait to see that baby." She stood to the side in the small front hallway and made room for Marie to push the carriage over the threshold. Marie was concerned about tracking in snow on the wheels.

"Don't worry about that," said Clara. "A little snow is good for the rugs – picks up the dirt." She smiled at Paulie and was given a happy gurgle in return. "Will ya look at him. What a happy fella."

"Yes, he's a good baby; fusses when he's hungry, lets out real good screams. But then, after a feeding, he settles right down. Likes to look around a lot." Marie noticed all the Victorian bric-a-brac in the front parlor. "Lookin' at all those pretty plates 'n things will keep him happy for hours – just don't let him near them – ha-ha."

Marie explained to Clara that she usually stayed at the Walkers' until six or six-thirty. Sometimes after their tea, they asked her to prepare a small supper for them and leave it on the stove, ready to warm up. She gave Clara the Walkers' telephone number. "Be sure to call me if you have any trouble with him," said Marie.

Clara took the slip of paper and put it in her apron pocket. "Pshaw – trouble? We're gonna have fun!"

Looking around the cozy room, Marie was inclined to agree. She smiled at Paulie and then Clara. "Thank you. I'll be back by six-thirty at the latest."

Marie stood a moment at the bottom of the outside steps to the Walkers' kitchen. Taking a deep breath, she walked up slowly, noting that the wind had blown most of the sand off the steps. Icy patches were exposed. For a fleeting moment she thought it might be easier if Harold Walker were to fall down these and break his neck. She gripped her pocketbook firmly and knocked on the back door as she opened it.

"Hello, it's me – Marie."

She was surprised to see Mrs. Walker in her

bathrobe.

"Hello Marie," said Trudy in a raspy voice. "How are you?"

Marie placed her pocket book on the wooden coat rack next to the back door, then put her overcoat firmly on top of it. "I'm fine. Doesn't seem you are."

"No," Trudy attempted to laugh. "Nasty cold's got me down. Just wanted to say hello." She poured some ginger ale in a glass. I'm going back upstairs. Mr. Walker's in the library; he'd love some tea."

Marie went to the kitchen sink and began filling the teakettle with water. "I can bring up a separate pot of tea for you."

"No, thanks." Trudy held up the glass of ginger ale. "This is all I can handle." She walked to the door connecting the pantry and library. "I'll tell Mr. Walker you're here, and – if you have time, could you make up a batch of those vanilla wafers, you know – the little ones you used to make…"

"I'll see what I can do," said Marie. "They won't be ready 'til tomorrow, though."

"Thank you," said Trudy. "And, Marie…how's your grandchild? A little boy, isn't it?"

"Yes, a boy. He's fine," said Marie, walking to the stove with the kettle.

"Good." Trudy hesitated at the doorway. "You do know how dreadfully sorry we are about your daughter?"

Marie simply nodded her head. "I'll take the tea in to

Mr. Walker as soon as it's ready."

"Yes, of course," said Trudy, understanding that the subject was closed. She went into the library to alert Harold of Marie's arrival.

Harold was tending the fire. It was smoking. "Useless wood. I ask that moron handyman of ours to bring in *dry* wood. Can he do it? No – of course not. Now I have to use all the kindling just to keep a little fire going."

"You fuss with it too much," said Trudy. "Marie's here. She'll be bringing your tea in shortly."

"Good. Has she got that kid with her?" Harold kicked a log further into the fireplace. The flames started going straight up. He was satisfied and went back to his chair. "I don't want to hear a lot of squalling."

"Keep your voice down," said Trudy. "She'll hear you, and no, the baby's not here. I don't know where he is. I didn't ask."

Harold put on the "Skater's Waltz" and resumed reading the newspaper.

Trudy walked over to Harold and poked at the newspaper. "I'm going back to bed. Please be civil and don't say anything about the child."

"You don't have to worry about *that*," said Harold, as he adjusted the newspaper.

Marie tiptoed over to the pantry door and opened it a crack. She was pleased to hear the music. It meant that Harold was settling down, waiting for tea. She went to her pocketbook and carefully removed one of the nose-drop bottles. She poured three ounces of hot water into a measuring cup, then put in three drops of her own liquid nightshade brew, watching it blend nicely. Checking to see that the silver teapot was warm, she poured out the water and then put in three carefully measured teaspoons of Darjeeling tea leaves, followed by a cup of boiling water from the kettle on the stove, and lastly the nightshade brew went into the silver teapot. She watched it blend with the tea before pushing down the silver lid. In lieu of cookies, she made two pieces of toast and put them on a plate with butter and jam.

Marie coughed slightly to alert Harold she was bringing in the tea. She pushed open the swinging door from the pantry to the library with her shoulder and walked straight to a drop-leaf table next to Harold's chair.

"Here's your tea. Ring the bell if you want more," said Marie.

Harold dropped the newspaper, ready to greet Marie, only to be looking at her back as she went in the pantry.

"Well – um, thank you. Nice to have you back," said Harold. He poured himself a cup of tea, enjoying the aroma. "Ahh – that's more like it."

The electric mixer made a lot of noise, particularly when it was creaming butter and sugar. Concentrating on getting the right blend, Marie was startled when the kitchen door opened and she saw Harold Walker marching in. She almost dropped the cup of flour she'd measured to put in the sifter.

"Didn't mean to scare you," said Harold, holding out the empty teapot. "Good tea; how about some more."

Marie turned off the mixer and took the pot. Harold stood in the middle of the kitchen, waiting.

"The water has to boil again; I'll bring it in," said Marie.

Harold looked at the cookie batter. "Guess the cookies won't be ready, ha-ha."

Marie turned the mixer back on. "No. Tomorrow."

Harold didn't know what else to say so he returned to the library. He assumed that Marie's abrupt answers had something to do with the loss of her daughter. Oh well, he thought, if it's not one thing, it's another with these people.

Marie continued creaming the butter and sugar for a few more minutes. When the mixture was light she stirred in the vanilla flavoring and flour, then, covering the bowl with a damp dishtowel, she put it all in the refrigerator. Once assured that Harold was back in his chair by the fire, she took the jar of nightshade tea from her pocketbook. Placing the teapot on the kitchen counter, she lifted the lid, preparing to put two more drops of her brew in with the Darjeeling tea. Suddenly, there was a crash at the bottom of the back stairs. Marie's hand shook, the nightshade brew spilled over the counter and into the sink. Panicked, Marie stuffed the bottle in her apron pocket and started running water in the sink.

Trudy stood in the back hallway, chastising herself for dropping the ginger-ale glass. "Honestly, I can't do anything today." She leaned over to pick up the broken pieces of glass and bumped her head on the door handle. "Ouch! Honestly – I'm useless."

"Let me get that. Sit down," said Marie. "I'll get you another ginger ale. I'm just fixing some more tea for Mr. Walker."

"Thanks," said Trudy, sitting at the kitchen table. "I'll just catch my breath. Boy – this is some bug I've got." She nodded toward the library. "Hope he doesn't get it. Then we'll *all* suffer."

Marie started sweeping up the bits of broken glass. "Don't worry, I'll give him lots of tea. Plenty o' fluids, that's what the doctors say." She put the glass shards in a wastebasket and went to the stove. Water in the teakettle was boiling over.

"Ha, no need to worry about Harold's fluid intake, said Trudy." They both heard the bell Harold insisted on ringing. "Oh for Pete's sake. Here, give me the tea. I'll take it in to him."

Marie moved to the edge of the sink, putting her hand on the teapot. "No, no – it's not quite ready; leave it to me."

"Okay, I guess you'd better, I'm likely to spill it." Trudy got up and headed for the back stairs. "Oh, I almost forgot," she said, turning around. "Ray Le Bec called, I have to tell Harold."

Harold was still reading the newspaper, and intermittently ringing the bell. He didn't look up when Trudy came in the library. "Put it right there," he said, pointing to the side table.

"Harold," said Trudy. "Stop ringing that bell. She'll bring it in when it's ready."

"Oh, thought you were Marie. What's taking so long?" He looked at her quizzically. "I thought you were – "

"Yes. I was upstairs. I came down to get some more ginger ale, then the glass broke." She sat on the edge of a chair opposite Harold. "I almost forgot, Ray Le Bec called earlier today. He wanted to know about Christmas bonus checks."

Harold slapped the newspaper into his lap. "Bonus checks? Is the man out of his mind?"

"No," said Trudy, "and that's not an unreasonable request – particularly this year."

Harold took a deep breath. "My dear Trudy, *this* year there's no longer a mill, or have you forgotten?"

Trudy's jaw dropped. Words failed her. She wanted to pick up the lamp and throw it at Harold. But just as she contemplated *which* lamp, the pantry door opened.

Without a word Marie walked in and placed the fresh pot of tea next to Harold. "I'll be back tomorrow at three."

"Thank you, Marie, for all your help," said Trudy.

"Yes, the tea's excellent," said Harold, "excellent

taste." He poured some in his cup. "Trudy, sure I can't give you some?"

Marie turned around abruptly. "No. That wouldn't be a good idea – not with your cold."

Harold looked at Trudy with a bemused expression, as if to say, *"since when is Marie an authority on colds?"*

Ignoring him, Trudy looked at Marie. "Thanks again. See you tomorrow." She opened the door to the front hall and walked up the front stairs without another word to Harold. Marie returned to the kitchen.

After wiping the counter to remove all signs of the spilled nightshade, Marie hung up the dishtowel; then, thinking better of it, she stuffed it in her coat pocket.

By the time Marie returned to Margarite's house, Clara Fawcett had left. She found Margarite asleep in a Victorian rocking chair with a very content baby in her lap. All thoughts of the Walkers' house and her activities for the past two hours vanished. She sat on the love seat. A Currier & Ives print hanging on the wall behind her was reflected in the gold-gilt-framed mirror above Margarite's head. Marie let herself lean back and let out the breath she'd been holding all afternoon.

Margarite opened her eyes. "Nice, isn't it?"

"Oh. I thought you were asleep," said Marie.

"No, just relaxing my eyes." She sat up, gently shifting Paulie, and pointed to the print. "I've always liked that Currier & Ives scene. The snow-covered cottage seems so cozy."

"Hmm, like this room," said Marie.

Paulie woke up. Margarite smiled at him and rocked back and forth in the chair. "I think you could be comfortable here." Paulie gurgled. "I know *he* likes it. Clara said he was as good as gold all afternoon."

Marie rose from the love seat and went to take Paulie from Margarite's arms. "I'm glad he was good, but now we have to go home."

Margarite handed him over. "How'd you like to move in here – permanently? Clara's moving to Walpole, and I'm not getting any younger. I'd appreciate the company, and the help." Before Marie could say no, Margarite put her hand up to stop any discussion. "Don't answer now. Just think about it. And no – I'm not senile. I'm simply realistic." Margarite didn't have to say what they both knew. With no paper mill to support it, the apartment building would soon be sold. All of the tenants would *have* to leave.

"All right," said Marie, "I'll think about it." She looked around the crowded room: lamps, bric-brac, china plates – all sorts of things a little boy could break.

Margarite followed her gaze. "All of that can be put away." She got up and walked to the door with Marie. "As for you – well, there won't be so many memories here."

"Yes, yes – I understand," said Marie, wishing at the moment just to be at home – alone with her thoughts. "I'll think about it."

~~~~~~~~

Trudy felt well enough to make herself some chicken soup and sit in the library with Harold. Marie had finished baking the cookies and poked her head in the library to tell them that the tea would be ready shortly.

"I'll stick with the soup," said Trudy. "Sure you don't want any?" she asked, looking at Harold. "Looks like *you're* coming down with something."

"I felt punk last night, kinda breathless," said Harold, "but it's not so bad now; tea will hit the spot." Harold called into the kitchen, "Give it some extra oomph."

Marie did not bother to respond. She'd already put a double dose of her nightshade brew in the silver teapot. Then, to mask any bitterness, she put in a few leaves of Lapsang Souchong tea. Her next step was to warm the teacup itself. The longer the tea stayed warm, the better; Harold would want a second cup, maybe a third. She swished hot water in the cup until it felt warm, dried it carefully, and put it on the silver tray next to the teapot.

Harold looked up from his newspaper. "Ahh, the best tea this side of Boston – ha-ha – glad they didn't throw this overboard."

Marie placed the tray on a table next to Harold. She turned to Trudy. "I have to leave now and pick up Paulie. I can come in after the weekend – on Monday."

"Splendid," said Trudy. "And you're welcome to bring…" Before she could finish the sentence Marie was gone.

"What are you *thinking*," said Harold. "The last thing we need is her bastard grandkid getting attached to us. I suppose Marie's already picked out a room for him."

"No, Harold." Trudy poured his tea and held out the cup. "Here, take your precious tea."

The phone rang. Trudy answered and listened as the caller announced himself. She put her hand over the receiver. "It's Ray Le Bec. He wants to talk to you."

Harold mouthed, "NO."

Trudy spoke to Ray. "He's busy at the moment, Ray. Can I have him call you back?" She put the receiver back on the phone. "Harold, that's just plain mean."

"I'm not interrupting my tea for him." He took a big gulp.

"You know darn well I'm not talking about tea. I think you can afford a few well deserved Christmas checks." Trudy got up and stood next to the fireplace. "It feels damp in here." She warmed her hands over the fire. "Now more than ever is the time to extend ourselves – *reach out* to the families."

"Extend – extend ourselves! My dear woman, *we* are extended. If the insurance company doesn't cough up something pretty damn quick, this house, and everything in it, will be on the auction block before you can say bankrupt." Harold got up and went to the liquor cabinet. "Where's the bourbon?" He settled for Irish whiskey and poured some into his teacup. "Thanks to that Canuck, Le Bec, the insurance snoops are asking questions about electrical failures at the mill."

Trudy turned to look at Harold. "Didn't Ray have trouble with the wiring months ago...long before the party? I thought something came up last summer."

"Listen," said Harold. "A: I'm not sure there ever was a problem. B: If there was, it was Le Bec's responsibility to fix it. Not mine." Harold finished the whiskey and poured more tea into his cup. "Besides, last summer he was seen talking to some of those Commie union organizers."

"What's that got to do with anything? You're not implying that he – "

"No," said Harold. "What I'm *saying* is...I don't trust the guy, I don't like the guy, and he's not getting one red cent from me." Harold wiped his brow with a napkin. " It's gettin' hot in here, and now I can't breathe." He took a deep breath and felt some relief. "Ah – that's better – see what this talk does to me?"

"I still think the mill should give some money to families who worked there; really, Harold, all those years – and now they have nothing!"

Harold poured more Irish whiskey in his teacup. "Save your sob stories. You might need them for us, particularly if our son, your boy prince, doesn't take that banking job when he graduates."

Trudy tightened the sash of her bathrobe. "I've had enough of this. I'm going back to bed."

"Enough of what? Pray tell...the good life in Bellows

Falls, Vermont? A maid in every household – a chicken in every pot?" Harold poured more tea and Irish whiskey into his teacup. "Boy – I tell ya that's class – not everyone can have the grandmother of a little bastard mill baby serving 'em tea every day – in china teacups no less." He raised the cup as if to make a toast and downed the tea in one gulp.

"For your information," said Trudy, "that grandmother has done more work than…" Trudy put her soup cup on the table. "You're drunk. Get your own damn supper."

"Yes, I believe I will." He finished the tea and mopped his brow again. "What could be a better end to afternoon tea than supper out in our fair city." Harold stood up, steadied himself on the back of the chair, then stared at the fire for a moment. "Ah yes," he said, placing the fire screen in front of the fireplace. "There, nice 'n tidy."

Trudy waited in the front hallway, wondering if she should try to stop him from driving in his drunken condition. But after a few seconds, she went up to bed, knowing it would be useless.

At first, Harold thought he'd go to the dining room in the Bellows Falls Hotel. It wasn't unusual on a Friday evening for his friends to congregate there for a drink or two and an early supper. On many occasions, he'd been there talking politics and banking with Sam Aldrich. Tonight, however, he was riled up over Ray Le Bec's phone call and wanted to set things straight with him. The bastard, thought Harold, he has no right to ask me for a Christmas bonus. Harold passed the hotel and continued driving down Main Street, then right onto Canal Street. From there he could see the lights of the Riverview Tavern. He guessed that Ray might be there. And sure enough, Ray Le Bec's car was in the parking lot.

The Tavern was filled with cigarette smoke. When Harold took a seat at the end of the bar, conversations around him all but ceased. He leaned on the bar to catch his breath.

The bartender took his time getting to him. "Slumming tonight, Harold?"

"I'll have Irish – on the rocks. And no, to answer your question, I'm here to see Le Bec."

Ray Le Bec was at the other end of the bar. "You've seen me, now get out."

Harold picked up his glass of Irish whiskey and walked down to Ray. "Not before I settle up with you."

Ray smiled and spoke to the attentive crowd at the bar. "Listen up, everyone: ole man Walker here is gonna tell us about how poor he is." He got off the barstool and stood within inches of Harold's face. "No Christmas checks, no compensation, no nothin' – in other words, t' hell with anyone who kept his firetrap mill goin'." Bits of sputum flying from Ray's mouth landed on Harold's necktie. "Why..." said Ray, playing to the crowd, "I betcha his own *gran*-kid won't see a dime."

Harold threw his drink at Ray. "What in hell are you talkin' about?"

Ray responded with a right hook to Harold's jaw. Harold staggered, but didn't fall. Ray snickered. "Nothin' new, ole man, nothin' new; it's an old story – rich kid – poor girl – and then…surprise, surprise – a baby." Ray snickered at Harold. "Only this time, Walker, the *rich kid* is *your son*."

Harold, taller and heavier than Ray, grabbed him by his shirt collar. "You son-of-a bitch! You spread any more rumors like that 'n I'll have you arrested."

Ray punched Harold in the stomach. "Get your filthy hands off me."

The bartender came out from behind the bar. "Okay, that's enough…both o' you – get out." He stepped between them, pushing Ray back from Harold.

"Yeah, it stinks in here," said Ray. He put a ten-dollar bill on the counter. "That'll take care o' my drinks. I'm gettin' some fresh air." As Ray walked to the door, the other patrons in the tavern clapped their hands.

Harold started after Ray, but he was too slow, he was having trouble breathing. Instead of walking, he shuffled. By the time he got outside, Ray was in his car heading out of the lot, and almost sideswiped Harold.

"Why you no good…" yelled Harold. He hauled himself into his car. Hurtling along the icy streets, chasing Ray, Harold's anger accelerated. He could feel his heart pounding in his chest. His mouth was dry, and his skin felt as if it would crack. As his rage mounted, his vision became blurry. He thought he was having a heart attack and told himself to slow down, but he couldn't. All he could do was hang on to the steering wheel. His foot hit the accelerator like a bag of cement. Suddenly, Ray's car became three cars, then none. Then no road, just a vast empty lot, and a lone streetlight shining on a brick wall. Harold thought that Ray was playing games, hiding behind the wall. He'd fix that crummy Canuck – he'd drive through the wall, get him on the other side. He'd beat the living crap out of him.

From the darkened side of the parking lot Ray waited in his car. He watched Harold drive full speed into the one remaining brick wall of the burned-out paper mill. "Good riddance." Ray remained in the shadows for a few minutes, then drove home and called the police station to report an accident.

The phone rang and woke her up. Trudy knocked the bedside lamp over. "Hello?" She heard someone clearing his throat. *"Hello!"*

"Mrs. Walker…?"

"Yes. Who's this?"

"This is Police Sergeant Davies – Bellows Falls. There's been an accident – "

"Oh no!" Trudy reached across the bed for Harold. He wasn't there. "Was anybody hurt?"

"It's Mr. Walker – he's in the hospital," said Sergeant Davies.

"Yes, I heard you," said Trudy. "He was drunk. I'll never forgive him if he ran into someone."

"Ma'am, he hit a brick wall – he's dead. Probably a heart attack, they said."

Trudy's hand started shaking. "Oh, I see… I'll be right there. Don't touch him – I mean tell them I'm coming to the hospital." She held the telephone in both hands and tried to keep her voice steady. "I'll have to call my son. He's in Hanover. Thank you for calling." Gently Trudy placed the phone in the receiver, almost as if it would break.

"Oh Harold, what were you doing? Why – why?" She looked at the alarm clock on Harold's side of the bed: nine-fifteen. Then, she wondered what time it was when he hit the wall. "Poor Harold, you never wanted to be here – with the mill – did you?" Trudy choked back a sob. No, she thought, cry later, call Hal now.

Trudy felt utterly helpless. She couldn't sit still. The doctor was attending other patients. After all, they were still living. What else could he do for Harold? Dr. Barnes had asked if she wanted to see Harold before they took him to the morgue. She said, "No. I mean, please leave him in his room. Wait 'til Hal arrives. We'll look at him together." She sat down and put her head in her hands. *I should have stopped him*, she thought. *Harold – what were you thinking! Just because we disagreed about the Christmas bonus – damn-it, you didn't have to kill yourself.* She twisted her wedding ring. *We really did get along –you and I – most of the time.*

From the hallway Trudy could hear Hal. "I *know* it's past visiting hours; I'm here to see my dad, and my mom. Where is she?" Ignoring the consternation of the receptionist, Hal burst through the door of the waiting room.

Trudy could not hold back her tears. She ran across the room to her son. "Oh Hal – he's gone."

"Whadd'ya mean *gone?* The message – my roommate said it was an accident." Hal put his arm around his mother's shoulders while she tried to stop crying.

"Yes, that's what I told him," said Trudy. "I didn't want to say it over the phone." She went back to the chair and pointed to the one next to it. "Sit down." Trudy looked straight ahead as she spoke. "Evidently he'd been drinking, became disoriented and drove into a brick wall. They are guessing he had a heart attack, either before or after." Her voice drifted off. "I…I don't know."

Hal swallowed a few times and pressed his forehead between his thumb and index finger. "I suppose we ask for an autopsy…?"

"Yes. Dr. Barnes told me the medical examiner does that." It was becoming an effort for Trudy to speak. She stood up. "Come on, let's say goodbye to your father."

87

~~~~~~~~

Because the medical examiner would not be in Bellows Falls for another week, thus delaying the autopsy, Trudy and Hal decided to have a memorial service for Harold within three days. A notice of the time and date of the service was in the newspaper the morning following Harold's death.

The Immanuel Episcopal Church was filled to capacity with Harold and Trudy's friends, some of Hal's, and most everyone who had worked in the mill, with the notable exception of Ray Le Bec. When the police questioned Ray about the accident, he made no bones about it, telling them the truth: how he and Harold started fighting back at the tavern, and then the jackass started chasing him all over town in his car. Ray said he hated the cheap son-of-a-bitch, but he sure as hell didn't make him drive into the wall. No sir, ole man Walker did that all by himself .

SIX

After the memorial service, Trudy and Hal hosted a reception at their house. Trudy was surprised when Marie declined to help serve the food. She wondered if it had something to do with the baby, and decided to pay her a visit in a few days.

Trudy's friends brought sandwiches and casseroles. When the last guest left, Hal took charge of cleaning up, hoping his mother would finally sit down. Of course she didn't. Nor did she stop talking. It seemed as if she was determined to plan the rest of their lives right then and there.

"Mom, whoa – I have to graduate first," said Hal.

"Of course," said Trudy, "what I'm saying is that *I'll* spend the next month or so in New York, until this house is sold, then…" she started drying the teacups Hal had been washing. "I think I'll redo my little house in Brownsville."

"Brownsville? Vermont?" said Hal. "Why not New York, or Boston?"

"Because, unlike your father, I really like Vermont."

She looked out the window at the gravel driveway and the large house next door. "You didn't know it, but I always wanted to buy an old farm, live in the country, surrounded by fields and hills." She waited for Hal to hand her the last cup. "Your father would have none of it. So…I made a life here."

Hal emptied the dishpan and watched the water drain out of the sink. "Well, you made a nice life – I liked it." The water in the sink became sluggish. He removed the strainer. "Huh, I didn't know you still had that house in Brownsville."

"You wouldn't remember, but in spite of your father's misgivings, I kept it after my parents died."

"Brownsville…that's Mount Ascutney. I've climbed up it a couple of times with some guys from the outing club – we had a race, nice trails."

"Good," said Trudy, "you can take me up sometime – at a slow walk."

Hal was still concentrating on the sink drain. "Something's clogged…"

Trudy leaned down. "What?"

"This'll work." Hal took a fork from the dish rack. He jabbed two swollen berries from inside the drain and held them up triumphantly. "There's your culprit: the bittersweet berries."

"How'd they ever get there?" said Trudy.

"Mom…you had 'em all over the house."

"Yes, but I didn't think – well, Marie must have put

some in vases." She pointed to a wastebasket. "Throw 'em away. Let's go sit by the fire."

Hal avoided sitting in his father's chair. He pulled a footstool next to the fireplace and sat down. Trudy noticed, but said nothing. She went to her usual chair.

"During the next few days, I'd like you to think about which pieces of furniture you'd like me to keep for you," said Trudy.

Hal shrugged. "I don't know. I don't even have a job – how am I supposed to – "

"Storage – I can put everything in storage until we both know what's going on." Trudy picked up a pad of paper from the end table next to her chair. "Which reminds me, I've got a few small things that I'd like to give to Marie."

The fire was getting hot. Hal stood up. "I noticed Marie at the service, standing in the back. I don't think she stayed long."

"No, she has that baby. I told you, didn't I? Yes, her daughter Jenette had a little boy and then, the poor dear... It's just tragic. I hate to think about it."

"What's Marie gonna do?" asked Hal, staring at the flames, unable to look at his mother. "I mean, you're moving – won't she have to work?" Hal was puzzled over Marie's silence. He wondered why she hadn't told everyone he was the baby's father. It might have changed things. Maybe *he* should say something. But, no, he couldn't spoil his mother's dreams for his future.

"Mercifully, Margarite Pierson's going to take her, and the baby. Marie will be a housekeeper – a caretaker."

"That's nice," said Hal, momentarily relieved.

"When are you going back up to Hanover?" asked Trudy as she started making another list.

"Tomorrow," said Hal. "Midterms start, and – um, well, I need to study."

Trudy put down her note pad and looked directly at Hal. "I know, dear. This has been hard on you, and it will be for quite awhile. There's no way around it."

"Just as bad for you," said Hal.

"Yes and no," said Trudy. She twisted her wedding band and gazed beyond Hal, at the empty chair. "I honestly don't know. I've never been a widow."

Hal smiled at his mother's way of putting it. "You're strong, Mom, you always have been."

"And so are you." Trudy wanted to change the subject. She clapped her hands and stood up. "Come on, let's have a house tour. You tell me what you'd like to see in that New York penthouse you'll have someday."

Hal put the fire screen up and followed his mother's lead.

The next morning, soon after Hal left for Hanover, Trudy put a few things in a basket for Marie: a small glass pitcher that Marie always admired, two miniature porcelain vases, and a silver sugar spoon – a souvenir from Montreal. Behind the back stairs, in a cardboard box, were some old toys of Hal's. Trudy had intended to give them to the church. She picked out a small wooden truck, rubbed off the dust, and put that in.

Marie did not welcome Trudy's visit. Right away, she said she was busy with Paulie, and had to get to Margarite's house.

Trudy stepped over the threshold into Marie's modest living room. "Margarite told me that you'll be moving in with her." Trudy held out the basket. "I thought you might like to have these. I know you admired them, and well, I'm going to be selling the house."

"You'll have to excuse me," said Marie, "Paulie needs his bottle." She walked over to the crib in the corner of the living room and picked up her grandson, holding him tightly, in a protective manner.

Trudy followed Marie into the kitchen and put the basket on the kitchen table. "Just a few things: the pitcher you used to like and – "

Marie, holding Paulie in one arm, silently turned her back to Trudy as she warmed the baby's milk bottle in a saucepan on the stove.

Trudy made one final attempt. "This is an old truck of Hal's. Maybe in few months your grandson would like it."

"No, thank you," said Marie, her back still to Trudy. "I won't have much room at Margarite's."

Paulie started crying. Marie had to sit down with him to give him his milk.

Trudy stepped around the kitchen table to get a good look at the baby. She smiled and reached out to tickle his tummy before Marie could react. "Hi there," said Trudy, "you're a big boy – hungry, aren't ya."

For a second Paulie stopped crying. He smiled at Trudy. In that split second of a smile Trudy saw her own son. *Oh dear,* she thought and instinctively gasped, and put her hand to her mouth.

Marie noticed Trudy's reaction. She stood up and walked into the living room with Paulie, holding him in a way that made his face less visible. "Paulie comes by his name for a reason; he's the spittin' image of his Grandpa Paul."

Trudy heard what she said, but all she saw was Hal. On a table next to the couch were framed pictures of Paul Senior and Jenette. Trudy bent down to look at them, willing herself to say something. "Yes, I guess you're right... Maybe a little Jenette too?"

"Jenette was a smaller baby," said Marie flatly.

"Of course," said Trudy, as she stood staring at the back of Paulie's head. "I assume the boy's father was big – "

"Yes," said Marie. "Don't forget the basket."

Trudy was at the door. "Why don't I leave it?" she said. "Anything you don't want – well, I can pick it up another time."

As soon as the door closed behind Trudy, hot tears burned Marie's eyes. Rage, then fear filled every pore of her body. Does she suspect something? Does she know how Harold died? No – the newspaper said *heart attack* – nothing else. But Paulie? Did she see the resemblance? She picked up her grandson and held him tightly. "No one can have you. We'll get money somehow. And we *do* have a place to live – that's a start."

Marie got up and put Paulie in his crib. "You stay there while I pack our things. Margarite's going to see us sooner than she thought." She took a worn leather satchel from the closet in her bedroom. The address label still read St. Jovite, Canada. Marie held it for a minute. *Maybe? No. Paulie will be better off here.* Paulie let out a squawk, as if to confirm her decision.

Marie opened the satchel and started putting her clothes in it. *What's done is done – no use in looking back.*

SEVEN

Trudy needed to keep busy with something repetitious, like wrapping cups and saucers and putting them in a cardboard box. On the kitchen counter was the autopsy report.

It stated clearly that Harold had died of a massive coronary – due in part to high blood alcohol. The injuries to Harold's body made it impossible to give a description of his overall condition. As best as could be determined, Harold had a small ulcer on his stomach lining, and traces of belladonna were found in his small intestine. The medical examiner went on to say that excessive use of cough syrup would explain the belladonna.

This puzzled her. Harold rarely used cough syrup. There wasn't any in the house. She'd checked their medicine cabinet – no cough syrup. As for the ulcer, she remembered that Dr. Barnes had specifically told Harold that *no* medication was the best remedy, that, and easing up on the booze and cigarettes. Maybe Harold kept a bottle of cough syrup at the mill for his scratchy cigarette-throat.

She stopped packing the china, took the report from the counter and went into the library. It was painful to read about Harold's death in such a cut-and-dried way, in plain black-and-white. He had lived, and now he was dead. A dead body with an explanation attached to it. This is morbid, she thought, and not the way to remember Harold. She got up and put the report in a carton labeled Medical, closing it firmly – out-of-sight, out-of-mind. Soon she'd call Hal and tell him that the autopsy confirmed the initial police report: his father died of a massive heart attack. And she would add what they both already knew – the tragedy at the mill brought it on. She would not mention the part in the report about traces of belladonna. Hal was too busy with exams to be troubled by any loose ends or inconsistencies. But the word was there, nagging at her – *belladonna* – it sounded Victorian, almost sinister. Trudy shuddered, as if to shake it off.

After giving herself a few more minutes to collect her thoughts Trudy called Hal. He received the information of the autopsy calmly, and was pleased that he could follow it with some good news. Thanks to Sam Aldrich, he had an interview scheduled with an investment bank in New York the following week. His midterm exams would be over, and he was going to use the break to get a job. In spite of her glum mood, Trudy smiled. Her wonderful Hal – he was on his way.

In the weeks that followed, Trudy emptied and sorted her household in record time. It was one of those funny quirks she had learned about herself long ago. She loved cleaning and organizing things, particularly the part that involved getting rid of stuff. And now, she admitted with a twinge of guilt, she didn't have to worry about saving Harold's *National Geographic* magazines, or Dartmouth College Bulletins. She'd checked with Hal. He had no interest in them. So, the library could have all of it – with her blessing. Next would be the furniture. That took a little more consideration. After deciding which pieces Hal might eventually like, such as Harold's desk, and what she wanted in her Brownsville house, Trudy planned to sell the remaining furniture and china to an antique dealer. After all, what was she going to do with four sets of china, sterling silver flatware – two complete sets, each with place settings for twelve, and enough crystal glasses for three banquets? With no daughters, it seemed silly to keep all of it. However, she thought, someday Hal will marry, and his bride might enjoy an extra set of china. The blue and gold Dalton – she'd keep that. It was pretty and elegant, the way she imagined a wife of Hal's would be. Wrapping the plates carefully in newspaper and placing each one in a cardboard carton, Trudy began to think more about Hal. His years at Dartmouth, the summer he went to Europe, the summers he stayed at home, working here and there, helping farmers with haying, or at the town garage, learning about cars. For some reason she couldn't remember what he did for fun. Did he go out in the evening? Did he date? Or was the work his fun? Funny, she thought, he never talked about girls, but he was gone a lot.

Goodness, when I was his age, she mused, I had a date every night. Last summer, I don't even remember Hal going to parties...he didn't mention any...

An inexplicable, uneasy feeling came over Trudy. She didn't like it. Why was she suddenly thinking about Marie and that baby? What did they have to do with anything? She stopped wrapping the china and put the water on to boil for a cup of tea. It was time for a rest, she reasoned. All this packing and planning – she couldn't think straight. She put some loose tea leaves in a small china teapot, poured in the hot water and let it steep, remembering after the fact that the pot had not been warm, but who cares.

She sat down heavily at the kitchen table. Nowadays, Trudy had tea here instead of the library. She was too lazy to make a fire, and it was easier to write lists at the kitchen table. It was lonely in the library without Harold. With her elbows on the table, she put her chin in her hands, sighing as she looked around the kitchen. A great big old drafty Victorian kitchen. Not much for convenience with five doors, and five – she counted them – *five* – four-by-eight windows. There was little room for counter space in this kitchen, but lots of room to walk. Just getting back and forth from the sink to the stove to the refrigerator was a day's exercise. She smiled, remembering times past. A lot of parties were prepared here. I wonder what changes the next family will make? Maybe knock out the pantry – put the table in there? Or make the whole kitchen a part of the dining room? Something she always wanted to do, but Harold said he didn't want to look at dirty dishes. Hmpf, she thought, as if he had anything to do with them. Well, by golly, she'd make herself comfortable in the Brownsville house. She'd serve small meals right in front of the fireplace, and...

The telephone's ring startled Trudy. It took her a minute to answer.

"Hello," she said, trying to sound pleasant.

"Hello, Trudy, this is Margarite."

"Oh, hello there," said Trudy, feeling better at the sound of Margarite's voice. "I've been thinking of you. You don't need anymore household knick-knacks, do you? I'm packing, and discarding all my worldly goods."

Margarite chuckled. "Goodness no. I'm doing the same thing, making room for Marie and the baby."

Again Trudy felt an odd discomfort. "Oh that's right, she's living with you."

"Yes, she has been for several weeks," said Margarite. "Clara moved to Walpole – her sister's house, and Doctor Barnes says I should have someone here, and well – you know, Marie needed a place to live."

"Yes, I know," said Trudy flatly, wishing she could be

more expansive, but the words weren't coming. After an awkward moment, Trudy remembered that Margarite had called *her*. "Well, Margarite, you don't want my knick-knacks, what else can I do for you today," she laughed, trying to sound light.

"I'm calling to ask you over for a cup of tea," said Margarite. "Marie's doing some errands and the baby's with her."

"Actually I've just had a cup," said Trudy, ungraciously.

"Trudy," said Margarite, "I'd like to talk with you. There are some things you should know."

"All right," said Trudy, in a friendlier tone of voice. "It's two o'clock. I'll be over in ten, fifteen minutes. First I have to call the funeral home, make arrangements for Harold's ashes. They keep them 'til spring…" Her voice trailed off.

Trudy put the phone back on the receiver and sat very still for a moment. Suddenly, she went to her desk in the library. The drawers were open and empty. Then, barely missing a beat, she went to the front hallway and started opening the cartons she'd packed the day before. The second one contained the family photo albums. The most recent were on top. Trudy dug to the bottom and pulled out a large leather-bound album. She walked to the lone chair next to the front stairs and sat down, putting the album in her lap. Ignoring the pit in her stomach, in the dim light of the front hallway, Trudy opened to the first page: Hal as a newborn. The picture showed a baby on its back screaming and kicking. Trudy turned the pages: Hal at four months. Oh dear, she sighed. The knot in her stomach tightened. Maybe it's a fluke, a coincidence – a lot of babies look alike. For a second, Trudy thought of taking the photograph from the album and...*and then what?* she thought. Part of her wanted to confront Marie, but, she reasoned, why not confront Hal? If he's the... This is ridiculous, she thought, Hal *is* the father – clear as day – he should own up to it. But her next thought was more pragmatic: why ruin his life? After all, you don't know for sure, and Hal hasn't said anything.

Trudy's mind was jumping all over the place. It was a simple matter. All she had to do was speak to Marie and promise to support the child. *Hmpf – not likely,* she thought. *Marie doesn't want to see me, or my money.* Trudy put the album back in the carton, with the snapshot in it. She realized that she wasn't making any sense, and told herself to stop jumping to conclusions. These things *do* happen and there *are* solutions. Trudy checked her watch. It was already ten past two. She grabbed her coat and went back in the kitchen to call Margarite.

"Hello, Margarite? It's me, Trudy. I'm just leaving, I got—"

"That's fine," said Margarite, "I'll be out back, pruning."

Pruning? What in the world...? Trudy shook her

103

head in wonder as she hurried along the snowy sidewalk. How old was Margarite anyway? The doctor said she can't be alone, but she's out in this weather pruning the shrubbery? Well, forget that, what are you going to say when she asks you if Hal's the father? Trudy had decided that that was the reason for Margarite's sudden invitation for tea. But darn it, why should it necessarily be Hal? And who's suggesting that? By the time she reached Burt Street and turned toward Margarite's house, Trudy had decided for the time being to be quiet. Let Margarite do the talking. After all, she realized, it's quite possible she just wants to talk about shrubs – maybe her grape arbor? Trudy slowed her pace. She walked up the sanded pathway to the front porch, wondering if Marie had done the shoveling and sanding. Then, seeing Margarite's footprints in the snow, she followed them around to the side of the house.

She called out, announcing herself so she wouldn't startle Margarite. "Hellooo – it's me – Trudy." She lifted her head and smiled, wanting to put aside her crazy thoughts and have a nice chat with her old friend. Someone who graciously welcomed her when she first came to Bellows Falls as Harold's bride. She spoke again, a little louder. "Yoo-hoo – anybody home…?"

Margarite was leaning on the grape arbor. She tried to speak but nothing came out. She waved her hand, the one holding the clippers. Trudy went over to Margarite, thinking she was just out of breath and needed help cutting something. Margarite was pointing to the nightshade vine twisted among the withered grapes, but Trudy saw only her friend's ashen face and her open mouth gasping for breath. "Margarite! What's happened?" Margarite coughed and grabbed one of the crystallized nightshade berries. Trudy wrapped her arm around Margarite's shoulders, supporting her as she gently pulled her away from the arbor. "It's too cold out here," said Trudy, "not the time to be cutting berries." She took the clippers from Margarite and put them in her coat pocket.

Margarite coughed again, clearing her throat. "Important," she rasped, pointing to the berries.

"I know," said Trudy in the tone of a dutiful pupil, "I remember you telling me once: they're deadly but important to the healthy growth of grapes." She took a small step forward, holding Margarite firmly. "Right now the most important thing is getting you inside." For some reason, Margarite looked at her wristwatch, then consented to go in the house. Trudy reassured her. "It's only two-thirty, still time for tea."

Slowly Trudy made her way back to the front of the house and up the steps with Margarite. The house was blissfully warm inside, the front parlor well lit and welcoming with a low flame burning in the gas stove installed in the fireplace. Trudy settled Margarite on the couch, taking her coat off and trying in vain to fluff up two small needlepoint pillows so she could lean back comfortably.

"Hmpf," said Trudy, regarding them with disdain, "I guess they're pretty, but..."

"My sister..." said Margarite, trying to smile, "she likes–"

"Oh dear," said Trudy, apologizing for her bluntness. "I'm sorry, I'll get some tea."

Margarite grabbed Trudy's skirt. "No – wait – no time!" She leaned forward, then fell back on the arm of the couch. She caught her breath and spoke, painfully. "Marie – the vine, it was..." She started coughing, spitting phlegm. "The baby – you must...understand why."

Trudy couldn't listen to this gibberish any longer. Margarite was slipping away before her very eyes. Keeping panic at bay, she pleaded with her, "Please – don't say another word. I'll call Dr. Barnes." She pried Margarite's fingers from her skirt.

"Tea," rasped Margarite. "It was tea." She sighed and stopped.

Trudy spoke gently. "Yes, I know, we were going to have tea together. "She reached for the phone. "But first I'm going to call–"

Margarite's hand shot out to stop her, her expression so intense that Trudy put the phone down. "Listen to me," said Margarite, the words spewing forth with a burst of energy. "Marie needs to take care of that boy." Then, shutting her eyes, she rested, and willed herself to go on.

"She made tea that day, the day Harold died."

"Yes, she always did," said Trudy, "and of course Marie will take good care of the baby."

Margarite knew that Trudy did not understand the meaning of her words. Finally she said, "Leave things as they are for now." Out the parlor window, she saw Marie pushing the carriage up the sanded pathway. "Soon enough you'll see." She shut her eyes. "I'll rest a minute."

At the same time Trudy picked up the telephone, Marie came in the front door. She was holding Paulie in her arms and didn't see Trudy. "We're back," she called.

"Margarite's in here," said Trudy.

"What's wrong," said Marie, stiff as a board, not intending it as a question – more a statement.

"She's short of breath, weak," said Trudy.

Marie saw the phone. "You've called Doctor Barnes?"

"Not yet. I'm about to," said Trudy, not happy with another interruption.

"Good. I'll take care of Paulie and get her some tea."

"I'm sure Margarite will be fine," said Trudy. "For some reason she was outside when I got here, clipping around the grape arbor. Do you know anything about that?"

"No. Why should I?"

"You live here. Margarite might have said something, why she wanted to cut the vines, now – in January."

Marie answered with a cold stare. The chill emanating from her eyes made Trudy shiver ever so slightly. She sat down in a chair next to the couch with her back to Marie, then deliberately picked up the phone and spoke to the telephone operator.

"Would you please ring Doctor Barnes' office? Thank you."

Marie walked over and put her hand on Margarite's forehead. "A nice pot of Earl Grey will make you feel better. I'll put Paulie down for his nap."

"No – don't go to any trouble, I just need to rest a bit," said Margarite.

"That's for sure," said Trudy. "The idea – cutting vines in January."

"I'll be in the kitchen," said Marie abruptly.

As soon as Trudy described Margarite's symptoms, Dr. Barnes rushed over to the house. He had been monitoring her heart closely for the past year, afraid of something like this. Ignoring Margarite's objections, he called an ambulance and had her taken to the hospital, citing the need for specialized medical care and complete rest. Margarite, of course, said that an ambulance ride was anything but comforting. Trudy agreed, but kept her thoughts to herself. As soon as the ambulance left, she said goodbye to Marie, reassuring her that she'd keep her informed about Margarite's condition.

During the short walk back to her house, Trudy tried to figure out why Margarite had called her in the first place. Was it about the baby, or the vines? No, it couldn't have been the vines, that's ridiculous. Margarite wouldn't invite her over to talk about a grape arbor; she wanted to talk about the baby – plain an' simple. But what about Marie? Why can't she just say that Hal's the father? Surely, Jenette would have told her own mother. Unless… Trudy paused and shook her head. Really – this whole thing is absurd. Marie's *got* to know who the father is. I'll ask her straight out and be done with it.

When Trudy got back to her house, she stood outside for a minute and looked up at her grand old Victorian. She'd be glad when it sold. It had really been Harold's house, big and rambling – the largest house on Atkinson Street. He wouldn't admit it, but he bought it just so he could outshine Sam Aldrich. It never occurred to him that Sam couldn't care less. Trudy chuckled to herself. Harold, Harold – appearances meant so much to you. I guess it's a saving grace that you never saw Marie's grandson.

When Trudy finished her musing and walked up the front steps, she heard the telephone ringing.

She pushed open the front door and ran to the phone in the library. "Hello…"

"Mrs. Walker?"

"Yes…" said Trudy.

"This is Doctor Barnes speaking, I'm afraid I have some bad news—"

"Margarite." Trudy sat down. "What's happened?"

"She died on the way to the hospital. There wasn't anything we could do. I'm very sorry to have to tell you this, so soon after Mr. Walker's..." He mumbled the next few words.

"She *died*? Are you sure?" Trudy sat down on the chair next to the telephone. "I'm sorry – I mean, how could she? Just the other day she was fine – this isn't right... Have you called Margarite's house? Have you spoken with her maid Marie?"

"No, you're the first person I've called," said Dr. Barnes. "I don't have her sister's number. Perhaps when you go back to the house you could get it for me."

"Yes, yes, of course, and, um – don't bother to call Marie. I'll go back right now and tell her, and Cynthia's number. I'll get that, so you can call her."

"Thank you," said Dr. Barnes, "and, Mrs. Walker, I am very sorry we couldn't help Margarite."

"I know you are," said Trudy. "Thank you. I – well, Margarite was a dear friend."

Trudy didn't call to tell Marie she was on her way over there. Instinct said not to. Marie would come up with some reason to leave. Well, by god, she has some explaining to do.

Trudy walked so quickly back to Margarite's house that she could feel her own heart pounding in her chest. She knocked on the kitchen door once and opened it. "Marie – it's Trudy Walker."

"I know who you are," said Marie, stepping into the kitchen from the dining room. "Why didn't you use the front door?"

Trudy stepped into the kitchen and shut the door. "Dr. Barnes called me about ten minutes ago. Margarite died on the way to the hospital." She took a deep breath and waited for Marie's reaction.

"I'm surprised that he didn't call me," said Marie.

"Dr. Barnes knows that *I* was an old friend of Margarite's. Quite frankly Marie, I'm not sure *what* you are anymore. This *assumed martyrdom* of yours was all well and good when Jenette died, but now –"

"How dare you!" hissed Marie. "You have no right coming in my house and talking about Jenette."

"*Your* house? As recently as this morning you were employed by Margarite Pierson as a *housekeeper* – there *is* a difference."

"Yes," said Marie with icy calm, "I know where I stand."

Trudy rolled hers eyes, dismissing Marie's apparent ignorance. "That's good. Then perhaps you can tell me, why was an eighty year old woman *outside – in January – cutting a god-damn vine?*"

"I don't have to listen to you."

Paulie was stirring in the playpen. Both women looked at him and lowered their voices. Suddenly Trudy lost her steam. She didn't want her last memories of Margarite to be a shouting match with Marie. "No, no you don't. Not now."

~~~~~~~~

After the funeral service for Margarite at Immanuel Episcopal Church, Cynthia and her husband invited

111

friends of Margarite's back to the house for tea and sandwiches. At first Trudy was going to decline, but realized that would only raise eyebrows and questions – questions she would not want to answer. Marie must have felt the same way. She was civil toward Trudy, and helpful to Cynthia, making sandwiches and serving tea.

When the guests were leaving, Cynthia asked Trudy to stay for a few minutes. She agreed, reluctantly. Aside from her troublesome thoughts about Marie, she was tired of talking about death and the past. She felt depressed and restless all at once. As people lingered in the hallway, getting their coats on, Trudy kept busy taking empty teacups into the kitchen. Marie had put a playpen in the corner of the room for Paulie. He was sleeping on his back, holding a small blanket next to his cheek. For an instant, Trudy felt tears welling up in her eyes. The blanket was in his left hand – just the way Hal held his "blankie." Marie noticed this, but said nothing, choosing instead to maintain a matter-of-fact tone.

"You can put the cups on the table. Thank you."

Trudy cleared her throat. "All right, I'll get the last few in the dining room." Then she nodded toward the playpen. "Good idea – get him used to it. Do you remem –"

Marie interrupted. "He's a good baby – no trouble."

"I'm sure he is," said Trudy. "Do you remember when –" Cynthia came in the kitchen.

"Well, now that we're all in here..." Cynthia said, smiling at Paulie, "why don't we sit down and relax." She picked up a neatly trimmed cucumber sandwich. "Hmm – these are yummy. Walter's gone to get some gas. He'll be back in a few minutes."

Trudy was in no mood for idle chatter. "Yes, they were good," she said. "Now, you said there were some things you wanted to discuss?" She looked at her watch. "I have to run along soon."

"It really isn't much," said Cynthia. She finished chewing the sandwich and wiped her mouth with the corner of the small linen tea napkin she had tucked in the sleeve of her blouse.

"Now that Margarite is gone, Walter and I will have to do something with this house." She looked critically at the old fixtures in the kitchen. "I don't think we'll live here – but then, maybe Walter can fix things up."

Cynthia hadn't noticed Marie's jaw tightening, and the haste in which she stood up. "Margarite left this house to me," said Marie. "I will be living here with my grandson."

"I don't believe that's possible – we were sisters," said Cynthia coolly. "Most of Margarite's things were part of our family. I mean – it's impossible." Now it was Cynthia's turn to tighten her jaw. "I'm not sure why you believe such a thing. Clearly you're mis-informed."

Trudy turned to Marie, waiting for an explanation.

Marie spoke calmly to both of them. "Margarite wrote an – an 'addendum' – I believe that's what it's called, to her will. In it, she leaves me the house, for as long as I wish to be here."

"That's perfectly ridiculous," said Cynthia, nervously patting her mouth with the linen napkin. "I'll see about that."

"I imagine you will," replied Marie.

Trudy stood up. "I'll let you two sort this out." She reached for her overcoat hanging by the back door and nodded toward both women. "Good bye. If you need anything give me a call. I'm going to New York next week, but I'll be back before my house is sold. Say goodbye to Walter for me."

"Yes, I will," said Cynthia.

Trudy was through the door and walking to her car when Walter drove up. Good. He can figure out who owns the house. The last thing I need is this mess.

EIGHT

Trudy returned from New York refreshed and ready to make the final push for her move to Brownsville. Hal came home for one night before going to New York. He felt confident about his midterm exams, and now with just a few more months of college he was eager to secure a job and move to Manhattan. Trudy had packed all of the china, as well as the kitchen utensils, so they went to the hotel for dinner. The Bellows Falls Rotary was finishing its monthly dinner in one of the small function rooms off the main dining room. Several of the members were milling around the lobby. They recognized Trudy and Hal and nodded a greeting in their direction. She smiled and kept walking, hoping to avoid any conversation. Hal wasn't so adroit. He hesitated just enough for Ray Le Bec to plant himself in the doorway to the dining room.

"Hear you're movin' on – to better things," said Ray, expelling puffs of liquor with each breath.

Hal tried to step back from him. "Yes, I have to find a job after graduation."

"Hmpf," said Ray, "not everyone can just leave town 'n start over."

"Yes, I know." Hal tried to walk around Ray to join Trudy in the dining room.

Ray moved sideways a step, blocking his way. "No, *you* don't know nothin' – leastways nothin' you want to admit." Hal could feel the sputum flying out of Ray's mouth. "…just like your ole man – mess up everything 'n leave."

Ray's buddy grabbed his arm. "C'mon, Ray, you've had enough – time to go."

"Yeah, I've had enough," shouted Ray. "I've had it up to here!" He gave Hal the finger and left with his friend.

Hal joined his mother at a table in the dining room. "That was a nice send-off. I thought he was a friend of Dad's."

"He was the foreman at the mill," said Trudy. "He and your father disagreed on things from time to time."

"Does he expect *me* to rebuild the mill?"

"No, don't be–" The waitress came by with menus. "Thank you." Trudy smiled mechanically.

"Is that what people think…?" asked Hal. "We're skipping town? Maybe I should – "

"Don't be ridiculous!" Trudy flipped open the menu. "Hal, listen to me. There's nothing you or I can do to resurrect the mill. Even if we could, it's too late. Small mills are a thing of the past."

Hal picked up the menu. "Yeah, I know, it's just

that…"

"Ray's upset and drunk, he'll get over it." Most of all, Trudy wanted *Hal* to get over it.

"I don't like people to think that we're leaving town," said Hal.

"Well, we are," said Trudy. "You've got a new job, a career to build. And I have to start a new life. These changes happen." She looked around for the waitress. "Let's have a drink. I'm not gonna let the likes of Ray Le Bec ruin our last evening in Bellows Falls."

"Yeah," said Hal. "I'm not exactly in a position to do much anyway."

"That's right," said Trudy, trying to keep the edge off her voice. The waitress came by to take their order. "We'll have a drink first. I'd like a martini – extra, extra dry; that means just a hint of vermouth." The waitress's blank face turned to Hal.

"I'll have a beer – Budweiser, thanks." She wrote the drink orders on her pad and left.

"Mom, do you think they really know how to make a martini here?"

"They should. I've been working on it for twenty years."

Within a few minutes the bartender personally delivered the drinks. "For you, Mrs. Walker, the perfect martini." He placed it in front of Trudy and bowed deeply. "And Monsieur, the perfect American beer."

Hal laughed. "Thank you – just what I wanted."

117

Trudy took a sip of her martini. "Exquisite. You've outdone yourself."

"Our pleasure," replied the bartender. "Michelle will take your order when you're ready."

When he left, Trudy held her glass up. "Here's to us!"

Hal responded and they clinked their glasses. "To the future!"

"So, tell me about Brownsville," said Hal, making an effort to cheer up. "I don't remember much about the house."

"It's small – well, 'bout half the size of this one – I mean, our former home. Comfortable, a mix of colonial, Federal, and..." she laughed, "plain frame farmhouse. I don't think you'd call it a classic." She warmed to the subject. "There are nice open fields around it, and a lovely view of Mount Ascutney, and...a small barn. I might even get me a horse."

"Do you know how to ride?"

"I used to, years ago. I'm sure it'll come back, like riding a bicycle. I tried to talk your father into buying a farm outside of Bellows Falls, but no; he wanted to be in town, in that big old house."

"It was fun growing up there; I loved my room on the third floor."

"Yes, of course," said Trudy, not wanting to spoil her son's childhood memories. "It's a beautiful period piece. I'm sure the new family will enjoy it." The waitress came by again to take their order.

"Sorry, I haven't even looked at the menu," said Hal.

"That's okay," said Trudy. "Let's have the lamb chops; they're always good here."

The waitress looked at Hal. He smiled and handed her the menu. "Sounds good to me. Two orders of lamb chops."

"Now..." said Trudy, enjoying her martini, "tell me about your plans for Manhattan, where ya gonna live, who do ya know..."

"In an apartment – somewhere, I guess. A couple of my friends have jobs on Wall Street. I suppose I can hook up with them."

"That'd be nice, ready-made friends," said Trudy.

"Yeah, but I don't know, I'm kinda sick of the roommate thing. A studio apartment – just me – would be a nice change."

"Hmm – true," said Trudy. The lamb chops had arrived. She smiled at the waitress. "Looks delicious, thank you."

"Would you like anything else?" asked the waitress.

"No, thanks, we're all set," said Trudy.

"Actually a place of your own *is* a good idea. You'll be more likely to branch out, meet people beyond the college crowd." She finished the last of her martini. "For starters, though, before you get a place, do you want to stay with the Butlers? Remember – we spent a Thanksgiving with them – so you could get a glimpse of city life. Duckie and Duncan Butler, they're on Sixty-

Eighth and Park."

Hal was busy with his chop. "Hm, Duckie – yeah, she took me roller skating in Central Park. I was the only boy with *girl's* roller skates. They're still alive?"

"I didn't know there was a difference in roller skates, and of course they're *alive* – Duckie's my age!"

Hal shrugged. "Well, Dad..."

"That's different," said Trudy. "He was under extreme stress. No one knew he had a heart condition. He kept it to himself."

"He didn't like the mill," said Hal. "Was that part of the problem – all the stress ?"

"I don't know, the autopsy revealed some..." Trudy stopped herself. "Some evidence of a weak heart." She didn't want to tell him about the traces of belladonna. It still bothered her. She saw no reason to trouble Hal. "Golly, hard to believe you'll be graduating in a few months. Think you'll miss Dartmouth – your friends? Maybe even a girlfriend or two...?"

"Nope, half the class is going to be in New York." The lamb chop slipped from under Hal's knife.

"Pick it up," said Trudy. "Much easier to eat. Don't miss the bone marrow, makes you–"

"Grow up big and strong," said Hal. "Marie always chanted that when I ate my meals with her in the kitchen." He stopped eating for a minute. "Umm, how is she? I mean with the baby 'n everything..."

"Fine," said Trudy a little too quickly. "She and her

grandson are living in Margarite's old house."

"Oh yeah, you told me…"

"It's good that you don't have any girlfriends," said Trudy, wanting to get off the topic of Marie.

"Oh…?" said Hal, wondering what his mother was getting at.

"I mean for now," explained Trudy. "You want to be independent; starting a career requires focus."

"Yup," said Hal. He looked out at the nearly empty street. "Boy, this town sure can look bleak; wonder what people are going to do for work, now that…"

"January's always a dreary month. Snow doesn't know what to do: melt – freeze – come or go. It's a good time to be someplace else." Trudy felt anxious, concerned that Hal might have second thoughts about going to New York. "Desserts aren't very good here. Let's finish the ice-cream at home."

"Chocolate and vanilla – right?" said Hal with forced gaiety.

"Yup, and paper plates and plastic spoons."

"Just like when I was a kid, and Marie didn't want me to dirty any more dishes."

"I'll pay at the front desk," said Trudy.

Hal awoke early Sunday morning. Out of habit, he went down the back stairs to the kitchen, half-expecting to smell bacon cooking. Except for packing cartons, the only thing in the kitchen was coffee. Trudy had wakened earlier and brewed a pot. Next to the stove was a loaf of bread, some butter and jam.

Trudy came in from the library. "Good morning! Sorry – this is it." She plugged in the toaster. "One or two pieces?"

Hal poured some coffee and sat at the kitchen table where he used to do his homework as a kid. He noticed some of the pencil indentations were still in the wood. "Just one, thanks. I'll eat later when I stop for gas."

They both drank their coffee in silence for a few seconds.

"It seems colder in here," said Hal. He pointed to the empty cupboards. "Less stuff – makes everything look colder."

"Yes, dreary really; I'm going to head up to Brownsville as soon as you go," said Trudy.

"What about all the furniture...and boxes?" asked Hal.

"Movers are coming tomorrow." Trudy rinsed the jam from a butter knife and dropped it in a carton next to the sink. "I'll come back in the morning."

"Oh," said Hal flatly. He pushed himself away from the table and rinsed his coffee cup at the sink. "Well, I guess I'd better get going..."

"Got your suit?"

"Suit?"

Trudy nodded and grinned. "Yes – a suit. Men wear suits in a bank."

"Oh yeah – the interview; I've got my sport coat."

"Uh-huh," said Trudy. "You need your suit – the pinstripe – it's hanging in your closet."

Hal groaned like a kid and started up the back stairs. Trudy patted him on the shoulder. "You look handsome in it."

While Hal collected his suit, Trudy gathered the few remaining clothes she'd left on her bed. The three skirts and blouses fit neatly in a dress bag, along with her favorite cardigan wool sweaters. She put her few toilet articles and wool bathrobe in a small leather overnight suitcase. Its corners were worn and the handle was almost off, but Trudy cherished this bag because it reminded her of her mother and the perfume she'd spilled on the linen lining many years ago.

She stopped at the head of the stairs and called up to Hal in his third floor bedroom. "I'm going to put some things in my car."

Hal scrambled down the stairs, his suit in one hand and some notebooks in another. "Need some help?"

"No," laughed Trudy, "but I'll hold the door for you."

Trudy stood on the front porch waving as Hal drove away. She had pretended to rush him out the door, saying that she didn't want to get all teary-eyed about his leaving. But in fact all Trudy felt was relief. Whew, she thought, he's on his way. Honestly, if given a chance he might have chosen to stay in Bellows Falls. She shook her head and looked around her lifeless house. Goodbye house... goodbye Harold. It's time for me to go, she whispered.

Instead of driving straight down Atkinson Street toward Route 5 North, Trudy turned left onto Burt Street. Maybe, with a different approach, she could get Marie to talk about the baby. And Hal. Marie used to like hearing about his activities. She parked out front and walked gingerly through the slush up to the house. It looked as if more vines had been cut from the grape arbor. How odd, she thought, with everything so frozen.

Marie answered the door after the first knock. "I saw you drive up."

"Yes – I guess you did. You were quick to answer." Trudy started to walk through the partially opened door. "May I come in?"

"I have to tend to Paulie," said Marie, "he's fussing."

Trudy peered into the parlor, where Paulie was sleeping peacefully in a playpen. "I won't bother him." She stood in the small hallway. "I'm moving to Brownsville. I wanted to say goodbye, and let you know where I'll be, in case you..." she glanced at Paulie, "or the baby need anything."

"We're fine," said Marie. "I don't need help."

Trudy chose her words carefully. "I can see that Paulie is fine, and I know you're a strong person." She adjusted her coat and stood up a little straighter. "I was thinking how we've both been through a lot together over the years, particularly recently. You're alone, and a grandmother, and I guess…well, at times it might be difficult, bringing up Paulie." Trudy smiled. "I remember when Hal could be a handful for me *and* his fa – "

"Yes, I am the boy's grandmother. I'm all he's got, and we'll manage, thank you," said Marie.

Trudy felt herself flush with the rejection, but remained calm "Here's my Brownsville number." She handed a slip of paper to Marie. "Call me if you think of anything."

Marie put the paper in the pocket of her apron. "Goodbye, Mrs. Walker."

Trudy wasted no time getting in her car. *Well, damn her*, she thought. *Stubborn, stubborn.* She jammed the stick shift of the station wagon into first, leaving a flume of slush in the air as she turned the car around in the middle of Burt Street and drove back out to Atkinson toward Route 5, and north to Brownsville.

After fuming for a few minutes, Trudy calmed down enough to think that maybe she was manufacturing problems. She only suspected things, and maybe she didn't want to know any more. It all came back to Hal; she was protecting him. *Protecting him from what? Damn it all!* Finally tears came. Frustration, anger, and a lonely, empty ache in her stomach. *Oh Harold, why did you die?*

By the time she got to her house in Brownsville, Trudy's tears had dried. She forced herself to put the past and her crazy imagination aside. She could do that. She'd always been able to will herself into a positive frame of mind. She blocked out the negative by concentrating on two good things: her house and its surrounding pastures, and the prospect of planting peas in the spring. She'd have a Fourth of July party: fresh peas and salmon. She wondered if Brownsville still had a parade on the Fourth. Hal would like that. He could come visit, bring some of his New York friends. Slowly the hollow, empty feeling receded, and when Trudy drove into her driveway she had to smile in spite of herself. It looked as if somebody had just shoveled it. *Lester*, she thought, *you are a gem.* The side door next to the garage was unlocked. Trudy wondered if Lester, anticipating her arrival, had left it like that to make things easier for her. She laughed. He probably remembered her difficulty with locks in general. She could never turn a key the right way. Trudy had called Lester in the morning to say that she'd be arriving in the afternoon. As soon as she entered the kitchen, Trudy felt some warmth in the house, not just the architectural charm – low ceilings, picture window, small brick fireplace, but actual heat from the furnace. Lester, bless that man. She checked the thermostat: right at sixty-four, where her dad always kept it. She shook her head in admiration. He'd probably called for a fuel delivery as well.

Lester and Louise had been living in the little brick house across the road – a narrow dirt road – as long as she could remember. He worked as mechanic in a local garage and drove the school bus for Brownsville. They never had children. Louise made hot lunches for the grammar school and took care of other people's pets when they went away.

Trudy could almost feel the house hugging her as she walked through the living room and up the front stairs. It was reassuring and familiar, the guest room at the top of the stairs, the small guest bath with a tub – no shower. Then the sitting-room, a large, sunny, south-facing room, so-called because her mother used to enjoy sewing in there, and on rainy days she read to Trudy and her brother Carl. Then there was Trudy's old bedroom, small and cozy, with wallpaper of tiny pink roses and white petit-point curtains. She smiled, barely noticing the faded brown spots on the paper. A little hallway led to the "new" part of the house, a larger bathroom, Carl's bedroom, and her parents' old bedroom. Within a few minutes, Trudy decided this would be her "wing": her office, bedroom, and bath. Hal and friends could be in the other rooms. Unlikely that she'd take up sewing, but, who knows, maybe someday there'd be grandkids to read to. Her mind flashed back to Marie and Paulie. *Stop it*, she thought harshly.

"Hullo – you here?"

"Yes! Be right down," said Trudy, as she took the back stairs down to the kitchen. She walked over to Lester and gave him a hearty handshake. "Hello-hello! And thank you so very much," she said spreading her arms out to take in the downstairs. "The house is nice 'n warm and..." she pointed to the fireplace, "...you even brought in some wood."

"Yup. It's winter and still gets cold at night," said Lester, "leastways in Brownsville, don't know 'bout Bellows Falls."

"I'm sure it's colder here, we're further north," laughed Trudy. She lifted the lid off a casserole dish Lester had placed on the counter. "What's this?"

"Louise was makin' some beans. She thought you might be hungry."

Trudy lingered over the open dish. "Hmm, they smell delicious. I can't wait to eat them." She pointed toward the living room. "I'm gonna make a fire and sit in front of it with the whole pot!"

Lester was pleased. "I'll tell her. She's been feelin' poorly, but it always makes her happy to be cooking somethin'."

"Oh, I hope it's nothing serious."

"No...don't think so, but to tell ya the truth, they don't know. She's just doin' poorly."

"Maybe it's a winter virus. Harold and I..." Trudy caught herself mid-sentence. "She's strong – probably be gone in no time."

Lester didn't seem convinced. "Hmm, prob'ly..."

"Tell her I'll pop in tomorrow afternoon, once the movers have gone," said Trudy.

"Movers?" asked Lester. "You bringing some things here?"

Trudy laughed. "Well, yes, I've sold my house in Bellows Falls. I'm going to be living here."

"Permanently?" asked Lester. "I mean, that's a big step. And Hal?"

"Hal's going to be in New York. Working. *This* will be my home," she said without elaboration. "Mine, and Hal's, when he has time off."

Lester got the point. He knew Trudy was her father's daughter. You don't ask too many questions. "Good 'nough. Them movers need any help you know who to ask."

"Thank you," said Trudy. "I think everything will be under control – the only problem's going to be all the stuff in this house. I don't want all of it."

"Have 'em put it my barn. Keep it there 'til the spring rummage sale."

"Really? That'd be great," said Trudy.

"Consider it done," said Lester. He opened the kitchen door. "I'll see ya tomorrow."

"Yes," said Trudy, "and, um, sorry I was a little short; it's been a long day."

"Don't mention it," said Lester with a smile. And he was out the door.

Well done, thought Trudy, you're getting off on the right foot – rude to Lester – right off the bat. She opened the cupboard next to the sink where her dad kept the liquor and saw a bottle of bourbon. *Thank God for small favors; now all I need is ice.* She opened the freezer door of the refrigerator and saw two ice trays – filled. Ahh – there is a God, she thought. From the kitchen window, Trudy could see the sun just beginning to go down over the hills west of her house. She mixed her drink: an ounce and a half of bourbon, lots of ice and a splash of water. A little early, but damn-it-to-hell, she thought, Harold died a little early.

~~~~~~~~

Trudy's visit had rattled Marie. Why did she come by again? Is there really a similarity between Paulie and Hal as a baby? Marie examined her face in the mirror above the couch in the front parlor. She confirmed the fact that her eyes were as blue as Paulie's. And he might even have my curly hair, she thought happily. Anyway, it doesn't matter. Trudy's never going to have Paulie. Marie went into the kitchen and started cleaning the kitchen cupboards. *But is she suspicious about Harold Walker's death? No. She couldn't be. The paper said it was a heart attack. And he was going to die anyway. God wouldn't let him live. He discarded my Jenette like so much rubbish.* Tears welled up in her eyes and a teacup fell out of her hands. She picked up the pieces and put them in the wastebasket. *I had to do it. The Bible says an 'eye for an eye, a tooth for a tooth.'* She knew it also preached forgiveness but that part of her was frozen; it was too late.

~~~~~~~~

With dry kindling, it didn't take long to get a fire going in her fireplace. Trudy sat in front of the large picture window in the living room, sipped her bourbon and watched the sun set. The twilight gave just enough light to silhouette the stand of spruce and hardwoods bordering the pastures south and west of her house. Finally the tension, the tightness in her body began to slip away. Trudy admired the fire she'd made. It was just right, gentle flames burning merrily, welcoming her home. She was pleased with her decision to move here.

A sudden ring of the telephone made her jump. For a second Trudy had to think about it, what-where...? The phone was in the kitchen, on the wall next to the back stairs. She put her drink down and hurried to answer, getting it on the last of her party line ring: two short and one long. "Hello...?"

"Mom...?" questioned Hal.

"Hal! Yes, of course it's me, who'd you think..."

"You sound different," said Hal.

Trudy laughed. "It's the same ole me. I was just surprised to hear the phone ring; took me a minute to remember the ring. This is a party line." She heard the fire crackling. "Hold on a minute, Hal, I've gotta put up the fire screen." Trudy put the phone receiver on the kitchen counter and hurried back into the living room to put the screen in place.

"Done," she said, picking up the phone again. "Well, sweetie, how are things in the big city? Where are you?"

"Right now I'm at the Biltmore, waiting for Tim Bradley to show up, then we'll probably go to his place on Seventy-Eighth Street."

"Nifty," said Trudy. "Will you be staying there?"

"Yeah, for now, then in June I'll get a place of my own."

"Great, but don't stay up too late, tomorrow's a"

"Mom," said Hal, "I know, and I didn't call about that."

"Of course," said Trudy hastily, "I'm just being…" she laughed, "…a mother."

"Yeah, that's okay," said Hal. "I called to say hi – to find out if you still like the house."

Trudy smiled. "It's perfect. Stop by on your way back to Dartmouth. See for yourself."

"Great," said Hal, "I'll be there Thursday."

"Okay," said Trudy, "that'll give me time to get things in order. The movers are bringing up everything from Bellows Falls tomorrow." She smiled at the thought. "By the end of the day I'll be an official resident of Brownsville."

Hal was silent for a couple of seconds. "Umm…the stuff in my room – in Bellows Falls – that's all going to Brownsville, right?"

Trudy was surprised that he asked. "Of course – everything, 'cept the heavy oak bureau and armoire; they're too massive for this house. I'm selling all of the oak pieces to Audley's Auctioneers. Don't worry about your room – it all goes."

"Good," said Hal. "There're a couple of boxes in my room…books 'n stuff – I want to keep."

"Don't worry, I'll take good care of them." Trudy could hear the fire crackling. She wanted to get back to it. "Good luck tomorrow; can't wait to hear all about it on Thursday."

"Okay, thanks, Mom."

Trudy hung up, feeling a momentary pang of loneliness. She brushed it aside and went back to the living room just in time to see the sun set, and put another log on the fire. Her mood of contentment was gone. She decided to make a list; she'd plan exactly how she wanted this house to look. Any piece of furniture 'out of place' would go to Lester's barn.

Trudy was on the road early. Her "to-do" list was on the seat of the car. On the way to Bellows Falls, she'd rearranged her Brownsville house at least three times. Bright orange tags would go on everything for the movers. She was already referring to her home of twenty-five years as the "old house."

It was eight o'clock. The movers would arrive at eight-thirty. Trudy raced through the house with the orange tags. In Hal's room she decided to tag the bed as well as the bureau; the twin bed in Brownsville wasn't long enough for him. At the foot of the bed were the two cartons Hal wanted. Trudy could see that they were stuffed to the hilt with books, papers, pens. It looked as if he'd dumped the entire contents of his desk into them. Oh well, she thought, it's his to sort out. As she started to fold the flaps of the boxes over one another, Trudy couldn't help noticing a pale blue envelope with neat, careful script bearing Hal's name and college address. There was no return address. She opened the letter.

Dear Hal,

It's been a whole day since you brought me home and our "vacation" ended. I'm still tingling with the memories of our Montreal 'escape.' Just like the movies, no one knew we were there! But more important than that, I loved being there with you – it felt so special. Wasn't it perfect? I know you have to finish college and that you'll be going to Europe this summer, but don't worry; I'll wait for you, and I promise you when the time comes to tell your parents about us, I'll make you proud!!!

Goodbye for now, and don't forget to study real hard!

Forever yours,

Jenette

The letter was dated January 2, 1954. Trudy sat on the edge of the bed and took a deep breath. Oh my... Hal, Hal, Hal, what did you get yourself into? Her hands felt clammy. She started thinking back to last summer; Marie had told her that Jenette was in Canada, visiting relatives. She'd be there until the fall. And then all of a sudden there was a baby... She put the letter down on the bed and stood up. *Get a hold of yourself – it's hardly the first time you've thought about this. If Hal knew for sure that baby was his, he would have said something.* Trudy felt a wave of panic. Damn it! she thought, this is just a silly letter, Hal's probably had lots like that – from different girls. Besides, he was busy all spring, then Europe...he would have said something. Trudy put the letter back in the carton and folded the top quickly and firmly; end of subject. After all, she reasoned, Marie had made it clear that she didn't want any help from the Walker family, and – Trudy was surprised she hadn't thought of this before – Jenette could have had a local boyfriend, a "townie," perhaps someone Marie didn't approve of. *Yes, no doubt that was the situation, so leave it alone. Stop looking for trouble.* Putting one box on top of the other, she picked them up and carried them to her car. It was cold outside. The wind seemed to whip around the end of her driveway. Trudy hoped the movers would be on time. Right now she wanted nothing more than to be in Brownsville.

~~~~~~~~

Either Lester was telepathic or plain nosey. Trudy didn't care; it was nice to have him waiting at the end of the driveway when she drove in with the moving van behind her. In no time at all he had the movers organized: outgoing furniture was hauled over to his barn, and the "new" stuff was put in place. Within three hours, favorite pieces from the Bellows Falls house became part of Trudy's new home. Then, before she knew it, Lester and Louise were on her doorstep with a large white azalea plant.

"A little bit of early spring," said Louise. "And you can plant it soon as the ground thaws." She pointed into the living room. "It'll do nicely outside that window, plenty of sun."

Her kindness brought tears to Trudy's eyes. She swallowed hard and walked toward the picture window with the plant. "It's beautiful and you're right, it'll do nicely out there, but for now I'll enjoy it right here." Trudy placed the azalea proudly in the center of the drop-leaf table in front of the window. "I can look at it every day."

Louise and Lester followed Trudy into the living room and stood staring at the plant. "It's gonna be thirsty, you might want a plate under it," said Louise. "Mine likes water prett'near every day."

"Yes indeed," said Trudy, "I'll get one in a minute. Can you sit down for awhile? I think I've got some tea in the kitchen…"

"Thanks," said Louise, "but I'm sure you've got plenty o' things to do." She had a big grin on her face. "We're neighbors – we'll be over lots."

"You bet," chuckled Lester, "we'll just wait 'til you get settled." He steered Louise toward the kitchen door.

"Okay, make that a promise," said Trudy. She followed them into the kitchen. "And thank you both for letting me store extra stuff in your barn."

"Glad to help," said Lester.

"And of course," Trudy added, "it goes without saying, if you want any of that stuff please take it."

Louise beamed. "Don't think we've got room for more furniture in our house, but my brother and his wife..."

"By all means," said Trudy, "have them take a look." She opened the kitchen door.

Louise stopped on the threshold. "Do you have enough to eat?"

"Louise..." said Lester, "I'm sure Trudy knows how to prepare food."

Trudy laughed. "Thanks. Yes, I have plenty to eat; still have some of your delicious baked beans, and I'll be going down to the store later."

Trudy sat down at the kitchen counter, resting her arms on top of cartons of china and silverware. It was already two o'clock. Boy, she wondered, where does the time go? She hopped off the stool. Suddenly she was hungry. A trip to the store *now* seemed like a good idea; unpacking could wait.

The Brownsville General Store was in the center of the village. A small school, the library, the fire station, and a church were dotted around it. Trudy had an exaggerated fondness for the school because of the one year she spent there. When she was nine and in the fourth grade, her father filled in for the regular general practitioner who was taking a year's sabbatical. His office was in the nearby town of Windsor. For Trudy, the entire school year was a wonderful adventure. The newness of a one-room schoolhouse, the grades divided by rows, was just part of the fun. Walking to school every day, lunch outside when the weather was good, and then having friends teaching her how to milk a cow was like a dream come true.

For a moment, she thought of stopping at the school, going in for a quick look before getting her sandwich at the store. But she was in a hurry; a trip down memory lane could wait The store had changed – for the better. It was larger, with a nice lunch counter along one wall. She didn't recognize anyone, but that was okay; in time she'd learn the new faces. She ordered a BLT on toasted white bread and a chocolate frappe. She told the girl that she'd like to take it home and asked if the sandwich could be wrapped in some wax paper. The high school girl behind the counter said sure, but the entire frappe might not fit in a paper cup. Trudy smiled and said that was fine, maybe *she* would like to finish it. The girl thought that was a swell idea.

Trudy picked up a small bag of potato chips at the cash register – something she rarely ate, but this little outing put her in a good mood; she wanted to extend it.

Back in her house, Trudy went right to living room with her lunch, having already decided that that was the place to sit and eat, particularly when she was alone. Everything in the room, especially the view from the picture window, made her feel happier. She sipped the last of the frappe and popped the remaining potato chips in her mouth. With her lists at hand, she prioritized: two hours to get the kitchen organized – fancy china in the cupboards, and the silver could go right back where it came from, in the sideboard, which fit nicely along the wall in the dining part of the living room. Silver candlesticks? That was easy: on top of the sideboard. And next to them, her pride and joy: a wooden bowl Hal had carved out of a knot from a maple tree and polished until he could see his face. He made it when he was ten, at a camp on Lake Fairlee. He gave it to Trudy for her birthday – said it took him all summer. She rubbed the bowl on her wool skirt a few times to brighten the shine and placed it carefully on the sideboard. She tried not to think of Hal, but couldn't help checking her wristwatch for the time. Three-thirty. I suppose the interview's over, wonder when he'll call. *When he's good 'n ready, stop your fretting.* But Trudy knew that Hal's interview wasn't the problem. It was that damn letter *and* Hal's tentative questions about Marie. For the next hour and a half she forced herself to unpack all of the china and get the kitchen entirely organized. It worked.

By five o'clock Trudy decided it was time for her shower and change of clothes. A habit she'd learned from her mother; at the end of the day it made one feel refreshed, lady-like, and ready for a pleasant cocktail with one's husband. Even with the absence of a husband,

Trudy saw no reason to change the pattern. She liked the routine.

Before laying a fire, she reviewed her choices for supper and laughed. Ha! Guess I'd better get to the market tomorrow. She took the leftover beans from the refrigerator and put them in the oven on low. Two pieces of Louise's brown bread would round out her meal. She mixed a drink – bourbon, and put some Triscuits in a bowl. She took extra care making a fire, breaking the kindling into smaller sticks, crumbling the newspaper, and laying three logs just so. When the fire was burning satisfactorily, she sat at the table with a pencil and pad of paper. Tomorrow, groceries would be the first order of the day. She looked out the window. The sun had set but she could still make out the lawn and the apple tree on the edge of it. A garden, she thought. I need to draw up a plan for my vegetable garden. The grandfather clock around the corner of the living room chimed. Five-thirty. Trudy checked her wristwatch to be sure. Well, Hal…you gonna call or not? She finished making the grocery list and started thinking about the garden. The only thing that came to mind was peas. She doodled on the paper. What do people grow? Tomatoes – lettuce, and parsley, I always need parsley. She eyed an ancient book of horticulture in the bookshelf. That might have something…

Just then the phone rang. Trudy listened. Yes, it was her ring. Oh, thank heavens, she thought. She picked up her drink and went to the kitchen to answer it.

"Hi, Mom, it's me! You okay?"

"Of course, why shouldn't I be?"

"You took so long to answer," said Hal.

"This is a party line – remember? I have to wait 'n see if it's my ring."

"You're kidding!"

"No, dear – two short and one long." Trudy pulled a stool closer to the phone and sat down. "Enough of that. Tell me about the interview. Did you get—"

"Yes, I did; I start the Monday after graduation."

"Congratulations!" said Trudy. "I'm really proud of you. Your dad would be too." Her own sense of relief was enormous. *He'll be in New York – away from Bellows Falls.* "Well, they don't give you much time, after graduation I mean. You'll need an apartment…"

"I'm way ahead of ya. My friend Sam Barnett – the soccer team captain? Graduated last year…?"

"Yes," said Trudy, waiting for further clarification.

"Well, he's decided to leave the real world for awhile."

Trudy was holding her breath. "And…"

"In June he's going to leave his job and bum around the world, and I get his apartment."

"That's nice," said Trudy, breathing again. "I mean that you get his apartment. I'm not sure about the other part."

"Don't worry, Mom, I won't do that – for awhile

anyway – ha-ha."

"Thank you, dear," said Trudy. "Now what time will you be coming through tomorrow? And will you spend the night, or go on to Hanover?

"Probably be there around supper time. Don't know 'bout spending the night. Can I let ya know then?"

"Sure. I'll get a leg o' lamb for dinner," said Trudy. "We can celebrate!"

Trudy put another log on the fire and checked the beans in the oven. A few more minutes, she thought. She mixed another drink. God almighty, what a day. *Now* I can relax.

She added some things to the grocery list: lamb, peas, onions, and potatoes of course, how could I forget – Hal loves roast potatoes. Dessert...maybe there's a good bakery in town. Apple pie would be nice.

By the time she'd finished planning the meal and adding odds 'n ends to her shopping list, Trudy was ready to eat and go to bed. Cleaning out one's house and moving into another was a full day's work, and then some, she decided. A good mystery story might help her forget, or at least not think about the emotional upheaval of the past few days. Days – hell – she'd been a wreck for well over a month, ever since that horrible fire. After Harold's death she knew that people expected her to fall apart; he was her husband for twenty-two years. But she couldn't collapse like a normal widow. She wondered, what's a *normal* widow? There's no such thing;

it's horrible for everybody – widows, widowers... She couldn't even stand the word: 'widow.' So – what the heck, forget about it, you've had to hold things together for Hal, and you'll continue to do so; life goes on. She stopped at the bookshelf in the upstairs back hallway. Her father had been a mystery buff, always on the lookout for unusual tales. Trudy picked one: *The Case of the Missing Teacup*. Perfect, she thought, this should put me to sleep in about ten minutes.

NINE

Hal didn't particularly like the drive from New York to Vermont. In good weather it took six hours; with snow, he figured it would be seven. He wondered if, in the future, he should leave his car in Vermont and take the train; but no, he wouldn't want to rely on others for rides. The whole situation: his new job, moving to New York; it all seemed so easy, and predictable. On the one hand he was pleased, but on the other he was resentful; everything had been dumped in his lap. People just assumed that he'd jump at the chance to work in a top New York bank. He knew that his father had planned on it long before Hal entered Dartmouth. But he did wonder why his mom was so gung-ho, why was she rushing him so. *The ink on my diploma won't even be dry.*

The traffic was light on the West Side Highway. He looked across the Hudson River at Palisades Amusement Park and remembered going there when he was ten with his Uncle Carl, his mom's brother. *I'll call him sometime; maybe he'd like to go again.* Carl and Hen, his wife, lived in Englewood, New Jersey. They were both physicians, and for some reason never had any children. That recollection – going to the park, made him think of Jenette's baby. *Yours, pal. He's yours. What are you going to do about it?* Hal squeezed his forehead. Thinking about Carl and Hen – childless, made him feel worse. He knew they would never turn their backs on a baby. God – Carl's the kid's great-uncle. Hal groaned. His head started to throb. "Okay, Walker," he muttered to himself, "get your facts straight."

A: Jenette didn't mess around with anybody else. B: The kid is yours, and Marie knows it. But Mom doesn't have a clue and you can't upset her now. That's one of the reasons you're taking the job, right…make her happy? The knot in his stomach was easing. Thinking about all of this – coming up with some kind of plan was better than doing nothing. First thing: talk to Marie; tell her he'd start working in June and could begin sending some money to her. Yeah, that's it – be straightforward. I'm goin' to be a banker; I can set up a special account for him. Pleased with his simple line of logic, Hal decided to stop in Bellows Falls before going to Brownsville. Why not, he thought. Might as well get things going. It was ten o'clock. He could be there by four, see Marie, and get over to his mom's in plenty of time for supper.

Hal turned off Route 5, drove down Main Street, and then to Canal Street before remembering that Marie had moved to Margarite Pearson's house. He stepped on the gas, not wanting to think about his last cowardly words to Jenette. Going down Atkinson Street toward Burt, he almost turned into the driveway of his old house. It startled him to see a car parked where he'd always put his car. He drove on, pushing away those memories as well. Burt Street came up sooner than he'd expected. Hal jammed on the brakes, looked in his rearview mirror after the fact, and turned a sharp left.

Hal wasn't sure if he should park in the small driveway next to Margarite's house or leave his car in the street. He decided on the street. The sidewalk was icy, but the short walkway up to the porch was free of ice and snow. Hal remembered how diligent Jenette's father had been about cleaning the sidewalk in front of their building – in all seasons. He straightened his coat and smoothed his hair before ringing the doorbell. No answer. He rang again. The curtains were drawn in the front parlor. Hal tried to look in between them. No luck.

"Hello – anybody home? Marie – it's me – Hal." No response. Maybe she's in the kitchen, he thought. He stepped off the porch and walked along the side of the house to the back door. Hal bounded up the back steps, ready to say hello and explain his plan to Marie over a hot cup of tea. After knocking on the door and calling out, he gave up; and walked back to his car.

Marie had watched him from an upstairs bedroom. Suspecting that he might try the kitchen door, she raced down the back stairs to lock it and close the curtains over the sink. Paulie was crying for his supper. Marie knew that Hal would hear the cries but she didn't care. For now she wanted only to keep the Walkers, and anyone close to them, out of her life. So far things were going her way, but she needed more time to figure out the future. The cycle wasn't complete. She went back upstairs to the front bedroom and waited until she saw Hal drive off.

As he got in the car, Hal looked up and saw Marie standing at the window. He started to wave and thought better of it. I'll write her in June when I'm working. Once she knows what I plan to do – that I care, she'll see me.

~~~~~~~~

Trudy was fussing about the kitchen, preparing Hal's favorite meal of roast lamb, peas, creamed onions and roasted potatoes. She didn't like cooking potatoes in the same pan as the lamb. Her mother always said that the fat drippings added flavor to them, but Trudy had her own recipe. She peeled the potatoes, cutting them into quarters, trimming the edges so they rolled easily in a pan with a little bit of butter. The result, after baking in the oven for an hour, was a tasty roasted potato – sans greasy fat. It struck her as odd that her father, a physician, had eaten her mother's fat-saturated potatoes with such glee. Oh well, at least *Hal* prefers mine. She took the mint jelly from the refrigerator and spooned some into a small cut-glass dish. Rather than set the dining room table,

Trudy thought it would be more fun to sit at the table in front of the picture window. It was big enough for two, and less formal. Hal was a small boy the last time he spent any time in this house. Trudy wanted him to enjoy it as much as she did. She lit the fire and sat for a few minutes, going over things in her mind. The cartons Hal requested from his room in Bellows Falls were upstairs in his 'new' bedroom. As for their contents, Trudy had decided to keep quiet. The whole business, Jenette, and the baby, upset her. So for now, the less said the better. Her overriding concern was Hal – keeping him on the right track. He had a job. Soon he'd be living in New York. She poked at the fire with the tongs. The clock chimed five. Trudy knew Hal would be arriving any minute. She put up the fire screen and went back to the kitchen. Emptying ice cubes into the ice bucket made her think of Harold, and in a funny way that calmed her down. She was following through with the plans he had made for Hal. Nothing else mattered.

Hal tooted the car horn as he drove in. Trudy rushed out to greet him. "Welcome – welcome home!"

Hal got out of the car with a big grin on his face. "Hi, Mom! I made it." He gave her a peck on the cheek.

Trudy returned it with a pat on his shoulder. "Get your bag and come on in." She held the side door to the kitchen open.

Hal was impressed as soon as he stepped in the kitchen. "Wow – this is great. It looks…" He continued walking into the living room. "Well, nicer than I remember."

Trudy laughed. "You just haven't been here for awhile." She motioned to the fireplace. "Look, I've even got a fire going."

"Yeah, my gosh, I didn't know –"

"That I knew how to make a fire?" Trudy replied happily. "I learned from my father – way back. Your dad just liked to lay the fires himself in Bellows Falls. C'mon, let me show you around." She headed for the front stairs. "You can have your old bedroom."

Hal followed Trudy, suitcase in hand. "Are the jigsaw puzzles still here? Remember when I did them with Granddad?"

"Uh-huh," said Trudy, "all of them, right in there." She pointed to a large cedar blanket chest at the top of the stairs. "In the bottom drawer."

"And Monopoly," said Hal, following Trudy into the sitting room. "Maybe I should play a few games, brush up on my banking skills."

"You were pretty good as I recall," said Trudy, "always beat Harry Wilkins."

"Hmm, that was tough. He was three years younger," laughed Hal.

"Ha-ha – never mind dear, you're all grown up now. And I can't wait to hear about your interview, the job – everything." They stood for a second looking out the windows at Mt. Ascutney.

"Wow...I remember racing up there during freshman initiation," said Hal, looking at the mountain.

"Put your suitcase down," said Trudy, pointing to the antique canvas and wood luggage rack. "Let's go enjoy the fire."

Hal glanced around his old bedroom, noticing the cartons on the floor. "Oh, thanks," he said, pointing to them. "I'll take care of that stuff later, you don't mind if it just stays like that for awhile?"

"No. Of course not," said Trudy, a little too quickly. "They're your things, just leave 'em there." She turned to go downstairs, and said over her shoulder, "Towels are in the bathroom."

"Okay – I'll be right down."

When he heard Trudy on the staircase, Hal opened one of the cartons, took out the letters from Jenette, and quietly put them in his suitcase.

The roast lamb was a success. Trudy watched contentedly as Hal ate with gusto. In between mouthfuls she plied him with questions about New York. She tried to be mindful of the balance between helpful and nosey.

"Do remember my brother, your Uncle Carl?" asked Trudy. "He lives in Englewood, not far from the city."

Hal finished the last of the potatoes. "Sure, it's not far from Palisades Amusement Park. Remember? He took me there."

"I sure do," said Trudy. "You came back to Englewood

green from so many rides on the roller coaster." She pointed to the green on one the rugs. "About that shade." She smiled at the recollection. "Well, anyway, if you're interested, you should call him sometime this summer. You know – get out of the city for awhile."

"Yeah," said Hal. "I was actually thinking about Carl and Hen this morning, goin' up West Side Drive." Before he even knew what he was saying Hal blurted out, "Why didn't they ever have any kids?"

"Well, ah – um... Goodness," said Trudy, laughing at Hal. "You come up with some doozies. I don't know... I mean – it's not something we talked about. I suppose they were too busy." Trudy didn't like that answer, but she was too taken aback to say anything else. "What ever made you think of that?"

Hal hadn't planned on mentioning his stop in Bellows Falls, but once again words tumbled out of his mouth. "I don't know, I was thinking about Marie...and, well..." Hal was quiet for a second. "Actually, I wanted to take a last look at our old house, so I stopped in Bellows Falls. I was thinking about the old days, kids I played with, stuff like that." He knew that none of this was making any sense but he stumbled on. "So I went by our house. Then I remembered that Marie was right down on Burt Street." He put a big spoonful of mint jelly on his lamb. "You know how you told me she had moved into Margarite Pierson's..."

Trudy, too tense to speak, nodded and waited for him

to continue.

"Anyway," said Hal, "I stopped at the house, knocked on the doors – front 'n back. She didn't answer." Hal stopped eating. "I know she was there, I saw her standing in the upstairs window. Guess she just didn't want to see me."

Trudy started breathing again. "That's not surprising. She doesn't want to see anybody, at least anybody *we* know." With a tone of finality, Trudy stated the facts as she saw them. "Marie has been through a lot. She's building a new life for herself. We, and others for whom she used to work, are no longer a part of that life."

Hal shrugged again. "I was just wondering how she was doing – with the kid 'n all."

"Hal," said Trudy, becoming annoyed, "listen to me: Marie is fine. And I'm sure the baby is too." She stood up and started clearing the plates. "We've got lots of other things to think about – like dessert. How 'bout your favorite – lemon meringue pie?"

The fire snapped and crackled, getting Hal's attention. "That'd be swell," he said, regretting that he'd mentioned his stop. *Must be hard on Mom*, he thought, *moving here without Dad.* He took the rest of the dishes into the kitchen. "Hey, Mom, got any good recipes – for canned goods? I just realized in a few months I'll be doing my own cooking."

Trudy handed a piece of pie to Hal. "That's what girlfriends are for," smiled Trudy. "I'm sure you'll have plenty."

"I hope they can make this!"said Hal, as he took a bite of the pie.

Light snow had fallen during the night. Trudy lay in bed for a few extra minutes savoring the early morning view from her bedroom window, the pristine fields and protective, bear-like Mount Ascutney in the distance. The mountain appeared to have two great arms ready to embrace the community. On the other side of the house she could hear Hal shoveling snow. *Well, I'll be... Guess I'd better get going with some breakfast.*

Hal burst in the kitchen, bringing the fresh smell of outdoors with him. "Oh boy, I'm starving. What's for breakfast?"

"Well, try bacon and eggs first," said Trudy. "Bread is on the counter, you can put a couple of pieces in the toaster. Forks 'n knives are in that drawer."

"I can't believe how organized you are. So quickly, I mean."

"Hmm," smiled Trudy, "I like it here. That makes it easy, and fun to put stuff away."

Hal wolfed down his food, and gave his mother a quick hug. "I'd better get going, the guys are waiting for me. We might go up to Tremblant for some skiing."

"Do you have time, all the way to Canada?"

"Classes don't start 'til Monday," said Hal happily.

"Of course, I've lost track of the days. Do you have enough money? I haven't put any in your account for awhile."

"Yup, plenty. Dad gave me some before..." Hal stammered. "Umm, before Christmas."

"That's all right, it's okay to talk about things before he died," said Trudy. "Now run along, and have fun." Trudy opened the door for Hal, who had his hands full with his suitcase and toast. "Say 'hi' to that funny friend of yours – Dexter? Dexter Bottoms...? Did he ever learn to ski?"

"It's Bottomley, and no, he still falls all the way down the mountain." Hal gave her a big grin and was off.

Trudy went to the window by the back stairs and waved as Hal drove away. Then she poured herself a cup of coffee and started to reflect on the last few days. Why did Hal stop in Bellows Falls? Simple, he was feeling a little disjointed – homesick, that's all. Not that unusual to want to see Marie – after all, she'd been with them for ten years. She warmed her hands on the coffee cup. He seems happy about his new job, and now he's off to have fun with his friends. And, for heaven's sake, he wants you to be happy. Trudy got up and rinsed her cup, trying to smile. She still felt as if the wind had gone out of her sails. Was it all the moving, getting settled? She rubbed her hands with a dishtowel, and then her eyes. She couldn't stop the tears. No, it wasn't just the move – it was everything. The fire, Harold's dying, which she didn't understand – he'd never had heart trouble, but then, as her father used to remind her, "Every human body has its surprises and secrets." And of course there was the baby. *Why* couldn't she confront Marie, or Hal? That's easy, she thought, you don't *want* to know the truth. She shrugged. There were so many thoughts. Harold was gone. She felt empty and lonely. Yes, Trudy muttered, but you're not the only widow in the world...get on with things! She refilled the coffee cup she'd just rinsed and started a new to-do list.

Just as Trudy got into it, the phone rang. She wasn't used to the different rings for the party line and let it ring several times before picking it up; even then she worried about interrupting a conversation. Her response was more of a question. "Hello?"

"Trudy...is that you?"

"Yes, who's this?" responded Trudy.

"Cynthia Luden, Margarite's sister."

"Oh yes, how are you?" said Trudy. "Nice to hear from you. Um – how did you know I was here?"

"I remember, after the service for Margarite, back at her house, you mentioned how you were planning to move to Brownsville," said Cynthia.

"Yes, yes, of course," said Trudy, not really remembering, but it didn't matter. "You'll have to come for lunch sometime. I'd love to show you my 'new' – ha-ha – part of Vermont."

"Thank you," said Cynthia, "that would be nice."

She hesitated a minute. "But I was hoping that we could meet in Bellows Falls, perhaps tomorrow?"

"I'm sorry," said Trudy, "I don't think that will – "

"Walter said that Marie's going to turn Margarite's house into an inn," said Cynthia without a pause. "She's going to take paying guests for the night and serve them breakfast."

"And how, pray tell, did Walter come by this information?" asked Trudy.

"At the Rotary – last night. They said she's applied for a hotel permit!" Cynthia's voice accelerated with each word. "She can't do that. I need to get stuff out of there."

Trudy's reaction was immediate. "Cynthia, I'm going to be busy here all day tomorrow, a carpenter's coming. And then," she hurried on, "I'm off to Boston for a few days."

"But couldn't you…?"

Trudy was having none of it. "Cynthia, I think you're worrying needlessly. Bar gossip from the Rotary is just that – bar gossip."

"Walter doesn't drink," said Cynthia firmly.

Trudy stifled a laugh on that one. "That's beside the point. I'm sure if you call Marie and ask her when it would be convenient for you to come by and collect some things, she'd be most accommodating." Trudy didn't believe that, but so what.

"I've tried. She won't answer the phone," said

Cynthia.

Trudy looked at her watch – ten o'clock, enough of this. She wanted to get on with the day. "Nothing in Bellows Falls happens quickly, Cynthia, particularly permitting for new businesses. It'll be spring before anything happens, if then. You and Walter will have plenty of time to visit Marie and collect your things."

"But Walter doesn't like Marie, that's why – "

"I'm sure you can work something out," said Trudy. "It was lovely of you to call, but I must go. Someone just drove in." Trudy hung up, staring at the phone as if it were infected. Good grief, she muttered, hard to believe that she and Margarite were related.

Trudy's string of white lies actually made her feel better. Unwittingly she'd come up with a plan for the next few days. Mo Dudley, her old boarding school friend, had been after her to come to Boston. So, why not?

Trudy called Mo and arranged the visit. The rest of the day flew by. She didn't think of Marie or Bellows Falls.

Before leaving in the morning, Trudy walked over to Lester and Louise's to tell them she'd be in Boston for two or three days. Lester gave her a wry look as if to say, 'Maybe livin' here full time ain't such a good idea?'

"I know what you're thinking, so stop. I have every intention of making this my permanent home," said Trudy.

"Yes, of course you do," said Louise. "Lester just worries; he was born that way. Why, I can remember – "

"I'm sure you can," said Lester, "but right now Trudy's on her way to Boston."

"Yes," said Trudy, grateful for the easy exit.

"We'll keep an eye on your house," said Lester.

"Thanks – bye," said Trudy.

After three days in Boston, Trudy felt refreshed and relaxed. Laughing, shopping, talking about frivolous things had helped. She could begin to feel the muscles in her face soften. Indeed, thanks to Mo, the rest of the winter was pretty well organized. Mo and her husband, Giles, said they'd be renting a house in Bermuda for the month of March. Attached to it was a small guesthouse. Would she like to visit? At first, Trudy dismissed the idea. Too much of a good thing. But then, with a little prodding by Mo, Trudy accepted. After all, what can you do during 'mud season'? There's nothing but mud and melting snow.

TEN

Home from Bermuda, Trudy was bursting with energy and new ideas for her house and garden. Peas had to be in by the end of April, lettuce plants should follow, and where could she buy strawberry plants? The fact that frost wasn't completely out of the ground 'til mid-April didn't faze her. The garden had to be planted immediately because right after that, the house needed to be sanded and painted; and who could she hire to wash the windows?

When Hal came down from Hanover, he was immediately put to work, either mowing the lawn or, much to his chagrin, washing windows. Lester made it known that he never took to that task.

"I don't wash windows," said Lester to Hal.

It was a Sunday afternoon. "Beautiful mowing job," said Trudy, as Hal turned off the lawn mower.

Completely unannounced, Cynthia Luden and her husband, Walter, came walking around the side of the house. "Yoo-hoo – anybody home?" chirped Cynthia, with Walter, head down, plodding behind her.

For a few seconds Trudy was nonplussed. She stared at them. "My goodness, we didn't even hear you drive in."

"Figured you didn't," said Walter, raising his head.

"Well, this is an unexpected surprise." said Trudy formally, "won't you..." Trudy motioned to the lawn chairs as Cynthia and Walter walked toward them.

Hal wasn't as gracious. "You startled us, where's your car?"

"On the other side of the garage, right there in your driveway," said Walter.

Trudy smiled stiffly, knowing the answer to the question she was about to ask. "What brings you here?"

"It's that crazy lady in Margarite's house," said Walter.

"What?" said Hal, suddenly alert. "Marie? Marie Furneau?"

"Yes – who else?" said Walter.

Trudy looked at Cynthia. "What's going on? I thought..."

Cynthia was clearly uncomfortable. "We'd planned on goin' by, like you suggested that time when I called...back in February."

"Just tell her," said Walter.

"Well, we couldn't go then. I got sick sumpin' awful. It lasted the longest time. Then, well, you know how time has a way of gettin' ahead – it takes charge."

"Yes," said Trudy, "and now you want to go to Marie's house?"

"We've done that," said Walter. "She won't let us in."

"What?" said Hal.

Walter looked directly at Trudy. "I know she's there, saw her pull the shades soon's we got out of the car."

Hal spoke up. "Cynthia, was she expecting you? Maybe it was a coincidence – her pulling the shade down."

"No," said Walter. "She knew damn well who we were."

"I called the day before," said Cynthia, "told her we wanted some things – like the tea set."

"Okay, and what did Marie say?" said Trudy.

"Nothing, really – she said she might not be home," said Cynthia.

"And she probably wasn't," said Hal. "Did it occur to you that somebody else might have been there?"

Trudy didn't like the tone of this conversation. "All right, I assume that you'd like me to call Marie and straighten things out?"

"Yup," said Walter, leaning back in the lawn chair.

"And," said Cynthia, "would you come with us next time?"

"There'll be no, *us*," said Walter. "I'm not goin' near that witch."

"She's not a witch," stated Hal. "She happens to be a hard-working lady trying to make her way in the world, and raise her grandson."

"Hmpf, and who's to blame for that?" said Walter. "I hear she doesn't even know who fathered the kid."

Hal stood up. "I suggest you mind your own business."

"Yes, Walter, that's none of our concern," said Cynthia.

"I'll call Marie tomorrow," said Trudy. "Perhaps something can be worked out for next week. I'll call you."

Trudy got up and started walking toward the driveway.

Hal barely waited 'til the car was out of the driveway. "Where the hell does he get off – saying stuff about – "

"Don't worry about it," said Trudy. "Walter's always been a blowhard."

"He has no right," said Hal, "I mean, he doesn't even live in Bellows Falls – how dare he!"

"Stop, don't concern yourself with his foolish blustery comments," said Trudy, trying to keep herself calm. "I'm sure everything will be fine. I'll call Marie. Cynthia and I will go over, have a cup of tea, and retrieve Margarite's china." She folded her arms together in a matter-of-fact manner. "No doubt Marie will be happy to get rid of it."

"So, you'll be going before graduation?" asked Hal.

"Yes, you heard me, probably next week," said Trudy. "You've got some hedge trimming to do, and, before you go, I want a guest list."

"Guest list?" asked Hal.

"Yes, remember? You wanted a party here – after finals – before graduation?"

"Oh, yeah," said Hal. He walked over to the edge of the field and started hacking away at the privet hedge. "I'll get it to you."

Trudy followed Hal to the hedge. "Hey! Take it easy. *Trim* – don't kill it. And I need the names today – as soon as you finish." She picked up the branches Hal had cut and put them in the wheelbarrow. "I just need a rough idea of how many of your Dartmouth friends will be here, then give me a list of your high school friends." Hal gave her a blank expression. Trudy was getting exasperated. "Earlier you were talking about Bellows Falls? Your friends?"

"Don't worry, Mom, I'll just call them." He stopped chopping the hedge. "Please don't mail invitations. This isn't a third grade birthday party."

"All right," said Trudy, keeping her voice even. "How many people – forty? Fifty? I will have to buy food, and beer."

"The guys'll bring the beer," said Hal, "and we can cook some hot dogs over there." He pointed in the direction of an old fireplace his grandfather had made on the edge of the field. It was a bunch of rocks and flat stones placed in a circle. When he was small, Hal used to put hot dogs on a stick and roast them over the fire.

"Hal, you said it yourself, this is not a kids' party."

"I know – I know, can we talk about it later? I'm kinda burnt out – finals 'n everything."

Trudy relented. "Of course. Dump that stuff and we'll have some ice tea before you go."

Hal took the wheelbarrow to the edge of the woods and spread the clippings from the hedge on a brush pile. Slowly it would flatten and blend in with the trees. He looked longingly at a small pine grove. He wished he could pitch a tent and stay there. *Why does Cynthia have to get her china now?* He knew he was being stupid. It wasn't the china, it was the kid – the way they were talking. Even his mother had that fake tone to her voice, like everything was fine.

Trudy called to him from the lawn, "C'mon – get a move on!"

Hal hurled some sticks into the woods.

Over their glasses of ice tea, Trudy kept the conversation short and sweet, nothing even remotely controversial. She was troubled by Hal's change in demeanor and was eager for him to leave, and get back to his routine at Dartmouth. *Walter and Cynthia took the cake.* Everything had been just fine 'til they showed up.

Hal put down his glass and got up to go. Trudy seemed not to notice.

"Mom...? Hello..." he said, waving his hand in front of her face. "Now who's daydreaming?"

"Oh my – sorry," said Trudy, "guess I'm sleepy. All this fresh air."

"I'm off – back to the books." He smiled at his mother. "I'll give you a party head count tomorrow – promise."

"Okey-dokey," said Trudy. She walked with Hal out to the driveway and waved as he got in the car. "Bye…"

Back in the house, Trudy fumed. Damnit, she thought, why *is* Marie being so difficult? And Cynthia! Arrgh! What a nitwit!

After mixing herself a bourbon and water, Trudy went to her favorite place in the living room – next to the picture window. A new telephone was now on the table next to her chair. She drummed her fingers on top of it. *I am not going to let this business ruin my summer!* Trudy felt like telling Cynthia and Marie to go to hell-in-a-hand-basket. The china was none of her business. However, she knew that Cynthia would not give up. She wondered what Margarite would have thought about all this fuss over a little china. Oh Margarite, if you only knew… Trudy stared at the phone. Okay, she thought, call her – get it over with. Trudy picked up the receiver and asked the operator to ring Marie's number. When Polly, the operator, said that she didn't know anybody in Brownsville who belonged to a number that started with 22, Trudy almost replied that she didn't either. "Oh," she said, "I'm sorry, I forgot to tell you that's a Bellows Falls exchange."

"That's okay, Mrs. Walker, everybody forgets to tell me when they call someplace else. Of course, most folks don't call that much – outta town that is – but you used to live there, didn't you?"

"Yes, that's right," said Trudy patiently, "now I'd like to telephone someone who *does* live there."

"Sure thing. Bellows Falls is easy to remember, it's always been 22," said Polly, "and what was your friend's number again?"

Trudy held her tongue and gave Polly Marie's number. While the call was being placed, Trudy decided not to mention Cynthia's visit. She'd just stick to the matter at hand: she and Cynthia would be coming to get Margarite's china.

Marie picked up after the first ring. "Hello – Burt Street Inn."

"Hello? Is that you, Marie? This is Trudy Walker."

"I know who you are," said Marie.

"Yes, I guess you do," said Trudy. "I didn't recognize your voice – the Burt Street Inn greeting. When did you open?"

"I'll be taking guests in June," said Marie.

"Good for you. That's nice," said Trudy. "Then I'm sure you're busy. I'm just calling to say that Margarite's sister, Cynthia, and I will be stopping by to collect Margarite's china. I believe it was a tea set that Cynthia wanted." Trudy didn't wait for Marie to balk. "I'll be in

Bellows Falls next Wednesday. We'll come by at two o'clock."

"Margarite had several sets of china," said Marie, "and I'm not sure–"

"Don't worry, Cynthia will figure out what's what." Trudy didn't leave time for Marie to reply. "See you Wednesday, at…" The line was dead. Marie had already hung up. Well fine, Trudy muttered, I didn't want to talk to you either.

Trudy went to the kitchen and got a can of tomato soup from the cupboard. While it was warming, she mixed another drink. She planned on having some soup, leftover chicken, and sliced cucumbers for supper. Then, she thought, I'll just go to bed. But it was early. If she went to sleep too early, she'd just wake up in the middle of the night and start worrying. So what, I'll risk it. With that resolved, Trudy decided to brighten her mood with some music. Using the same record player that she and Harold used in Bellows Falls was comforting. At first, she thought of playing the "Skater's Waltz", but no, that would be too much. Instead, she put on Beethoven's violin concerto and returned to the kitchen to stir her soup.

~~~~~~~~

Marie was furious. How dare they? Trudy Walker just thinks she can do whatever she pleases. *"Oh, Marie how are you? How's the baby?"* she said sarcastically. Well, if she only knew! Marie looked at Paulie, who was playing

169

happily in the playpen in a corner of the kitchen. "Granny will be right back, I have to go to the attic for some things." Paulie grinned at his grandmother, shaking a small baby rattle as if to say, "I'll be fine."

As soon as Margarite died, Marie put the Wedgwood china in the attic, thinking in time that she would sell the whole set and use the proceeds for renovations. She hadn't counted on Margarite's sister wanting it. Her thoughts raced ahead to other family heirlooms that Cynthia might be after. Margarite had always kept the Georgian silverware in a safe in the back of the front hall closet, bringing it out once or twice a year. Cynthia probably didn't know anything about it. Good, she thought, that's worth plenty. Looking around the attic, Marie decided to bring down two tea sets: the Wedgwood and the Dalton, and some fancy vases that Margarite always used for her roses. Carefully she carried the boxes downstairs and put them on the floor in the living room. "Tea sets, vases," she mumbled, "now...what else?" She looked around the living room. Her eyes fell on two figurines on top of a Victorian corner shelf. "I don't need these foolish-looking dogs." She put two porcelain English Spaniels in the box with the vases. Then, eager to make the collection look bigger, she started to take more things off the corner shelf. No, she thought, best to leave it all there, with an empty carton waiting to be filled – like I don't care what she takes. Marie eyed a silver mint dish. "I'll keep that, thank you. It'll be nice for cookies when I serve tea to my guests." She took the dish into the kitchen and tucked it in a drawer of dishtowels. Paulie was shaking his rattle, dropping it, then picking it up with glee. "Yes, young man, we're gonna have a good time – you wait 'n see."

~~~~~~~~~

The quickest way for Trudy to keep her mind off her troubles was to get a spade or a rake and start working in her garden. Lester had helped her dig up an area on the edge of the field, about ten feet long by five feet wide, and now she enjoyed turning over the soil with a spade, getting it ready for planting. Lester had teased her about the diminutive size, asking, what kind of tiny vegetables did she have in mind? Trudy replied that she wasn't feeding an army. She wanted a small garden that would behave, and follow the rules in the gardening book. Lester had no further comments.

A large tangle of honeysuckle and wild barberry bushes was spilling over onto the edge of the garden. Tired of digging and raking, Trudy started chopping away at them with the hedge trimmers. Lester came upon her as she was yanking at the vines of a deadly nightshade plant.

"You'd be smart to put gloves on for that," he said.

Trudy looked over her shoulder. "Oh, hi – I could use a hand, this stuff is horrible."

"Worse 'n that," said Lester, "it can kill ya."

"I'm not gonna eat it, I just want it away from my

garden."

Lester picked up the spade. After a few quick jabs with his foot on top of this sharp-edged shovel, he'd loosened the roots of the plant. "No good getting the vines, they grow back 'fore ya know it."

"Thanks," said Trudy. "I was told once that these berries protect grapes – keeps deer and other animals from eating them."

"Hmph, maybe, but not every animal is smart 'nough to stay away. Two of my brother's calves died eating this stuff." Lester kicked the plant away. "I'd wash that juice off my hands if I was you."

Trudy wiped her hands on her pants and looked at them. "You're right, it doesn't want to come off. I'll use soap when I go in." She motioned to the small pile of brush and nightshade vines. "What am I going to do with all of this – if it's so deadly?"

"I'll burn it," said Lester.

"What – is that safe?" asked Trudy. "I mean, ya burn poison ivy and people catch it from the smoke."

"I ain't gonna be inhaling the stuff," said Lester. "Besides, I'll wait'll it rains."

Trudy shrugged. Lester had his ways and opinions. She wasn't going to change them. "How 'bout my beautifully raked garden? I'm already to plant." She tapped her foot on one corner of the little plot. "Peas will go here, then tomatoes, and then some lettuce and green beans, and carrots at the end!"

Lester couldn't resist a chuckle. "Don't overdo it; two servings of beans might tip the scales…"

Trudy laughed with him. "Think strawberries will like it over there?" She pointed to a sunny spot in the field near the apple tree.

"Yup, but so will the deer and every other critter," said Lester. "You'd be better off puttin' 'em right here near your garden and we'll put a fence up around the whole thing."

"But then I won't be able to look at everything," said Trudy.

"Sure ya will – it'll be chicken wire – high and then spread flat on the ground, 'bout three feet out. Deer won't want to walk on it."

Trudy groaned. Visions of a picture-perfect garden were diminishing. "Well, if you say so, but it has to be sturdy and upright. I don't want chicken wire flopping all over my lawn." Her hands were beginning to feel sticky. "I'm going in to wash off this berry stain."

Lester was pacing off an area for the strawberries. "You'll want to get a couple dozen strawberry plants."

Trudy was about to object to the large number, but she heard the telephone ringing, two short and a long. "That's mine, be back in a few minutes…" She ran to get it.

"Hello," said Trudy, slightly breathless.

"Oh dear – you were doing something," said Cynthia.

"Yes," said Trudy recognizing Cynthia's whiny voice.

"I can call back," said Cynthia.

"No," said Trudy, "I'm here, and I was actually going to call you, this evening."

"Oh, that's nice," said Cynthia.

Trudy rolled her eyes. "I called Marie; it's all set. I'll meet you there Wednesday afternoon – two o'clock."

Cynthia wasn't prepared for such efficiency. "Umm – what if I get there before you? Could we meet at the hotel or someplace, and go together?"

"Cynthia," said Trudy, trying to keep her patience, "Marie won't bite. Park out front and wait for me if I'm not there."

"You are planning on being there?!" screeched Cynthia.

"Yes, Cynthia – I will be there, and I'll bring some empty cartons. I've got plenty of them."

Cynthia was mollified. "Thank you, okay – I'll see you at two on Wednesday."

"That's correct. Goodbye," said Trudy.

She went to the kitchen sink, and washed her hands. Boy, Lester really doesn't like this stuff, she thought, looking at the nightshade stains on her hands. *Two* dead animals, hard to believe that nightshade was the cause... She felt herself shiver and rubbed the back of her neck. Ouch, too much digging. Time for an ice tea break. Trudy took two glasses from the cupboard and got a pitcher of ice tea from the refrigerator.

"Yoo-hoo – time for a break," called Trudy, sitting in one of the lawn chairs. Lester put down the shovel and came over to join her. They decided that Trudy should go into Windsor and get the strawberry plants right away. He would have the "patch" ready when she returned. Lester said they could "have 'em all in 'fore suppa time." When Trudy suggested that they hold off on the planting, he reminded her that "spring has a way of runnin' ahead – likely to be summa 'fore ya know it – then, by golly, fall." Trudy laughed and told him to slow down. "Stop – I want to enjoy spring!"

Driving to Bellows Falls, Trudy couldn't help noticing all of the lilacs in bloom and thought of Lester's remark about spring running into summer. He's right. It's already the middle of May – two more weeks 'til Hal's graduation, and the party. I should start calling people. I haven't even called Carl and Hen.

Meeting with Marie and Cynthia was the last thing she needed. Well, it shouldn't take long, thirty minutes at the most, unless Cynthia wants to go through the whole house. Fine, I don't have to stay there; I'm sure Marie will be happy to see me leave. I might even have time to see the Barnards. Harold always liked Sissy and Jack. It'd be nice to invite them to Hal's party. And of course the Aldriches, Sam will want to hear all about Hal's new job. Thinking about the party and her old friends, put Trudy in a better mood. She felt quite chipper as she drove down Atkinson Street. For the heck of it, she decided to drive past her old house, to see if the new people had made any exterior changes. She saw a familiar figure walking briskly on the sidewalk near her house. Sam Aldrich going back to work after lunch.

Trudy was delighted. She tooted the car horn and called out. "Sam – hi! It's me, Trudy."

Sam stopped walking and looked in her direction. "Who…? Why, Trudy Walker – I haven't seen you in a coon's age!" He rushed to the car window and gave her a peck on the cheek, then stood back appraising her. "Well, how are you? We were just talking about you the other day. "What brings you to the big city?"

"To see you, of course," said Trudy with a smile, as she folded her arms on top of the rolled-down window. "Actually, I'm here this afternoon to help Margarite's sister get some things out of the house. Marie Furneau's living there now."

"Oh yes, I know, she's been after me – the bank that is, for a loan." Sam frowned. "It's tough – she says she owns the house, but I've never seen any papers, no title – no nothin'." He gestured with his hands open and shook his head. "Do you know anything about it?"

"Marie said that Margarite left the house to her in her will. Cynthia's gonna be there, she probably has the will."

"Cynthia?" asked Sam.

"Hm, Margarite's sister, she wants the china," said

Trudy flatly.

"Oh," said Sam, not understanding. "If you could ask Marie about the will, that would help."

"Sure," said Trudy, eager to change the subject. "Tell Susan that I'll be calling this evening or tomorrow." She smiled broadly. "Hal's graduating, and – as you know, he got the job in New York. We'll be celebrating!"

"Susan'll be delighted to hear from you," said Sam, patting her arm as a goodbye gesture. "And you tell Hal that we can't wait to see him."

Trudy laughed in agreement, and pulled away from the curb.

Three minutes later, she was parked in front of a sign announcing the opening of the Burt Street Inn. Well, I'll be, thought Trudy, Marie isn't wasting any time. It's fairly attractive too. The wooden sign hung from a post a few feet in front of the house. It was painted beige with purple block lettering. A small, 3 x 8 inch removable slat read: June Opening. Trudy inspected the sign more closely when she got out of the car. It looked brand new.

Marie had been observing her from the side yard.

"Don't touch it, the paint's still wet!"

Trudy turned quickly at the sound of her voice. "Marie! I didn't see you." She pointed to the sign. "It's nice."

"Yes," said Marie. "Ray Le Bec did it for me."

The mention of Ray's name a slight jolt for Trudy. The memory of his animosity toward Harold was still fresh. "I'm a little early; Cynthia should be along in a few minutes."

"That's good," said Marie, walking after Paulie, who was crawling rapidly across the side lawn. "I've put everything in the living room. Hope she takes all of it, I need the space – what with guests."

"Yes, I hear you'll be doing some renovations," said Trudy.

"Where'd you hear that?" snapped Marie over her shoulder, as she continued after Paulie.

Oh boy, here we go, thought Trudy. "I just saw Sam Aldrich. He said that you were asking for a loan." She saw Marie's back stiffen. "I assume it's to fix things up, and – well, he told me that he needs some legal documents – ownership – that kind of thing, and since I was coming over here he asked me to mention it.'

Marie whipped around and almost spat the words out. "Margarite gave this house to me!"

"Yes," said Trudy, regretting that she'd even brought it up, "but banks need more than hearsay. Sam suggested that a copy of Margarite's Will might be proof enough."

Trudy's attention diverted to Paulie, who was reaching for the grape arbor. "No-no – don't touch that." In two strides she was between Paulie and the nightshade vine. "Whew – these things are deadly, you'd better get rid of 'em." She kneeled down next to a smiling Paulie. "No-no, little fella, mustn't touch." Trudy reached out to the baby, who returned her smile.

Within seconds, Marie was between them, scooping Paulie up into her arms. "I'll take care of him, thank you."

Ignoring Marie's rudeness and the quick pang of disappointment over not being able to hold the baby, Trudy continued to speak her mind. "I know Margarite believed the berries kept little critters away from her grapes, but nightshade vines are poisonous. My neighbor told me that two calves died after eating them." She looked at the puny grape arbor. "I don't understand why Margarite pruned everything so heavily and left this stuff." She kicked the nightshade.

Marie turned on her heels and headed straight for the house. Trudy remained in the yard a few seconds, increasingly annoyed that she'd agreed to come here. Where *is* Cynthia? Anymore of this nonsense – she and Marie can whistle Dixie – for all I care.

Just then Cynthia drove up, tooting her car horn.

"Yoo-hoo," said Cynthia, "it's meee."

"I see," said Trudy, grinding her teeth.

Marie raced upstairs and put Paulie down for a nap in his crib. Trudy's questions about a will had upset her. She assumed, after Margarite's absent-minded lawyer gave a copy to Cynthia, that everything was in order, that all of it, including the Addendum, was buried in a file somewhere. Any bank review of Margarite's Last Will and Testament could be troublesome, and she certainly didn't want Sam Aldrich talking to Cynthia. Marie's thoughts raced ahead. Without a loan she'd need to sell Margarite's Georgian silver sooner than later. Coming back downstairs, she stopped in the front hallway and locked the closet door.

Marie smoothed her apron and opened the front door for Cynthia and Trudy. "Come in." She held the door open with one hand and motioned to the front parlor with the other. "Everything's in there."

Cynthia was still chirping about the sign. "I didn't realize you'd be a real inn – I mean Walter said the permits 'n things—"

"Walter doesn't live in Bellows Falls, does he?" said Marie.

Trudy saw an argument in the making. "Marie is talking about permitting – how it probably varies from town to town."

Cynthia was doubly confused and defensive. "Well, I don't really care about any of that. All I want is my sister's china. After all – it's my right." She babbled on. "I can't believe that Margarite expected total strangers to be living in her house."

Marie, worrying that Trudy would ask Cynthia about the will, turned on her charm as best she could. "Margarite always told me how much she wanted you to have the Wedgwood tea set. Of all the people she knew, she thought you'd be the one who'd take the best care of it." Marie smiled. "And see that corner cupboard? I hope you'll take everything in it." She paused for effect. "They were some of Margarite's favorite things."

Cynthia looked like a child let loose in a candy store. She picked up each dish and figurine, oohing and aahing.

Marie smiled, satisfied with herself. "Take your time, I'll make some tea. Do you like lemon or milk?"

"Lemon," said Cynthia, fondling the china pieces.

"Nothing for me, thanks," said Trudy. "I've extra cartons in the car. From the looks of things I think you'll need them."

Trudy didn't waste any time going to the car. Marie's behavior was puzzling, almost creepy. Why the sudden change? Why was Marie being so accommodating? She opened the trunk of her car, and stood there for a minute, looking at the side lawn with the grape arbor, then the house, and the new sign. Clearly, Marie was making an effort to spruce the place up, nothing wrong with that. The flowerbeds were tidy and pretty, and it looked like she'd have some roses in July. The house could use a coat of paint; that would explain the need for a bank loan. Trudy put the cartons on the sidewalk, and closed the trunk of her car. Maybe it's just me, she thought, that chat with Sam Aldrich – memories of Harold. It's depressing. I shouldn't come here anymore. I don't have to, Marie's got what she wants, and… Trudy stood by the car for a second, slowly following her own thoughts. Yes, that's it, of course. Marie's happier because she has direction, she knows what she's doing, and you, Trudy Walker, are still...still what? Trudy picked up the cartons and hurried back to the house. She was anxious to leave Burt Street.

Two teacups and a plate of cookies were on a side table in the parlor. Marie offered some to Trudy. "How about some before you go?"

"No – no, thanks," said Trudy, "I've given up tea in the afternoon." And then out of the blue she added, "Ever since Harold died...I've lost my stomach for it." Trudy heard the words but had no idea what prompted her to say them. Just the other day she had a cup of tea.

She tried to make light of it. "So busy getting things organized in Brownsville – no time to sit, let alone have a cup of tea."

Cynthia stopped wrapping the china figurines long enough to accept the teacup Marie handed to her. "Why, thank you, Marie," she said sweetly. "Hmm – what a lovely aroma, what kind is it?"

Marie dismissed the question, her eyes still on Trudy. "Nothing special – some leftovers of Margarite's."

"Well, my sister always had a taste for the unusual," said Cynthia. She finished what was in her cup and resumed packing.

Trudy, aware of Marie's stare in her direction, realized that she was still holding the empty cartons. "Oh – here, you might want these." She put three boxes next to Cynthia. "I've got to get back to Brownsville.

ELEVEN

With classes over and his senior thesis completed, Hal had a lot of unaccustomed free time on his hands. He couldn't remember anything like it, certainly not in the past four years. With a full load of classes, sports and parties, he'd barely slept. Now he sat on the bed in his room, chucking textbooks into a box. His roommates had taken off for a couple of days, assuring him they'd be back by Friday, in time for the party in Brownsville. They said they wanted to climb one more New England mountain before heading back to their home territory – the great Golden State of California. Both roommates had tried to convince Hal to get a job in San Francisco instead of New York, constantly telling him that the best-looking girls were on California beaches. "And," they said with great confidence, "anything new in this country will start out there." Well, maybe, thought Hal, but he had some ideas of his own, best kept to himself, for the time being. He sighed, wondering what he was going to do until Friday. Frankly he'd like to skip the whole thing – the party, *and* Saturday's graduation. It would be just as easy to drive to New York right away. But, maybe he could go Saturday afternoon – right *after* graduation. It'd be good to get settled on Sunday – before starting a new job. Yeah, Mom would go along with that. And Carl and Hen will probably stick around for the whole weekend; she wouldn't feel lonely Saturday night. Although when he thought about it, he didn't think moms worried about what they were going to do on Saturday nights.

Hal knew that his mother wanted him to have a good job, something solid, with a future. He would go along with that idea for a few years, but sooner or later he would make other plans. He owed it to Jenette, and his son. "Son" – the very word made him nervous. He was surprised that he actually said it. Guilt began to wash over him, beads of sweat formed on his forehead. He got up quickly and finished packing. Don't be such a wimp. You've got a plan. You're gonna write Marie, ask to see her, and explain how you'll send money. He threw the rest of his books and clothes into an empty laundry bag.

After loading his car, Hal wrote a note for his roommates reminding them to be in Brownsville by six o'clock on Friday.

~~~~~~~~

Trudy was still thinking about Bellows Falls and Marie when she pulled into her driveway. It took her a second to recognize Hal's car. She had mixed feelings about his being there. Usually happy to see him, she had looked forward to being alone. She needed time to sort out the afternoon, and the disquieting behavior of Marie. Oh well, maybe it's a good thing; I can pin him down about his guest list for the party.

When Hal came bounding out from the kitchen like a big friendly dog, her glum mood vanished. "Hi, Mom, guess what?"

"What?" replied Trudy with a smile.

"Everything's over – finito – all done but the clapping." Hal took the last box from his car. "Your son's college career has ended and I've emptied my Dartmouth room."

Trudy eyed the overloaded carton. "The contents of which are going…?"

"Not to worry," said Hal. "I've already chucked a lot of stuff."

When Trudy got out of her car she realized how tense she'd been. It took a minute to stand up straight.

Hal was surprised. "You okay?"

"Hmm – just a little stiff. Margarite's sister, Cynthia, wanted help getting things out of the house, which evidently is now Marie's."

"Oh," said Hal, sensing that it wasn't a pleasure trip.

Hal put down his box and held the door open for Trudy. "She couldn't do it herself?" he asked, following her into the kitchen.

Trudy tried to make light of it. "Oh sure, it's just that Marie had been a little prickly about things." Trudy put her pocketbook on a chair in the living room and stretched her arms, then rubbed the back of her neck.

"Why would Marie even care?" asked Hal.

Trudy wondered why *Hal* cared. "Oh God, I don't know – I suppose she's feeling proprietary – now that it's going to be an inn."

Hal placed the carton on the kitchen counter. "An inn?"

Trudy wasn't in the mood for questions. "Yes. It's a good idea. She's going to get a bank loan." She went to the refrigerator and took out an ice tray. "Which reminds me, I have to call Susan Aldrich." She smiled sweetly, and tapped the carton on top of the counter "And now would you mind taking this upstairs so I can mix myself a drink?"

Hal knew when to back off. "Yes, ma'am." He grabbed the box of books and papers. "Be down in a minute. Any beer?"

"Yes, and bring down a schedule of events for Saturday, if you have one," added Trudy, knowing that it would be unlikely for Hal to be that organized.

Hal came back down with a bunch of papers in his hands. "Events? I don't know – I think it's just graduation." He put the papers on the table next to Trudy and went to get a beer.

Trudy could see from the stationery that most of the papers looked like Dartmouth College information pertaining to graduation. "This will do. Thanks." She turned to Hal as he came out of the kitchen. "Would you grab my pocketbook? I need my address book. I told Sam that I'd call Susan about the party on Friday."

Hal handed the pocketbook to Trudy and sat in the chair on the opposite side of the window.

"This'll just take a second," said Trudy. As she picked up the phone to call Susan Aldrich, she heard Lois Dufane's voice.

"I'll be through in a minute, Trudy," said Lois.

"No hurry – sorry to trouble you," responded Trudy.

Hal was laughing. "I don't believe it – my God, what if you had an emergency?"

"I'd tell her," said Trudy, "and she'd hang up."

Hal drank some beer and settled back in the chair. He was still curious about Trudy's visit to Marie's house. "Umm – so Marie's really gonna have an inn? Did she talk about it – I mean about needing a loan?"

"No," said Trudy, with a small sigh, "Sam Aldrich did. I saw him briefly – he was taking his usual walk. I had stopped to look at our old house – wondered if the new people had made any changes." Trudy got up, and went into the kitchen to get some Triscuits. "Anyway – Sam, in his usual way, got talking, and one thing led to another."

"Well, how did the house look?" asked Hal.

"What? That's funny, I was so preoccupied I forgot to look."

Trudy had no intention of mentioning the matter of Margarite's will. She held out the basket of Triscuits to Hal. "Want some?"

"Um, sure," said Hal absently. He looked at the Triscuits, but his thoughts were a thousand miles away.

Trudy stopped holding them and put the basket on the table. "Yoo-hoo – are you there?"

"Oh, sorry," said Hal. "Um – no, thanks." He stared out the window. "Boy, that'll be a lot'a work – for Marie, I mean."

"Yes, I imagine it will," said Trudy. "Sam was delighted when I told him that he'd have a chance to see you on Friday. Speaking of which – how many friends have you invited?"

Hal forced himself to stop thinking about Marie. Looking more closely at his mother, he could see that she was tired. Being in Bellows Falls must have dredged up memories, particularly when she drove by their house. He felt guilty for asking so many questions and decided to pay more attention to the party.

"About fifteen guys. I left a note for my roommates – reminding them about it. They're climbing Mount Adams now."

"No girls?" asked Trudy, surprised.

"Well, maybe – hm – hadn't thought 'bout it. Yeah, I suppose some of 'em will bring dates."

"And what about your friends from Bellows Falls?" asked Trudy. "Have you been in touch with any of them?"

"Nah," said Hal abruptly, "that wouldn't work."

Trudy wasn't going to press it. She picked up the note pad that was always next to her chair. "Okay. Tomorrow you can get the beer." She wrote down a few things and looked up at Hal. "I gather you're spending the night here."

Hal took a handful of Triscuits from the basket. With his mouth full he answered, "Uh-huh – and I'm starving. How 'bout we go over to the mountain for supper? I saw a sign out – the restaurant's open."

Trudy laughed. "No, I'm too tired. How 'bout some leftover meatloaf? It'll just take a second to warm up." Trudy got up and headed for the kitchen. "In the meantime you can write down on that list how many bags of potato chips, pretzels, and stuff that we'll need to buy."

~~~~~~~~

Hal had agreed to stay home for a post-graduation luncheon buffet, but he was eager to get going. Friday night's party, the graduation ceremony, and now lunch. It was time to go. He didn't think his mother would mind a quick exit. Carl and Hen would be staying until Sunday and they'd be nice company for her. Everyone was anxious to give him the best route into the city. He listened patiently, not bothering to mention that he'd driven to New York many times.

Hen was trying to pin him down for a weekend in Englewood. "We're usually there in July; August is our

189

month on the Cape."

Hal tried not to make any commitments. "I'll call you when I get settled."

Hen started looking at a calendar in the kitchen. "How about the second weekend in July?" she asked.

"I get him for July Fourth," said Trudy.

Then Carl chimed in, laughing, "You'd better go, Hal, before these gals have your whole summer planned."

"You bet – I'm off." He gave Trudy a hug. "I'll call you tomorrow night," he said over his shoulder as he went out the kitchen door.

Trudy smiled and gave him a wink. "Yes, and have fun."

Hen wasn't one to dilly-dally. "My – look at all this food, and the cake! Hal hardly touched it."

"We didn't give him a chance. Don't worry, I'll eat most of it," said Carl.

"Oh no, you don't," said Hen, poking his stomach. "Now come on, let's help Trudy pick up, and then we can all go for a walk."

Carl shrugged and threw up his arms in mock despair. "Hey Tru," said Carl, using Trudy's childhood nickname, "tell her that we always finished our cakes *before* walks."

Trudy laughed and joined Hen in the clean-up. "She's right. It's a gorgeous afternoon for a walk, then you can have some tea and cake."

~~~~~~~~

Marie did not let herself relax until she saw Cynthia's

car reach the end of Burt Street and turn left onto Atkinson. She locked the front door and took the empty teacups to the kitchen. Then, taking great care, she washed the teapot, being sure that all the leaves fell into the tin and enamel strainer in the corner of the sink. She could hear Paulie cooing upstairs in his crib and hoped he'd stay happy for a few more minutes while she put the tea leaves outside in a garbage can next to the garage. Cynthia's hunger for Margarite's belongings was worrisome. Now that she'd had a good look around the parlor and dining room, Cynthia began to remember other things. Eventually the Georgian silver would come to mind. Marie slammed the lid back down on the garbage can and walked quickly back into the kitchen. *Calm down.* No need to get upset. You've come this far; Cynthia's a small hurdle. Well, maybe not so small. You just don't want Sam Aldrich asking her about the will. But why would he...unless... No. They never see each other. But what if...?

Oh, you silly woman. Marie knocked the side of her head. It's so obvious. The bank won't need to look at anything because you're going to withdraw your request for a loan. Sam Aldrich will have no reason to talk to Cynthia about the will, even if they do happen to meet. Unless... Marie stopped on the back stairs up to Paulie's room, thinking of all the possibilities. What if Margarite put some of her accounts in Cynthia's name? Marie thought back to the days prior to Margarite's death when, during her afternoon naps, Marie pored over Margarite's bank statements. Nowhere had she seen Cynthia's name. There had been no joint accounts. Cynthia would not become a problem. Marie nodded her head calmly. Yes, all she had to do was keep the Georgian silver out of sight. Paulie was becoming impatient; his cooing had turned to squawks and kicking feet.

"Granny's coming – hold your horses," said Marie.

~~~~~~~~~

Trudy poured herself a glass of ice tea and went outside to sit, and enjoy her yard. Carl and Hen had left early, wanting to be in Englewood by mid-afternoon. It was going to be a warm day. The air already had that still, sticky feeling. Trudy moved her chair under the willow tree. She began to unwind. The pasture to her right, her lush green lawn stretching out in front, and a pretty garden just beyond made it easy to relax. She'd done it: Hal was launched and now she could plan her future, not that it needed a great deal of planning. All I really want to do, she thought, is finish unpacking, have some new curtains made for the living room, and then, she laughed, keep Lester from putting chicken wire around everything in the garden! Trudy's gaze fell on the peas in her vegetable garden. Yes, that'll be fun – fresh peas and salmon for the Fourth of July. Then she looked at the strawberry patch, and wondered how to rush them along. A delicious summer meal has to be followed by strawberry shortcake, and lots of whipped cream. Trudy remembered the last time she ate strawberry shortcake. Marie had made it. Hal loved her shortcake – we all did. Marie said it was an old family recipe. Harold used to make lame jokes about it, saying that her shortcake was the French Canadian's form of bribery; a way to keep the lumberjacks working during the black fly season. One thought led to another. Trudy looked at the clump of nightshade vines Lester had pulled out. She wondered if Marie would heed her advice and remove the vines from Margarite's grape arbor. Then she leaned back in the chair and put her face up to the sun, welcoming the warm heat. She shut her eyes and let her thoughts wander. *Surely she'd keep the baby away from them.*

"Slackin' off, are ya," said Lester as he came around the corner of the garage.

Trudy's eyes popped open. "Oh hi," she said. "I guess I dozed off. The sun feels so good."

"Yup, it does now – keeps the black flies away," confirmed Lester.

Trudy didn't see the connection, but she let it go. "Do you think I'll have strawberries by the Fourth?"

"Prob'ly – a few," said Lester. "New plants – you're not likely to have bushel baskets."

"I just need a few," said Trudy. "I want to make strawberry shortcake for Hal. It'll be fun – along with my peas."

"Thad'be nice. Louise makes wicked good shortcake…"

"That's good to know," said Trudy, "because mine's nothin' to write home about."

Lester chuckled quietly, remembering that Louise always made the shortcake for Trudy's parents. He walked over to the nightshade vines. "I'll take these outta here – I'm gonna burn a pile a' brush." Trudy, feeling the heat of the bright sun, started to say something about starting a fire in the middle of the day. Lester explained, "Not 'til tonight – it's gonna rain."

"Good," said Trudy. "Need any help?"

"No," said Lester, picking up the rotting vines, "just keep small dogs and children away – ha-ha."

Trudy got up and walked over to the clump of bushes in which the nightshade grew. "It's kinda like a parasite, isn't it – needs other plants to cling to."

"You might say that," said Lester, "but then again, it serves to protect 'em. Any critter worth his salt ain't comin' near it."

"I thought you said two calves died from eating the vine."

"Like I said, 'those critters worth their salt'...musta been dumb calves, couldn't stay away from the shiny berries."

Thoroughly puzzled, Trudy stood there shaking her head. "I just don't understand how little black berries and green leaves could be so strong..."

Lester didn't know any more about deadly nightshade than the folklore he'd grown up with. "Cows

– calves – guess they kinda get the poison concentrated, chewing their cud 'n all."

"Hmmm," said Trudy, "maybe that's it." She looked up at the perfectly blue sky. "Well, it's not Monday, but it's an ideal day for hanging sheets on the line." Lester wasn't sure what she meant.

"*Monday* – that's wash day – according to my childhood nursery rhymes," Trudy explained.

"Oh," said Lester, "I see. You had quite a house full over the weekend. How's the college graduate doing in the big city?"

"So far, so good," said Trudy. "He starts his job tomorrow."

"Hope he likes it. Don't understand city life myself." Lester picked up the vines and walked around the edge of a lilac bush. "More of the fool stuff in there." He nodded toward some nightshade. "I'll cut it later. Gotta get rid o' this." He headed back to his yard across the street.

"Right-o – thanks," said Trudy.

True to her word, Trudy went inside and gathered up the bed linens. In Hal's room, she noticed that he'd put the cartons from Bellows Falls in the back of his closet. For a minute, she thought about checking to see if the letter was still in one of them. She held the closet door open, pretending to decide which sport coats of Hal's should go to the dry cleaners. For heaven's sake, Trudy –

mind your own business, she thought, and shut the closet door.

Trudy loved hanging clothes, sheets, towels – anything. This clothesline ran from the side of a tool shed to the branch of a maple tree. The back yard in Bellows Falls had been too crowded with lilacs and hemlock trees for a proper clothesline. At Marie's suggestion, Harold had put up a small store-bought contraption that stuck in the ground and blew down in a light wind. Trudy stood back, watching the sheets flutter in the breeze. A sudden puff blew one of them up so high that its edge caught in the privet hedge behind the clothesline. Pulling it from the tangle of leaves and fragrant blossoms, Trudy inadvertently grabbed more nightshade vines. She shuddered, and dropped them. *It's everywhere!.* She shook the sheet as if it had somehow been contaminated, then wiped her hands on her Bermuda shorts. Well, so much for peaceful thoughts. First Margarite warns me about it, and then Lester with his old wive's tales. What *is it* about this stuff? Trudy realized that it would drive her nuts if she didn't find out.

On top of the bookshelf in her living room was a complete set of *Encyclopedia Britannica*, the eleventh edition (1911). Trudy reached for volume 19: Mun–Odd. Nightshade – nightshade – hmm... She read quickly, looking for pertinent facts. Okay, here we go: *regular nightshade has ovate scarlet berries; large doses can poison children.* Trudy thought for a minute. She'd seen some vines with red, and some with black berries. The ones near her garden were black, by the privet they were red, and Margarite's were black. Huh, wonder what the difference is. She read on: *Deadly nightshade, or belladonna, has a shiny black berry. The entire plant is highly poisonous.* She reached for volume 3: Aus–Bis. *Belladonna: from the Italian – bella donna – the berries having been used as a cosmetic. Belladonna is widely used in medicine on account of the alkaloids which they contain…* Trudy's pulse quickened when she saw the word "alkaloid." Dr. Barnes mentioned it, something about cough medicine…? She scanned the page and stopped after reading phrases describing a *lethal dose* and *death from combined cardiac and respiratory failure.* Her mouth became dry. She swallowed hard, closed the volume and put both books back in their place. The antique clock on the corner table chimed. It was four o'clock. Without thinking Trudy looked at her wristwatch, as if the old clock couldn't possibly be right. Had she really wasted an hour looking in ancient encyclopedias? She checked the date of publication: *New York – The Encyclopedia Britannica Company 1910, published in twenty-nine volumes.* Hmpf, she thought, probably all out of date.

She looked at her watch again: 4:02. Too early for a drink, and Lord knows, I don't want a cup of tea. Next best thing was laundry – there's plenty more of that. The washing machine was next to the kitchen, under the back stairs. She quickly stuffed some bath towels into it, banging her head on the stairs in the process. Ouch! Trudy straightened up, and then almost tripped over the laundry basket. What are you doing? Before you lose your mind completely, why don't you call Carl and Hen? They're doctors, I'm sure they've heard of belladonna.

Before asking Polly to dial her brother's number, Trudy wondered how to bring up the question of deadly nightshade. On the off chance that Polly listened in for a minute or two, she didn't want the whole village of Brownsville thinking she was nuts.

"Hi, Carl – it's me…just checking up on you two. You made it home safely?"

"Yes," said Carl, "we got here a couple of hours ago. Easy drive home. Stopped for lunch outside of Hartford." Carl had a big smile on his face. "Hen and I spent the whole time rehashing the visit. Your ears must have been burning, Tru, all we did was talk about you."

"All good…" laughed Trudy.

"Everything was splendid: you, Hal, and your new surroundings. You made a good choice – moving to Brownsville."

"Oh thanks, Carl, your approval means a lot to me."

"Well, it's true; you're a strong gal, always have been – ha," he chuckled, "you were always defending me against that bully Scranton Lewis… Oops – Tru – can you hold on a second?" Carl put down the phone and held the kitchen door open for Hen, who was coming in with an armload of flowers from the garden. He pointed to the telephone. "I'm telling Trudy how great she is," he said to Hen.

Hen nodded in agreement. "I second the motion."

"Okay," said Carl, "I'm back – flowers are on their way to a vase."

Trudy laughed and decided to get to the point of her phone call. By now, Polly and anyone else on the party line would be bored with their family chatter. "Carl, I do have a question, something that might require medical knowledge."

"Fire away," said Carl, "I'm all ears."

"What do you know about belladonna – from the plant deadly, nightshade?"

"It can be deadly – no pun intended," replied Carl, "and, in small doses – very, very small – it was used cosmetically. In Victorian days medical powders were made from belladonna. Sometimes ladies would use it to enhance their pupils, hence the name – 'beautiful woman' – belladonna."

Trudy nodded in agreement. "Umm – but the deadly part – why is the plant called 'deadly nightshade'?"

Carl laughed heartily. "Why, sister dear, are you planning to do someone in?"

"No, *I'm* not," said Trudy, "it's my yard – I mean, there's a lot of deadly stuff growing in it."

"Cut it – pull it up, and wash your hands with soap," said Carl in a matter-of-fact tone.

"That's what Lester told me to do, but he also said that two calves died after eating the vines. Can it really kill a cow, or calf?"

"Sure," said Carl, "and people too – in big enough doses – over days. Don't you remember those stories we used to read as kids – Victorian London – belladonna was often the cause of death, self-inflicted, or otherwise."

"No...I guess we didn't read the same books. You were the budding doctor."

"As long as you don't mistake the berries for grapes or cherries, I'm sure you're safe – even if you don't pull up every last vine," said Carl.

"Okay," said Trudy, trying to sound cheery, "and I guess I'd better not buy any cows."

"Noooo," laughed Carl, "leave that to the dairy farmers."

Hen came over to Carl and took the phone from him. "My turn now," she said to Trudy. "Just want to reiterate what Carl said: we had a grand time, and I can't wait to have Hal out here. We'll get a few young people together before they go off to summer jobs."

"I'm sure he'd like that," said Trudy, now completely distracted. "It was lovely having you both here. Bye..."

Trudy hung up the phone and remained in her chair for a good five minutes. She thought back to the report from the medical examiner: cardiac failure. And then Doctor Barnes' explanation: "Trudy, his ticker gave out." But why did he mention finding alkaloids in Harold's blood? And then he asked me if Harold had ever complained of chest pains. No, he hadn't, ever. He was always healthy. The sun was still streaming through the picture window, but Trudy felt a chill. She reached for her sweater on the back of the chair. It wasn't even dark out, but all she wanted to do was go to bed. She didn't want think anymore. She knew the truth. Marie killed Harold. And now what was she going to do about it? She felt sick to her stomach.

TWELVE

The telephone rang. It might be Hal, thought Trudy, she'd better answer it.

With an effort Trudy made her voice sound light. "Hello..."

"Hi, Mom, this is your hard-working son reporting in," said Hal.

"My, my, has the bank got you working on weekends?"

"Almost. They've given me a manual three inches thick that requires full understanding by tomorrow," said Hal. "I'm on page four."

"Well, do your best," said Trudy sympathetically. "I'm sure they don't expect you to memorize every word."

"Mmm – maybe not...but I'd better not forget rule number three: 'Executive dining is on the top floor; employees *must* go downstairs – to the cafeteria.' Wonder what happens if we're caught eating a hot dog outside..."

Trudy missed the humor in his voice. "Wouldn't you want to eat with your colleagues, even if it is in a cafeteria?"

"Sure – sometimes. I'm just laughing over the

minuscule details of this 'Handbook.'"

"Oh," said Trudy.

"You okay?" asked Hal. "You sound kinda...flat."

"Oh, do I? Heavens – I'm *fine*. Just thinking about the wonderful weekend – gosh, it was fun. And I've got some more good news. You'll be getting a call sometime soon from Hen. She wants to introduce you to the Englewood set – young people, of course."

This is more like Mom, thought Hal, trying to organize his life. He laughed and let her 'arrangements' roll over him. "Swell – I'll look forward to it."

"Right-o," said Trudy. "Call me at the end of the week."

"You bet. I'll tell you all about the banking world."

Trudy went to bed, hoping that tomorrow would be brighter. She simply couldn't cope with her own thoughts. The only good thing right now seemed to be that Hal was happy in New York.

~~~~~~~~

Hal grabbed a beer from the refrigerator. It took him a few minutes to find an opener. There's gotta be one here, he thought. Above the stove on a narrow shelf he found a cigar box filled with utensils. He dumped the contents on the kitchen counter – a 2' x 2' piece of plywood squeezed in between the sink and the stove. Church key – church key – where art thou? He poked through a random assortment of forks, knives and spoons. A-ha! He picked up a rusty beer can opener and returned the other items to the cigar box. Then he hauled one of the two battered oak Mission chairs up to a sturdy rectangular table, four feet long by three feet wide, the top of which was an inch and a half thick. Hal figured that all of the furniture must have come in through a window – or was mysteriously placed in the apartment before they built the narrow stairs and doorways.

He sat on the old cushion stuck to the seat of the chair. At one time it might have been real leather, but years of spilled beer and food had taken its toll. After a long swig, Hal started writing. He knew exactly what he was going to say to Marie. He'd thought about it during the long drive from Brownsville to New York.

Dear Marie,

I am now working and living in New York City. Soon, I will have money of my own. With your permission, I would like to open a bank account for Paulie. I know that you will not forgive me for the past, but it is my hope that you might let me help, if only financially, in the care of your grandson. If you give me his full name, I can send the money directly to an account I will open for him. You can be the guardian.

I will be back in Vermont for a weekend in July. May I stop by your house and discuss this with you at that time? I can let you know ahead of time which day.

Yours truly,

Hal

Hal purposely referred to Paulie has *her* grandson, not his son, because he knew in Marie's eyes that he had given up that right when he turned his back on Jenette. His eyes began to sting as he remembered what he wrote to Jenette last fall. What did she think of his words? *I'll make it right, I'll make it up to you.*

~~~~~~~~

Marie was still wrestling with the problem of Cynthia. It was a rush against time, to sort through Margarite's possessions, and hide the things she wanted to sell or use when she opened the Burt Street Inn.

"*No one wants to be greedy...*" said Marie, mimicking Cynthia. My foot! If anyone's cornered the market on greed, it's that woman. She'll never use half of this stuff. I'm the one who needs it: a tea service for my guests – *and* the breakfast dishes. Marie was in the process of lugging the Georgian flat silverware up to the attic when the doorbell rang. The ringer was persistent. *Hold your horses!* From the landing at the top of the stairs, she looked out the window facing the driveway on the side of the house. Well – the nerve! She recognized Walter's truck. Hastily she shoved the mahogany box of silverware under her bed, then ran down the back stairs to the kitchen. Two large silver platters she'd just polished were on the counter. She wrapped them in a linen tablecloth she was planning to keep and put them in a laundry basket under a pile of Paulie's clothes.

Paulie had been playing happily in the playpen Marie had set up in the front parlor. After observing his grandmother angrily moving things about, he let out a sharp wail as she rushed by without stopping. For once, Marie was happy to hear his cries – all the more reason for her to appear flustered when she opened the door.

"Oh Marie," gushed Cynthia, "this is probably inconvenient for you, but Walter was coming this way in his truck today so we thought...well..."

"She wants to get the rest of Margarite's stuff," interrupted Walter.

Paulie's screams were getting louder. Marie held the door wide open so they could get an earful. "I'm very busy now. If you have a couple of boxes, you can take the figurines on that table." Marie pointed to the Asian carved wood and marble-topped table in the parlor. "And those leather-bound books on the shelf behind them – you're welcome to those."

"Oh, are we now..." said Walter sarcastically. "Glad to hear that you're allowing my wife to take what's rightfully hers."

Marie gave Walter a scathing look, and turned her back to him as she spoke to Cynthia. "On Tuesday afternoons, I leave Paulie for a couple of hours with my friend across the street. Why don't you come by then and have some tea with me? We can have a nice time packing the things you'd like to have."

"I won't have much time Tuesday," said Cynthia, reaching for a date book in her pocketbook. "I have to go shopping in the morning, then a hair appointment – "

"You go to Shirl's Curls, don't you?" asked Marie.

"Yes…" answered Cynthia cautiously.

"She's just two blocks over," stated Marie. "You can come here afterwards."

"Yes, yes, I suppose I could."

"And if we can't finish packing everything, you can come back on Wednesday," said Marie. "I know how important it is for you to have all of Margarite's favorite things out of here, now that this is my house."

Cynthia looked wistful. "Yes, yes. The attorney sent me the documentation. That's what Magarite, apparently, wrote in her will." Cynthia looked around the parlor. "I always thought…well, you know, we were sisters. It's funny, she never said anything about the house…"

"Should've stayed in the family," said Walter, "doesn't make any sense."

Marie felt beads of sweat forming on her the back of her neck. She leaned over and picked up Paulie, letting his blanket brush against her face. Any response would only provoke more questions. She focused her attention on Paulie. "There-there-there, little fella – what's the matter? Are you hungry?" She started for the kitchen. "I'm going to get him some juice, why don't you pack up those things." She pointed to the figurines.

Cynthia looked at Walter helplessly. "Do you have the cartons?"

Walter made a show of his empty hands. "No – does it look like it? Forget it – the little things will just break, rattling 'round in the back of the truck. You can get them Tuesday." He walked to the front door. "I'll be in the truck."

"Yes, Tuesday, I guess Walter's right," said Cynthia, reluctantly putting a figurine back on the table. She stepped gingerly around the playpen, as if she might catch germs from it, and called to Marie in the kitchen, "Bye, Marie – see you the day after tomorrow."

"And do *not* park in the driveway," Marie called out. "I have deliveries that day – park in front – on the street." Her real reason for wanting Cynthia to park out front was security. She didn't want Cynthia popping in the back door unannounced. She couldn't lock that door, and the pantry, with its myriad shelves and cubbyholes, was too much of a temptation for Cynthia's prying eyes.

Usually Marie had no need for an alarm clock, Paulie started each morning with the birds, but before going to sleep, she set it for 4:30 a.m.. Monday would be a busy day. She had to go through the whole house, removing every item of Margarite's that she wanted to keep and storing them safely in the attic. After which, it would be imperative to arrange all of the remaining knick-knacks, china, and silver pieces on shelves and in cupboards. She wanted everything to appear untouched, as if Margarite had arranged them herself.

By the time Paulie woke up at 6:30, Marie had found

a safe hiding place for the silver and china, a dark corner in the attic, behind a built-in closet. It was unlikely that Cynthia even knew about the attic, but Marie was taking no chances. She left a silver candelabra, a sterling silver Paul Revere bowl, and Margarite's 'everyday' silver flatware smack in the middle of the dining room table, sure that Cynthia would be riveted. She put the entire set of Georgian silver in an old steamer trunk in the attic. The trunk was tin-lined, bulky, and covered with dust. Once she'd filled it, Marie sprinkled a new layer of dust over the top.

After giving Paulie his breakfast, she surveyed her handiwork, satisfied that everything looked much the same as it did when Margarite was alive. Paulie looked at Marie with wide eyes. It was time for an outing. "Okay, okay, Granny's all set." Marie carried Paulie to the front porch, where she'd left the baby carriage. It was becoming a struggle to hold Paulie in one arm while pulling the carriage down the porch steps with the other. Paulie squawked at being held so tightly. "I suppose if I were smart I'd let you crawl around on the ground while I did this – then we'd both be happy," said Marie. Paulie's answer was to squirm, and reach out for the carriage. "Hold on – you almost knocked me over!" Marie plunked him in the carriage and sat down on the steps to catch her breath.

Just then, the mailman came bustling down the street waving a letter in the air. "Yoo-hoo, Marie – got something special for ya." Norman Bowes, the postman, ran over to the porch, his long grasshopper legs knocking at the knees. "It's a letter – certified," he said breathlessly, "ya gotta sign for it."

Marie was almost as surprised as he was. "Certified? I don't know anybody who'd – "

"Somebody knows you – it's from New York City," stated Norman proudly, as if anything from New York City was automatically important. The return address was simply a street number with an apartment number next to it. No name. Marie held the envelope in her hand. She had a feeling who'd sent it, and was grateful that he'd not written his name at the top of the address. She got up from the porch step. "Do you have a pen?"

Norman gave Marie a pen and watched her sign the piece of paper taped to the envelope. Marie tore off the signed receipt, and handed it to him. Norman stood there a second longer than necessary, only to be disappointed when Marie put the letter in her skirt pocket and said to him with a smile, "Thank you, Norman." She put her hands on the carriage, ready to push off. "Paulie is ready for his carriage ride."

Norman jumped out of the way, just missing the carriage wheels. "Sure thing – ha-ha – don't want to keep the little fella waitin' – bye now." He waved to Paulie as Marie headed down the sidewalk pushing the carriage at a good clip.

Marie waited until she reached the end of Burt Street

before taking the letter from her pocket. With a quick glance back to make sure that Norman was out of sight, she opened the envelope. Her heart was keeping time with the crazy thoughts racing through her head. Marie knew the letter was from Hal. She recognized the handwriting. But why certified mail? Why the hurry? Was he plotting to get Paulie? Trudy had seemed awfully interested in him. Or was it Margarite's house – that business about the will?

Paulie didn't like the sudden halt of his carriage. "Shh," said Marie, as she unfolded the one piece of lined paper she'd removed from the envelope. Holding the paper open in one hand, she turned the carriage, and slowly pushed it on the sidewalk running along Atkinson Street. Within half a block, she'd read Hal's words twice. At the end of the block she stopped and read the letter a third time. She felt weak with relief.

Marie spoke to Paulie. "Well, young man, this puts a different light on things. Except the money is going to be in my name, not yours." She folded the letter and put it back in her skirt pocket. "Don't worry, I'll save most of it for you. I just can't have folks at the bank asking questions."

Marie wasn't much of a letter writer. Her reply to Hal was simple. Yes, she'd see him when he comes. They could talk then. Rather than wait for the mailman to pick it up in the morning, she made time later that afternoon to walk downtown, and slip it in the letterbox

212

in front of the post office. Paulie was delighted to be in the carriage again, looking about and returning the smiles from folks greeting him with a shake of his rattle. Each silly cooing noise from an adult produced a hearty laugh from Paulie. Marie smiled, but kept walking, saying she needed to get back to the house in time for Paulie's nap. He'd already had his nap but the last thing she wanted to do was answer a slew of questions about her plans for the inn. Clearly, they all knew she was living in Margarite's house. That's all the information anyone needed for now – or ever, as far as she was concerned.

Marie stayed up later than her usual nine o'clock bedtime. She needed to clear her thoughts. The money from Hal might be enough to eliminate the need to sell Margarite's things right away. However, Cynthia wouldn't let up 'til she thought she'd removed every valuable item from this house; she'd take the shutters if she could, and Walter would help her. Marie reviewed the list of the things she'd put in the attic. During her travelling days, Margarite had amassed a sizable collection of china. She doubted that Cynthia knew about every purchase. After all, thought Marie, as sisters go, they really weren't that close, they never seemed to do much together. The only loose thread was Margarite's will, and the Addendum. If Cynthia ever looked at it closely, her plans might go up in smoke. No, Marie decided. That *will not* happen. She felt the letter in her skirt pocket and smiled. Knowing Hal as she did, she knew that he'd be in Bellows Falls before the month was out.

In the morning, Marie felt energized and eager to set her plans in motion. First thing was to call her neighbor across the street, and ask if she could leave Paulie there an hour earlier than scheduled. Cynthia would be arriving shortly after two. Marie wanted time to artfully arrange the less appealing pieces of china and glass figurines in Margarite's collection. Her intent was to make the parlor look crowded, as if she'd unearthed every last "collectible" in the house. She made a fresh batch of cookies and chose a particularly bland-looking teapot, one unlikely to attract Cynthia's attention, for their afternoon tea. Fortunately, the cartons which Margarite had used to store the china in, were still good. Marie took them out to the back steps, tapped them upside-down on the railing, and brushed any lingering dust off the sides. She put four of them and a stack of old newspapers on the kitchen floor. The rest she put in the garage. Marie thought it would be more convincing if Cynthia had to make several trips to Bellows Falls, proving that she, Marie, wanted Cynthia to have all of Margarite's belongings. The clincher would be the mink stole Marie had found in Margarite's bedroom closet. At first, Marie had thought of selling it, but the desire to placate Cynthia won out. Marie actually giggled to herself when she thought of Cynthia's expression upon seeing it. Paulie giggled, too, when he watched his grandmother put it over her shoulders and prance around the bedroom. "Don't you think Granny looks pretty?" Paulie was sitting on the floor looking up at the fashion parade as Marie took more clothes from the closet and put them in a cardboard box. She paused before discarding a thick wool sweater. "Now, this is something I could use. How 'bout it – good – yes?" Paulie kicked his legs in appreciation. Marie smiled at him. "Okay, we'll put this in the cedar chest for safekeeping from the moths – and Cynthia."

Marie was proud of herself. The mink stole on the arm of the velvet Victorian love seat was the perfect touch. Cynthia would be drooling. The tailored suits, tweed and wool chenille she left on hangers on a chair in the hallway. Unlikely that Cynthia, a few dress sizes larger than Margarite, could wear them, but that's all right; she knew Cynthia would take them anyway.

While Paulie ate a banana, happily squashing most of it on his high chair, Marie made the rest of his lunch: little bits of a hamburger and cooked carrots. At eight months, he had lots of teeth and seemed capable of chewing most anything. However, worried about the possibility of choking, Marie preferred to cut his food into tiny pieces.

"There you go, mister," she said, placing the food directly onto the tray of the high chair. Paulie stared at the spread before him, and then at his grandmother.

"Nope, no bowls for you," said Marie, "I've learned." Paulie inspected the food, wondering what his grandmother was up to. Marie was amused. "It's food – I just saved you a step; you don't have to dump it out of the bowl." Paulie started eating some of the well-cooked hamburger, pausing occasionally to throw some carrots at the cat, Felix, a stray who'd wandered into the yard a week ago. He was without a collar, and seemed in no hurry to leave. Marie decided to feed him, and named him after a pet kitten she'd had as a child. Felix dutifully ate the carrots and waited patiently for the meat course.

"Oh no ya don't," said Marie, as Paulie started to throw the hamburg pieces. "You eat your lunch, young man. This fella's goin' outside." She opened the kitchen door and dropped Felix onto the porch. "And you stay out of here if you know what's good for you." Felix, all black with four white feet, was a quick study. He made a beeline for the garage. Paulie, less understanding, started bawling.

"Oh now, now," said Marie, "don't worry about Felix." She gave him a Zwieback cookie to take his mind off Felix.

By the time Marie deposited Paulie with her friend across the street, her cookie dough had chilled enough to slice small rounds from the roll she had wrapped in wax paper. She put them in the refrigerator. The recipe, calling for lots of butter, chopped pecans, sugar and a little flour, was foolproof. All it required in the fussy department was flattening the rounds with the bottom of a small glass, over which she placed a damp dishtowel to keep the dough from sticking. While one cookie sheet was in the oven, she filled up the second one, timing the baking to be completed just as Cynthia was due to arrive at two o'clock. And to preclude any poking about in the kitchen, Marie decided to put everything in the parlor ahead of time: cookies, teacups, milk, sugar, and lemon. Cynthia could be out of the way, salivating over her new riches in the parlor while Marie prepared a nice pot of hot tea for her enjoyment.

"I see you've been very busy," said Cynthia between mouthfuls of cookies. "I knew my sister had a lot of rare pieces of china, but never realized the extent." Cynthia had the mink stole over her shoulders as she moved about the front parlor, admiring herself in the gold-gilded mirror as she spoke to Marie, who was in the kitchen. "Everything she ever bought must be in this room. I don't know if I have enough cartons."

Marie smiled to herself. She poured hot water from the teapot, satisfied that it was warm enough for a proper pot of tea. After putting in the tea leaves, she removed the kettle of boiling water from the stove and poured half of it into the teapot, saving some for a refill. "I'll be right there. I'm just letting the tea steep for a minute." She covered the pot with a worn tea cozy, crocheted with blue and green yarn years ago. Her Great-Aunt Marie, after whom she was named, gave it to her as a wedding present. Marie knew it would make Cynthia comfortable – seeing Marie with a worn, ordinary teapot. This way, Cynthia could rest assured that she was getting all of the "good china."

Marie stretched her mouth into a big grin. "Here we are – a nice pot of tea." She placed it on a tray with a faded floral design, next to the plate of cookies. "Why don't you sit down for a minute? A cup of tea will be refreshing. You'll need energy to go through all of this." Marie chuckled inwardly at the stole over Cynthia's shoulders. "That looks nice on you."

"Thank you, Marie," replied Cynthia, expecting nothing less than a compliment. "I expect to wear it a lot. But maybe not this summer – ha-ha, it's kinda warm for mink."

"Hmm," said Marie. "Put it over there – next to those suits." She filled a teacup and held it out for Cynthia. "Lemon – sugar…?"

Cynthia took the tea absently – still eyeing the suits. "I hadn't noticed those – "

"Yes, they were Margarite's," said Marie. "I put them – "

"Well, *of course* they were Margarite's," said Cynthia, gulping her tea. "Ooh – my – that's hot." She put the cup down, and ate another cookie. "But good – nice 'n strong – the way I like it."

"Yes, well – drink up – you've got a lot to do," advised Marie. "It might be a good idea to make two trips, take what you can today, and get the rest tomorrow. I can probably find more cartons. And of course, you can empty those when you get home and bring 'em back for a refill." Marie leaned back in her chair and smiled. "Might as well get everything while you can, before I open for business."

"Absolutely. It wouldn't do to have my sister's things exposed to strangers." She drank more tea. "I still don't understand why she changed her mind – leaving the house to you. I mean, having that little baby is no reason..." She saw Marie stiffen. "Oh, Marie – I know it's not *your* baby, it's not as if you could've done anything."

"Paulie is my grandson," said Marie, keeping her temper in check. "I'll help you take these things to your car."

Cynthia put her cup on the tray. "Thank you," she said formally. "And by the way, the cookies were very good. Is that an old family farm recipe – from Canada?"

Marie ignored the question. "If you're here tomorrow at two we can finish this."

"In time for another lovely cup of tea," said Cynthia, trying to smooth things over.

After a few trips back and forth from the house to the car, Cynthia decided that she had enough cartons for one trip.

Marie cleared the tea things from the parlor. She rinsed the teapot, leaving it to dry in the dish rack. Carefully, she removed the soggy tea leaves from the strainer in the kitchen sink, and put them in the garbage can. The few cookies Cynthia did not eat went into the cookie jar. What a pig, thought Marie.

~~~~~~~~

Trudy guessed that she'd had about four hours of sleep, in spite of the fact that she'd been in bed since seven the previous evening. It was now six a.m. She woke up with the birds at 5:30, then mercifully dozed for another thirty minutes. Lying in bed staring out at the mountain, she forced herself to sit up and get out of bed. You've been here long enough, she grumbled to herself, ten – twelve hours – ugh, disgusting. In one swoop, she put her legs on the floor and stood up, sort of testing to see if they still worked. Once they seemed okay, she proceeded to the next step: shower.

Sometime during the night, Trudy decided to stop kidding herself. There was only one thing to do: confront Marie – reveal her suspicions about Harold's death, and the identity of Paulie's father. Furthermore, she realized, she had to explain all of this to Hal, just when and how, she didn't know. That part still eluded her. Should she speak with Hal first, and then confront Marie? What if Marie denied everything – then what? She had no proof, of the poisoning anyway. And the child? Well, that is easy; one look at that baby, and you know who the father is.

Trudy started to make some breakfast, but decided on a walk instead. It was hard to think straight with the rings of early morning phone calls on her party line. Her neighbors were ever vigilant about matters that might have occurred during their sleeping hours. She put the bacon back in the refrigerator and turned off the coffee. Anyway, she thought, breakfast would taste better after a walk up the hill to the old cemetery. She'd walk back home across the freshly-mowed field. All of the hay bales had been picked up; the grass would be short and crunchy underfoot. She decided to wear sneakers instead of sandals.

Louise was already in her flower garden in front of the small brick house she and Lester shared. She was tending an exceptionally tall delphinium, gently tying it to stakes, hoping to keep the brilliant blue flowers from flopping over. Trudy was reluctant to disturb her concentration, but Louise spoke first.

"Mornin', Trudy," she smiled, "nice time o' day for a walk."

"Yes," agreed Trudy, "before the sun gets too hot." She paused at the corner of the picket fence where Louise was working. "What a gorgeous delphinium – I've never seen one quite so tall. How long have you had it?"

"Five years. Bought it at the church plant sale five years ago May." Louise stood back and admired her handiwork.

"You have a good eye for quality," said Trudy as she waved and walked on.

Sticking to her resolve to sort things out while walking, Trudy began to make a mental list of priorities as she started up the road.

Number one: Ask Hal if he's the father. He'll be up here July 4th weekend – that's only two weeks away.

Number two: If he says yes, then they'd both talk to Marie about his obligations. And *mine* too; after all, I *am* the other grandmother.

Number three: The poisoning. Yes, Harold *is* dead, but you have no hard proof that Marie was responsible – that she actually poisoned him with deadly nightshade. It could very well be your imagination working overtime. And what good would it serve to start accusing Marie? Who would believe such a wild theory? Hal would probably think she was off her rocker. Trudy stood at the top of the hill, catching her breath. She remembered how Hal used to *run* up the hill when he was a little boy. Then her thoughts went back to the baby. Who would take care of him, if Marie couldn't? Trudy had to stop herself right there. *No*, your whole nightshade idea is preposterous. Put it out of your mind! She turned abruptly, and started walking back across the field to her house. What you *need* to do is come up with a plan to help your grandchild. It's up to you *and* Hal. And, most likely, Hal will feel better once things are resolved. He won't have to worry about keeping everything from me. He can go about his life, see the child occasionally, and, who knows, maybe someday he'll marry. Trudy hoped that she was at least partly right.

~~~~~~~~

Cynthia had phoned Marie early in the morning, saying that Walter was feeling poorly – probably something going around – and didn't know if she could get to Bellows Falls that afternoon. Marie insisted that Cynthia stick with their plan to pack the rest of Margarite's things at two o'clock. There would be no other convenient time.

Concerned that Marie might not welcome her in the future, Cynthia decided to leave Walter for awhile and go to Bellows Falls. Once there, she settled herself comfortably on the love seat in the parlor, in a proprietary, lady-of-the-manor sort of way.

"I know it must be a relief for you to have these fine things of my sister's out of the house. Unless one is brought up with them, it's hard to know…" She shook her head in a patronizing manner. " Well, you really wouldn't know what to do with them."

"Yes," said Marie succinctly. "I see you've brought back the empty cartons. Good. We'll fill them up." She passed the cookies to Cynthia. "Please, have some. I'll get the tea."

"Why, thank you, Marie. I could use a pick-me-up. I've been feeling kinda tired myself; I hope it's not Walter's bug." Marie went into the kitchen while Cynthia continued talking. "That man – he always gets just a little sick, then passes the worst of it to me." She prattled on, "Pretty soon, though, *you're* goin' to have to watch for germs…"

"How so?" said Marie, not sure what Cynthia was talking about.

"Your little one – you know – how babies get sick," said Cynthia.

"I'm sure I can handle that," said Marie. She poured tea into Cynthia's cup. "This is a little stronger today, you might notice a different taste."

Cynthia took a sip with relish. "Hmm – even better than yesterday." She held the cup in her hands, ready to drink more. "One thing did occur to me as I was driving over here: photo albums. I'm sure Margarite had some…." Her eyes scanned the room and stopped at Margarite's Hepplewhite desk. "Ah – I bet they're in there."

Marie was pleased with herself. After retrieving the loose change, the spare tens and twenties that Margarite had kept for emergencies, she purposely left Margarite's garden journal, personal letters, and the photo album just where Margarite had always left them. "That's a good idea, why don't you look."

Cynthia put her cup down and went to the desk. "Of course – here they are, and look, here's her garden journal." She picked it up tenderly – feigning sentiment. "How sweet, I can read about all the flowers she loved." Cynthia placed the photo albums and the journal in one of the cartons. "But wait a minute, didn't my sister have a checking account?"

Marie thought quickly. "Check with the attorney.

I'm sure he has all of that information."

Cynthia looked at her wristwatch. "Well, time's a-wasting, and now I'm beginning to feel tired." She rubbed her throat. "Darn Walter anyway – his ole germs."

"Why don't you sit down for a minute. Have some more tea," said Marie. "I'll wrap up the rest of the china plates, and carry the cartons to the car."

Cynthia liked that idea. She poured herself another cup of tea and started directing Marie's packing. "Don't forget that vase on the table – wrap that – I know it was one of Margarite's favorites. I think it had belonged to mother."

Marie chuckled quietly to herself. The vase had been given to Margarite by the hospital volunteer association. It was a thank-you gift for all of her help. She never liked it, and brought it out only when one of the volunteers stopped by.

Within ten minutes, Marie had the car packed and Cynthia in it ready to drive away with her loot. There was no mention of a return visit. Both women were content.

THIRTEEN

Hal was walking down West 78th Street with his seersucker jacket over his shoulder and his necktie loosened. It was 5:30 Friday afternoon and still very hot and muggy. People were sitting on the stoops in front of the old brownstones, fanning themselves with newspapers. His block, between Amsterdam and Columbus, was mostly Puerto Rican families, college students, and young college graduates like himself just starting out in the business world. Hal was friendly with the kids playing on the street and the sidewalk. Today they'd somehow opened a fire hydrant and were running through the gushing water, daring Hal to get wet. He laughed and chased them around the hydrant. They loved it when Hal's shirt got soaked. He smiled and waved hello to their mothers, who sat watching the play from their stoops. In three bounding strides, Hal was up the stairs in front of his brownstone. At the front door, he feigned alarm when one of the boys threw a water balloon after him. Hal caught it in mid-air and threw it back. The kids broke out in hilarious laughter. Hal made a big deal about opening the front door, and rushing inside.

Dripping with water, he checked the day's mail. Usually his box, number two, was empty, so it was a surprise to see a single white envelope sitting there. The postmark was clear: Bellows Falls, Vermont. A return address wasn't necessary; he knew it was from Marie. Hal raced up the stairs to his second floor apartment. Ignoring the water dripping from his shirt, he tore open the envelope. Marie's message was not a glowing invitation, nor was it a rejection. Simply put, she would be willing to see him when he came to Bellows Falls again. Hal gave a sigh of relief and smiled. That's Marie, he thought – gets straight to the point, no beating around the bush. He put the letter on his desk and went into his bedroom to change his wet button-down shirt for a short-sleeve cotton knit, one of the two casual shirts he'd remembered to pack. His khaki pants were still dry; he'd kept those on and removed his cordovan shoes for some more comfortable loafers. In a while, he'd be joining some friends at Michael's Pub on Madison Avenue for beer and maybe a hamburger.

He was in a good mood. Things were falling into place. He could see Marie on his way to Brownsville over the 4th of July weekend. He had enough money in his New York checking account for an easy transfer of funds to the bank in Bellows Falls as soon as Marie wanted it. Hal picked his wet shirt up from the floor, and hung it over the shower rod in the bathroom. It was still early. He opened a can of Budweiser, and sat by the window. Looking down at the kids, Hal wondered if Marie would let him play catch with Paulie when he was the age of those kids, or would she just accept the money, and tell him to get lost. The ring of the phone broke into his thoughts.

Hal reached for it on the desk. "Hello," he said, hoping it wasn't one of his friends changing their plans. He was in the mood to go out, and talk with people. Now that he knew Marie would meet with him, he didn't want to think about it. The enormity of the situation still frightened him.

"Hal…is that you? This is Hen – in Englewood."

"Yes – hi Hen. This is Hal," he laughed. "How are you?"

"I'm fine – so's Carl," replied Hen. "Listen, I've just got a minute, but we wanted to catch you before your calendar gets too full."

Hal laughed to himself. He remembered his mother saying how Hen always prefaced a phone conversation: *"I've just got a minute."*

"We're having a party on the 4th and would love it if you could come. A fun, casual thing – badminton, volleyball, and of course fireworks."

Hal thought quickly. He had to get to Vermont, but the 4th wasn't 'til Tuesday. He could still go up on Saturday, just come back a day early, on Monday. "Sure –

tha'd be great – umm, what time?"

"That's swell – I'll tell Carl you'll be his badminton partner. Come at four." She started to hang up. "Oh – Hal, do you know how to get here?"

"No," laughed Hal, "it's been awhile, when I was back in high school."

"Don't worry then – I'll send you a little map. And give our love to Trudy. Bye." And she hung up.

"Okay, Walker," said Hal out loud, "I guess you're going to meet the Englewood set."
He finished his beer, and put the empty can in a wastebasket in the kitchen area of his apartment. Checking the time, Hal realized he'd better get going. Tomorrow he would call his mom and tell her about the shortened weekend. She'd be disappointed, but he knew that the party at Carl and Hen's would make up for it.

~~~~~~~~

Trudy was on her way out the door to play tennis in Woodstock when the phone rang. It was her ring. "Now, who's that?" she muttered. She put her racket on the counter and reached for the phone. "Hello," she said hurriedly.

"Mom...? It's me. You sound rushed," said Hal.

"I am a little – on my way to play tennis with Patsy Strong. She's punctual, and lets the world know it." Trudy sat on one of the kitchen stools. "But that's okay. I'm ahead of schedule – talk away," she said with a smile.

"I've got good news and bad – well, not *bad* – just not

as *good* news. Hen called late yesterday and invited me to a party in Englewood on the Fourth–"

"But I thought you'd be coming here," interrupted Trudy.

"I can still come to Vermont," Hal quickly explained. "I'll come up Saturday, and leave Brownsville Monday instead of Tuesday. It's just one less day; I'll be back up in August."

Trudy was mollified. "Hmmm – all right, and that's nice – you'll be meeting some young people in Englewood."

"Maybe," said Hal. "I think Uncle Carl just wants a strong badminton partner."

"Ha-ha," laughed Trudy, "I'm sure that's not the only reason." She looked at the kitchen clock. "I'd better run now – let me know what time to expect you on the first."

"Will do," said Hal. "I'm expecting to see lots of tennis trophies."

"Right-o," said Trudy as she hung up. The phone started ringing again. It was her ring; she ignored it and rushed to the car.

Hal had a lot of planning to do regarding this quick trip to Vermont. But the first thing was to write a short note to Marie. He'd be there Saturday, July first – right after lunch.

~~~~~~~~

Trudy had just come back from the General Store with the Sunday paper, and was looking forward to immersing herself in it, along with several cups of coffee, four strips of bacon, and three pieces of toast and jam. This was a treat she saved for Sunday mornings.

Bacon cooked to the right crispness, homemade raspberry jam – compliments of Louise – and a strong pot of coffee. Trudy was very content. Then the telephone started in. She barely listened, sure that it was not for her. None of her friends would think of calling at this hour on a Sunday morning, and Hal certainly knew better. The ringing persisted.

Who in the world…? Thought Trudy staring at the phone. She gulped some of her coffee and picked up the receiver. "Hello," she said icily. Nothing – no sound, then a slight cough that sounded like someone clearing his throat. "Hello," she repeated impatiently.

"Is this Trudy Walker?" said a scratchy voice.

"Yes – this is she. With whom am I speaking?" said Trudy in her haughtiest tone.

"This is Walter – Walter Luden – Cynthia's husband."

Trudy sighed, thinking, now what? "Yes, good morning, Walter. What can I do for you?"

"Sorry to bother you so early – it being a Sunday – I tried callin' yesterday."

"That's all right," said Trudy, lying, but trying to be patient. "How are you?"

"Well – umm – I'm callin' to tell you that Cynthia is dead," said Walter with an uncommon softness in his voice.

"Cynthia died – she's dead? Why – why, what happened?" said Trudy, trying to recover from her bluntness. "When did it happen – I mean…how?"

"Thursday evening," said Walter. "She got home from Bellows Falls, tried to fix supper, said she was feeling poorly…she looked kinda peaked too. Of course, I'd been sick myself, so I figured – "

"Yes," said Trudy " and you called a doctor?"

"Not right off. Cynthia didn't want me to – said it was nothing, just a touch of what I had."

"Oh," said Trudy, "you had the flu, or something like that."

"Not exactly, you see, I could breathe – it got so Cynthia suddenly couldn't. Then I called the doctor."

"And…?" said Trudy.

"When the doctor came, he said her heart had failed. He'd known for some time that she had a weakness there. Same as her sister. It runs in families," he said. "Weak hearts, it's what they have, sometimes." Walter blew his nose. "She died while I was holding her head up." He cleared his throat. "Didn't Margarite have the same problem – with her heart, I mean?"

"Yes, I think so," said Trudy, remembering Margarite's breathless condition before she died. "I'm very sorry, Walter. Is there anything I can do? When are you going to have a service for her?"

"Tomorrow at two o'clock – at Christ's Church here

in Walpole. And – umm, thank you for your offer of help, but the church ladies are taking care of things, they'll be making sandwiches…" His voice trailed off.

"All right," said Trudy gently. "Thank you, Walter, for calling me. I'll be at the service tomorrow." She put the receiver down. Oh dear – poor Walter. The stuffing has been knocked right out of him.

Reading the newspaper was no longer pleasant. Instead, Trudy went outside to weed the flowerbed in front of the house.

After the funeral service, Trudy went to the hall in the lower level of the church, where friends of Cynthia and Walter's were gathering for coffee and sandwiches. She took some coffee, and a small egg salad sandwich, and waited in the short line to express her condolences to Walter. The general opinion seemed to be that Cynthia's extraordinary love of sweets was the cause of her heart attack. And, as one lady reminded people, "Cynthia had two trips in a row 'tween Walpole 'n Bellows Falls and she *always* ate candy in her car, an' boom – her heart just said 'enough.'"

Trudy wasn't sure of the logic in this premise, but refrained from commenting. Just before it was her turn to shake Walter's hand, she put her empty coffee cup in a nearby wastebasket. One of the ladies thanked her, and offered her a piece of strawberry rhubarb pie. It looked good, but after that dissertation about sweets, Trudy declined.

Walter seemed to be holding up well. He gave Trudy's hand a firm shake. "Thank you for coming, Trudy. Cynthia appreciated your help with sorting out Margarite's things, and now...well, I guess it's too late to for her to enjoy them."

"I was glad to help," said Trudy, hoping to sound neutral. She nodded toward the flowers, and all of the food on the table. "It's nice that you have so many friends, they'll be a great support." She saw no point in staying any longer. "Don't hesitate to call if I can do anything."

"Thank you," said Walter with a quiet dignity. "I will."

On her way out of the church, Trudy thought about the change in Walter's manner. Clearly, he enjoyed the attention of the church ladies. At the very least, he'd be assured of a warm casserole in his kitchen every few nights.

~~~~~~~~

Thursday turned out to be a banner day for Marie. She read in the obituary section of the *Bellows Falls Gazette* that Cynthia Luden died on June 14th, and then she had a letter from Hal Walker. The paper said Cynthia died in her home of heart failure, and that there had been a family history of heart problems.

Good, thought Marie, that was short and sweet, and no more Cynthia pokin' around here. Putting the newspaper aside, Marie opened Hal's letter. She read exactly what she'd expected, and then some. Hal's visit would be sooner than she'd hoped for.

Paulie was playing happily in the playpen in the corner of the kitchen.

"You don't know him, and maybe you never will, but it's your papa who will be paying for the upkeep of this house." Marie surveyed the kitchen critically. "Yes, we've got a lot of work to do."

~~~~~~~~

Hal had written to Marie that he'd be at her house at one o'clock on Saturday, July 1st. It was only 12:30 when he got to Bellows Falls. He didn't want to get off on the wrong foot by arriving too early, so he stopped for a hot dog at Joey's, a lunch place on the corner of Main and Bridge Streets. From the window of the luncheonette, he saw the burned brick shell of his father's paper mill. Looking at it, lots of questions came to mind. Mostly "whys" and "what ifs." He wondered for a moment. Absently, he put more mustard on the hot dog he'd ordered and allowed himself to dream.

The waitress's voice interrupted his thoughts. "Aren't you Hal Walker?" she asked.

Hal turned toward her. "Um – yeah – yes, I am," he said, wondering who she was.

"I'm Ginnie Monroe. I'm a...well – I *was* – a friend of Jenette's." She was refilling a napkin holder on the lunch counter and turned shyly toward Hal. "I recognize you from a picture Jenette had."

Hal stared at her. Picture…? What picture?

Ginnie saw his puzzlement. "A little one." She bent her thumb and forefinger into a small circle. "You two were at a fair – one of those carnival booths."

"Oh – oh yeah," said Hal, not remembering, and feeling ill at ease. "Ah – yes – um – I – that is, my family and I were very sorry about her death." He hated the insincere ring of his voice. His mouth felt like sawdust. "The whole thing, it was terrible."

"Yes, it was…" Ginnie studied the napkin holder. "I hear that her mother is takin' care of the little boy…"

Hal struggled to finish his hot dog, then checked the time on his wristwatch. "Yeah – that's what I hear too." He stood up. "Well – I'm kinda in a hurry, how much do I owe for the hot dog and Coke?"

"You pay my mom. She's over there." Ginnie pointed to a woman sitting by a cash register at the end of the counter.

"Okay – thanks," said Hal. "Um – nice meeting you."

"Yeah – sure," said Ginnie.

Hal checked his watch again. He still had a couple of minutes. Why did I go in there? Now I suppose it'll be all over town – "Hal Walker came back to survey the damage and…he dated Jenette Furneau." Hal didn't look up at the waitress, standing at the window. Driving north on Main Street, he turned onto Canal Street, and stopped at the door of Jenette's old building. Silently he promised her, *again*, that he'd watch out for their son.

Marie was waiting on the front porch when Hal drove up. She waved, but didn't get out of the wicker chair that she was sitting in. It was exactly one o'clock. "I see that you've learned to be on time," she said when Hal stepped out of his car.

"Yes, have to – now that I'm working," said Hal, walking up the porch steps. He stood in front of Marie, and extended his hand for a formal handshake. "Hello, Marie, thank you…"

Instead of shaking Hal's hand, Marie pointed to a chair next to hers. "Sit down, and tell me what you have in mind. In the letter you said something about opening a bank account for my grandson?"

"Yes," said Hal, sitting in the chair Marie had indicated.

"Why the change of heart?" asked Marie. "Last fall, you didn't want anything to do with him."

Hal thought he'd explained everything in the letter. For a second, he felt a flash of resentment, but he remembered another letter – the one he wrote to Jenette. "I told Jenette – before – before she died, that I'd make it up to her."

Marie knew full well what he was talking about – it was the letter she'd intercepted – but she wasn't going to let him off the hook so easily.

"Just 'cause it suits you now to admit fatherhood, don't think for a minute that you're gonna have a say in how the boy's raised."

"I'd like to – "

Marie interrupted again. "Only thing people around here *know* – or care about – is that Paulie's my grandson. Period. And that's the way I like it, so when you open that bank account, you put *my* name on it." She sat back in the chair, tilting her head toward the window opened to the front parlor. Paulie was beginning to stir from his nap. She ignored his little squeaks.

Hal had not planned on this. The whole idea had been to open an account for his *son*; he was acknowledging his duty – his concern. This was the right thing to do, he *wanted* to be the father, even if it was a remote fatherhood, and now Marie was saying "no" – he should pay but be quiet about it. She had him over a barrel. If he didn't go along with her wishes, he'd never get to see his son.

"All right, I'll wire money next week. I'll need your full name, and new address, which is here, I presume," said Hal, pointing to the sign in front of the house. "I can put in a hundred dollars to open the account, then fifty dollars the first of each month."

Marie looked skeptical.

"As soon as I get a raise," explained Hal, "hopefully in the fall – I can send more."

Marie nodded as if that's what she expected.

At a very young age, Paulie was becoming a peacemaker. The awkward silence following Hal's explanation was broken by his squawks and rattling of the playpen. Hal peered in the open window.

"Can I go in and say hi?" he asked.

"I guess it won't hurt," said Marie, getting up from her chair. "He wants his juice and cracker. You can come in while I get it."

Hal didn't hesitate. He jumped up, and followed Marie into the parlor. He'd never thought about the size of a baby, but he was surprised to see how big Paulie was.

"He's so big," said Hal proudly. "I mean, are all babies so tall?" He held his hand over the playpen just above Paulie's head.

Marie leaned down, and picked up Paulie. "You were big," she said, looking him up and down. "Ya still are." She walked to the kitchen, and put Paulie in a high chair while she poured some apple juice into a small baby bottle. Hal watched, fascinated, as Paulie grabbed it and started drinking.

"If he throws it, hand it back to him," said Marie, stepping aside. At the end of the kitchen counter in a corner between the door and the back stairs, Marie had created a "business workplace", necessary, she believed, when her inn was up and running. In it, she'd placed a stand-up desk, a writing tablet, and ink, and a fountain pen. After checking to make sure the pen had ink in it, she slowly wrote her full name: *Marie Anne Louise Furneau*. Then, just as carefully: *23 Burt Street, Bellows Falls, Vermont*. With equal care she used an ink blotter before folding the piece of paper.

"Here," said Marie, "this is what you can give the bank."

Hal had been fixated on Paulie, wondering if there was a right way and a wrong way of handing a dropped bottle back to a baby. Reluctant to give up his job of bottle retriever, he took the paper from Marie, glanced quickly at her careful penmanship, and put it in his pants pocket. "Okay," he said, stepping away from the playpen, "I'll set up an account the end of next week, or early the following week."

Marie had been disappointed to see her carefully scripted name and address so casually stuffed into Hal's pocket. Hal mistook her frown for distress over the timing of the account opening. "You see, July Fourth – that kinda messes things up – everything gets backlogged – but I'll do it as soon as possible."

"Of course. I know you will," said Marie as she opened a box of Zwieback biscuits for Paulie. "You must be busy – new job – new friends." She took the nearly empty bottle of juice from Paulie and handed Hal the biscuit. "Would you like to give it to him?"

"Sure!" Hal extended the biscuit to Paulie. Paulie gurgled and smiled, and took the biscuit, putting most of it in his mouth.

"Do you have a girlfriend, yet?" she asked, still looking at Paulie.

Hal felt himself flush. "No – ah – no, I don't."

Marie knew the question made Hal uncomfortable, but she didn't care – she wasn't in the business of making people feel comfortable, she had scores to settle. Making Hal Walker wince was just part of it.

"Well – I imagine you will – in time. Children too." She pointed to Paulie. "But this one's mine. You remember that when you tell your mother about this meeting."

"I might not tell—" said Hal, feeling anxious and cornered.

"Yes, you will," interrupted Marie. "You're much too soft-hearted, least you were before…" Her expression hardened. Her voice changed to steel. "People like you Walkers… Someday, you'll learn about pain."

For an instant, Hal felt like a ten-year-old boy back in his old house on Atkinson Street. Then he was angry, and defensive. After all – he'd lost someone too. He looked over Marie's shoulder, through the screen in the back door – wishing to be outside, but Marie and Paulie were in the way.

Marie could still read his mind. She walked over to the screen door, pushed it open and stood there. "You can come by from time to time to see Paulie. Let me know ahead of time; I'm very busy."

Hal wasted no time in leaving. "Thank you," he said. I'll try to get the account set up by next Thursday – or Friday at the latest." He turned towards Paulie. "Bye, big guy."

Marie nodded silently. Be patient, she told herself. Things were in motion.

During most of the drive to Brownsville, Hal felt sad. He wasn't sure exactly what he'd expected. Maybe a little more enthusiasm from Marie? Marie's certainty that Hal would tell his mother about the visit, annoyed him. Of course she was right. Mom would be hurt, and mad, if the news came from someone else. Maybe he wouldn't tell her about the bank account. But Sam Aldrich would find out, and tell her. Oh boy. Hal wondered what his mother had planned for dinner, and if she'd bought some beer.

A new sound greeted Hal as he drove in the driveway: barking – a dog's barking. He turned off the motor, and before he could open the car door, a springer spaniel jumped up to the open window. Following this uncontrolled, wriggling, drooling canine was Trudy.

"Cinders – heel! Down! Cinders – sit!" Finally she pulled the dog by its collar, so Hal could open the car door.

"Cinders?" asked Hal, as she struggled to get free and jump up to him.

Trudy laughed helplessly. "Yes, Cinders, a thoroughly pedigreed Springer Spaniel, and thoroughly untrained. Midge Forbes dropped her off this morning. She thinks I need a pet."

Hal knelt down to eye level with Cinders, and the dog continued to pant. "She's great," he said. "Just think, you might even be able to train her for bird shooting – take her out hunting like Granddad did. What was it – grouse, or woodcock he used to shoot?"

"Woodcock, I think," said Trudy, recalling the days of tramping over the fields with her father, "but I think this bird dog has a way to go." With that she released her hold on the dog, and Cinders went bounding out across the pasture.

"Will she come back?" asked Hal, as he watched the liver-and-white spaniel race out across the mowed field.

"Oh yes, at least I think so – this is where she's fed. Speaking of which," Trudy added, "get your bag and come on in, and...how 'bout a hug?" She gave Hal a quick embrace. "It's been awhile – can't wait to hear everything."

Trudy opened the refrigerator, and pointed to the Budweiser. "Get a beer and come on outside. That way, I can keep an eye on the dog, and she can see us."

"Do you think she'll *remember* us?" laughed Hal.

"Stop it," said Trudy. "Springers are supposed to have a good homing instinct; that's what I've been told, anyway."

"I know nothing," smiled Hal, opening a cupboard next to the sink. "Got any nuts? I didn't have much lunch."

"On the top shelf," said Trudy, "take the can."

They sat on the lawn chairs Trudy had placed under the willow tree. From there they had a good view of Mount Ascutney, and the pasture. For a few seconds they were quiet, enjoying the view, and watching Cinders chase imaginary rabbits. Trudy leaned back in her chair.

"It appears that New York agrees with you – or vice-versa. You look well," she said. "I guess food in the employee dining hall is edible – your clothes aren't hanging off you."

"Yeah, when I have the time, I try to fill up at lunch; lately I've been too busy to have more'n a sandwich," said Hal. "But then," he laughed, "I make up for it on the way home. I meet my friends at Michael's Pub and put away two or three cheeseburgers – and a couple of beers."

Trudy raised an eyebrow in mock admonition. "Every night...?"

"Don't worry," said Hal, "we're all pretty moderate during the week."

"I'm sure you are," smiled Trudy, "and I know it's nice to relax with friends." She reached for some peanuts, and scanned the field for Cinders. "What time did you leave the city – you're earlier than I expected – which is lovely."

"Oh – I don't know," said Hal, "eight or so – I woke up early. I kinda took my time, stopped along the way." Hal finished the beer, and stood up. "Mind if I get another one?"

"No, of course not – help yourself," said Trudy. "Then you can help me pick some peas." She got up and headed for the garage, while Hal went in the living room door. "I'll get my vegetable basket. Would you bring out that blue bowl that's on the kitchen counter? We'll need it for the peas – after we shell them."

"Sure thing," said Hal.

Hal tossed the empty beer can in the kitchen waste basket, and looked at the kitchen clock. He'd planned on telling Trudy about Paulie during dinner, but all of a sudden, he felt apprehensive about the whole thing. This'll screw up everything for her. Maybe, I shouldn't say anything. He got another beer from the refrigerator and walked into the living room. Hal noticed the family photographs Trudy had arranged on a bookshelf. He peered closely at them, particularly the one in which he was standing next to a canoe holding a fishing rod, and his first fish. That had been one of those rare days his father had taken him canoeing on the Connecticut River. They cleaned the fish – an eight-inch perch, made a little fire, and cooked it right there. Hal squeezed his forehead. His mouth felt dry. He stared at the picture with a mixture of panic and determination. Someday, he thought, that's going to be me and Paulie. It has to be – the kid has to have… His thoughts were broken by Trudy's voice.

"Yoo-hoo – out here – remember?" called Trudy.

Hal hurried out the living room door. "Here I come." He put his beer on the table, and went over to the garden to help pick the peas. "I was looking at the pictures you've put out. They're nice."

"Hmm, yes, it's fun to look at them – a time long ago. You're all grown up now," said Trudy. "Did ya bring the blue bowl?"

Hal looked at his empty hands, laughed, and headed back to the kitchen. "Nope – forgot all about it."

"Before you do that, maybe you'd better run out to the field and get Cinders," said Trudy. "I'm beginning to think she's off on a toot."

"Will do," said Hal. "Do you have a leash?"

"No, Midge forgot to drop it off. Just pick her up if you have to."

Hal laughed and went running off after the dog.

For a couple of minutes, Trudy's thoughts followed Hal. He seemed distracted – not quite at ease. She wondered if it was something about his job, or maybe adjusting to life in New York. No…he probably likes *everything*; it's coming back to the country that throws him off. She'd have to reassure him that he's not obliged to spend every holiday here.

After they filled the basket with peas and were sitting back in the lawn chairs, Hal began eating peas as fast as he could shell them. He looked at the near empty bowl on the table. "Oops, sorry," he said with a mouthful.

"Uh–huh," said Trudy, "save some for supper. We're

having lamb chops."

"Great – I haven't had any since…well…since we were last in Bellows Falls."

"Yes, that was when we had dinner at the hotel, and Ray Le Bec caused a scene." She shook her head. "Mercifully, that seems like a century ago."

Hal drank some more beer. "Yes and no," said Hal quietly. "I stopped in Bellows Falls before coming here; I went to see Marie."

Trudy felt her eye twitch. She blinked, pretending something was in it. She was afraid to speak, almost feeling what Hal's next words would be. But then, she heard herself prattle on about the house, and Marie's plans to make it an inn. "That's nice – I mean that you stopped by. It must have been fun to see the changes. I suppose she'll have to enlarge the kitchen. I wonder if Sam ever gave her a loan – the porch could use some paint. But she has to show him a deed first – if she – "

Hal interrupted her. "Mom, I went to talk about the baby – Paulie. He's – a… well – I'm the father."

Trudy gasped, put her hands to her mouth. Peas fell on the ground, and tears welled up in her eyes. "I'm sorry," she said, reaching in her pocket for a nonexistent handkerchief.

"*I'm* the one who's – " said Hal.

"No-no," said Trudy, waving her hand, "I mean about getting weepy, it's just that…" She took a deep breath and reached out for Hal's hand. "I always kinda suspected

248

that was the case."

Hal stared at his mother. His eyes welled up with tears.

Trudy sat up straight, and nodded her head knowingly, as if to confirm her faith in Hal. Then she explained. "Way back – when I first laid eyes on Paulie, I saw you."

Hal rubbed his eyelids.

"Yes," said Trudy, "moms can spot things like that."

Hal didn't know what to say. He'd been prepared to explain everything, starting with Jenette – his love of her, then the confusion, and guilt when he turned his back on her. Had his mother known all along about their dating? Why didn't she say something?

"Oh Hal," said Trudy. She gave his hand a pat, and leaned back in her chair. "First let me say how proud I am of you."

"But, I – " stammered Hal.

"Wait," said Trudy, "let me finish. As I said, I've suspected all along that you were the father." She put her hands in her lap, twisting her wedding ring. "But...I was cowardly; I didn't want anything to upset your future – your job in New York. I talked myself into believing that your job was more important than..." Trudy paused, and took a deep breath, "...than the baby. I guess you could say I swept it under the rug." She gave Hal a weak smile. "And Marie made it easy. She didn't want anything to do with me."

249

"Marie doesn't like us – or me – much. Can't say I blame her; I was pretty cruel to Jenette. I mean she'd still be here if I'd – "

"Stop that," said Trudy. "Your actions then were a direct result of torn loyalties between your father and me, and Jenette. Where could you turn?"

"I wrote Jenette a letter – before she died. I told her I'd send money, and that things would work out as soon as I got settled in New York. I never thought…well – I didn't want to be a father, and Jenette probably hadn't planned on having a – "

"I know," interrupted Trudy, "but these things happen, and when they do we don't always know how to react. If I could take back all the dumb things…" She caught herself. "I'm sorry."

"I've been thinking about this for a long time," said Hal. "My plan is to open a bank account for Paulie. I'm going to start with fifty dollars a month. And when I get a raise, I can increase that amount, maybe to sixty dollars. It might be awhile though," he added, "before the bank thinks I'm ready to move up."

"I see, and you stopped in Bellows Falls to tell Marie about your plan. How did she receive you?"

"She was expecting me. I'd written her ahead of time. She answered, and told me to be there at one o'clock."

Trudy let it pass, but when did Marie have the right to order her son around? "And I'm sure you were punctual," she said, with a bit of an edge to her voice.

"You bet," said Hal, "you know Marie."

"Yes."

"Well, we got right down to business," said Hal, feeling more relaxed, almost excited about his decisions. "Marie accepted my offer of opening a bank account for Paulie. It was all pretty straightforward, except – she wants the account to be in her name."

"What? The money's for Paulie – your son, for heaven's sake!"

"Yes," said Hal, "I know – I know who he is, and the money *is* for him. It's just that Marie doesn't want people to know I'm the father. She thinks people will find out if the account's in his name."

"Nonsense," said Trudy, "somebody's gotta be the father."

"I know – I know," said Hal. "I went along with it so I can see Paulie from time to time. All he's got is Marie, and she's his *grand*mother – who is old. The kid's gotta have somebody else…" The fishing photograph was still in Hal's thoughts.

"Well," said Trudy, "I'm his other *grand*mother – what about my rights to the child? Or is she calling the shots on that, too? And who's to know if the money will go for Paulie? She'll probably use it for that bizarre little inn she plans to open." Trudy's anger was accelerating, and she didn't care. "Really – a grandmother, with a little baby – running a business – an Inn – no less, with strangers around!"

He tried to deflect Trudy's vehemence. "I gave him a biscuit. The kid has quite a grip. He held it all by himself."

"I should hope so," said Trudy, "he's ten months old; you were feeding yourself by then. Is he crawling?"

"I guess so. I don't know, he was in a playpen," said Hal.

"Of course," said Trudy, "that's where he was the last time I saw him. She keeps him penned up all the time – be lucky if he walks by the time he's two!"

"Mommm," pleaded Hal. "Give her a chance – in time she'll come around. Right now she's still mad, and...well, it hasn't even been a year since the fire. It's hard on everyone..." Hal looked at his mother's clenched jaw. Oh great, he thought, now I've done it. He picked up the old tennis ball Cinders kept dropping at his feet, and tossed it across the lawn. "Look, I'm sorry – I've made a mess of everything. I know Dad would probably be disowning me about now."

Trudy forced herself to calm down. "No dear, it's your ole ma who's in the wrong." She reached for more peas to shell. "Simply put, I'm a tad bit jealous. I'd like to see the boy too." She struggled to fight back a tear. "But, you're right – best to wait. Maybe sometime in the future I'll be able to play with my grandson." Cinders came back with the tennis ball, dropping it this time at Trudy's feet. Trudy patted her absently, ignoring her pleas for another toss. "As I said a minute ago, Hal, you've done the right thing. I am very proud of you, and your father, after his initial blustering, would have stood by you. We always knew what a fine man you'd be." With that said Trudy stood up, and slapped her hands together. "There – that's enough praise for one day!"

Hal knew that the discussion was over. Trudy's abrupt rise, and quick slap of her hands was the signal. For as long as he could remember that was his mother's method of signaling guests that the party was over. If that didn't work, she started taking plates into the kitchen. In this case, it was the bowl of peas.

For the remainder of the afternoon, Trudy busied herself with dinner preparations. At five o'clock, she decided it was time for a cocktail. The cubes in the ice tray were stuck. Trudy stood at the kitchen sink holding it under hot water. Out the window she watched Hal playing with Cinders. Her heart ached – for the past – for what might have been. Stop it! she muttered. But her mind wouldn't quit. What kind of boy will Paulie become? Smart – nice? After all, she'd never said more than "hello" to Jenette. Had she been a bright girl? Hmpf – guess not, she thought cynically, or none of this would have happened. The hot water almost scalded Trudy's hand. "Ouch!" See – that's what you get – *you're* not being nice. Annoyed with herself, Trudy dropped three ice cubes in an old-fashioned glass, and put the remaining ice in the freezer section of the refrigerator. After pouring a jigger of bourbon in her glass, she added a splash of water, and stirred it with her finger. Now just calm down, she repeated, your son is doing the right thing – it's good to have it out in the open. But *is* it out in the open? No, of course it isn't. Why is Marie so adamant about keeping it a secret? What's she up to? Will she use that little boy to bleed Hal dry – take everything he earns? And why is she shutting me out? If she's really going to make that place an inn, you'd think she'd *welcome* some help. Outside, Hal's hoot of laughter over the dog's antics brought her thoughts back . Maybe Hal's right. Marie's daughter is dead. She's grief-stricken, *and* angry. But no, that couldn't be the whole story. I've lost people too – my husband, for Pete's sake. And Margarite – she was a good friend, yet I'm not mad at the whole world – sad, yes, and lonely. Inexplicably that same uneasy feeling was coming back. Trudy dismissed it. You're becoming a suspicious, jealous old woman, she muttered.

It was warm enough to have dinner outside. They sat under the willow tree, quietly watching swallows dive back and forth. Occasionally, a meadowlark would grace them with a song. Hal fell under the spell of the soft summer evening. He actually felt relaxed. He'd never thought about "relaxing" before. In college, the routine was study, play sports, go to parties, drink beer, and fall asleep. In New York that had modified to work, drink a couple of beers – sleep.

He helped himself to another lamb chop. "Boy, these are good."

"Well go to it," said Trudy. "That's why I bought them, but don't forget your peas…"

"Don't worry – all that shelling – I'm not leaving one," laughed Hal. He put an extra-large serving on his plate.

"Speaking of work," said Trudy, "tell me more about yours – think you'll make it to the executive dining room by the fall?"

"Not likely," laughed Hal. "I think what happens is, that after this summer's training period the work load accelerates – be lucky if I have time to eat a sandwich – let alone go to a dining room. Some older guys told me that it's not unusual to work Saturday mornings."

"Ooh – that'll put a cramp in your style," said Trudy.

"Yeah, I hadn't really thought about it. I don't know how many weekends I'll be able to get up here. I'll have to figure out something – in order to see Paulie."

"Your work comes first," said Trudy, "you can't take time off willy-nilly. If it's the baby's welfare you're worried about…well, I can…" She stopped, hearing the hardness in her voice. "What I mean is – "

"I know, Mom, thanks, but I'll work it out."

Trudy felt hurt, and wanted to pursue it. This mess involves me as much as anyone.

They both heard the phone ringing. Hal jumped up.

"Don't bother – it's for Phyllis Berryfield – her son always calls her at supper time," said Trudy.

Hal stood – ears cocked. "Is yours two longs and a short?"

"Yes."

"Then it's for you," said Hal, waiting for instructions.

"Darn it all – why doesn't Polly tell them we're not here – she knows I like to be outside in the early evening."

"Well – should I get it?" asked Hal.

"Yes – you'd better, she won't quit."

Seeing the empty chair, Cinders jumped up to it, expecting at the very least a lamb chop bone. "What do you think you're doing – get down! And dogs aren't supposed to eat these bones," said Trudy, "it'll split, and you'll choke." She cut off a small piece of meat and handed it to Cinders, almost losing her fingers in the process. "Hey – careful! And don't get used to it – lamb is too costly for the likes of you." Cinders responded with a friendly slobber in Trudy's lap. "Yes…you're a good dog – you'll keep me from getting too cranky, won't you?"

Hal was standing on the front steps, holding the telephone in one hand and waving the receiver with the other. "Mom – it's for you – Uncle Carl. He wants you down there for the party…"

"Hold on…" Trudy smiled and got up.

"The phone won't stretch any further," said Hal,

handing it to her at the front door.

"I know – thanks. Go finish your chops before Cinders grabs them."

"Cinders?" queried Carl, on the other end of the phone line. "You have a pet?"

"Sort of," said Trudy, "a friend dropped her off yesterday – for a trial run. She's a lumbering springer, but quite lovable."

"Sounds perfect," laughed Carl, "but give her back for a couple of days so you can come down for our party. No need for you to stay up there while everyone's here."

"Aren't you sweet," said Trudy, "but I've made plans to go to Falmouth; Margo and Thadd are having a 'do.' I think I'll stay for the week. When do you go down? Maybe I'll still be there."

"Not 'til the second week in August. Darn – that's too bad, sorry to miss you, both here and Falmouth, but I'm glad you'll be having fun. And Hen's tickled that Hal will be here. She's lined up all sorts of young people, you know – ever the matchmaker."

"Sounds lovely," said Trudy, "and many thanks for thinking of Hal. He's been straight out with work. Your party will be a nice change."

"That's what we're aiming for," said Carl. "Call us when you get back from Falmouth."

"Okay – bye," said Trudy. She hung up and realized that she felt better. Good ole big brother Carl, she thought, he's still rescuing me – from myself.

Hal was at the door with his hands full of plates. "I don't believe that dog – I hope you'd finished eating."

Trudy opened the door and let him in. "The lamb chops? Did she get those?"

Hal handed her the plates. "Yours was empty when I got to the table..."

"Oh dear – let's hope she chews well, otherwise..."

"Great, she'll be losing it all night." Hal looked back at Cinders. "She's eating grass now – she'll be throwing up in a minute."

"Where'd you learn those pearls of wisdom?" asked Trudy.

"Dartmouth. The fraternity had a mascot for awhile – a beagle – it ate grass all the time."

"Oh. Well – keep an eye on her. I can't leave her out all night."

"So," said Hal, "I guess I'll see you down in Englewood...?"

Trudy started putting the dishes in the dishwasher. "No – I've made plans to go to Falmouth – the Baldwins."

"Huh? I thought you were celebrating the Fourth here," said Hal.

"I was, but then when your plans changed I decided to change mine. You know, I'm not without resources of my own," said Trudy, smiling at her son's confused expression. "And besides, Falmouth is more fun in the middle of the summer than Englewood."

"You're right there, but compared to Manhattan, Englewood'll seem like the wide open country," said Hal.

Trudy handed him a dishtowel to dry the pots and pans and the salad bowl. "You're leaving half the stuff *out* of the dishwasher," said Hal.

"Hmm-hm," said Trudy, "that's a crystal salad bowl and these pans get cleaner when I wash them. The pans go over there – on the shelf above the stove."

Hal was watching Cinders from the kitchen window. "There she goes."

"That's good – at least she won't be in trouble all night," said Trudy. "Why don't you call her in, I'll get some water."

When Trudy was filling the dog's water dish in the garage, Hal went over to the bookcase with the photographs on it. He picked up an album from the bottom shelf, sat on the couch, and started looking at the family pictures. Most of them were of himself – as a baby, young boy and high school student.

"Do you want to take a few of those to New York?" asked Trudy, walking in from the kitchen.

"These…" said Hal, holding the album up. "Oh no, I – um – I was just looking, I wouldn't want to keep anything – um – anything good in my apartment." He closed the album, and put it back on the shelf. "Actually, I need some more shirts," he said, tugging at the one he was wearing. "Are there any more upstairs?"

"Yes, and socks – your dresser drawer is full of them.

Did you take *any* to New York?" She looked at Hal's feet as he walked past her to the front stairs. "What are you wearing? I hope you're not going sockless..."

"Nope – I've got a couple," said Hal.

"That's nice...do you ever *wash* them? And take that madras shirt – it looks nice on you. You can wear it to the party."

Trudy heard the dog scratching on the screen door. "Hold on – here I come." When Cinders came bounding in, Trudy had to smile in spite of the watery trail she left behind. "What a happy dog you are; maybe I *should* keep you." Cinders wriggled and grinned. "Ha-ha – yes, you're a good dog – we'll have lots of fun," said Trudy, "but you *will* have to learn some manners."

In the morning shortly after breakfast, Hal piled shirts, socks, and more of his 33 LP records on the back seat of his car.

"Don't you want a box?" asked Trudy.

"Nah – then I have to get rid of the box, the landlord doesn't like stuff left in the hallway," said Hal.

Trudy shrugged, not quite sure what that meant. "Hmm – okay." She leaned in the car window, and gave him a peck on the cheek. "Drive safely and have fun at Carl and Hen's."

"I'll try," said Hal with a big grin.

FOURTEEN

"Yoo – hoo – Hal – over here…" Hen was waving to Hal from the other side of the badminton net. She came running around the net to give Hal a big hug. "We're so glad you could come!" She took his hand and walked over to a small bar Carl had set up on a flagstone terrace. "Everybody – the guest of honor has arrived," declared Hen.

Carl laughed, and shook Hal's hand. "Don't worry – she'll calm down in a minute." He turned to a young couple just getting a beer. "Jamie – Karen – this is my nephew, Hal Walker. Hal, meet two of Englewood's rising young physicians."

"Hi," said Hal, accepting a beer from Carl. He nodded thanks, and started to ask Jamie and Karen some questions about the medical field when his eyes fell on the most beautiful hair he'd ever seen. For a few seconds he stood stock still, staring at the reddish-golden curls of a young woman standing on the other side of the terrace. She had her back to Hal. All he could see was sparkling wavy hair going every which way when the girl moved her head.

Karen followed Hal's gaze and laughed. "That's Christy Enders. Would you like to be introduced?"

"Oh. Well – no…" said Hal, "I mean…"

Jamie helped him out. "Sure, come on – we'll introduce you. Her father's chief of surgery. We run into her from time to time in the hospital."

"Is she a doctor, too?" asked Hal, feeling a little awkward.

"Oh no," said Karen, "she's a candy striper – volunteer work. I see her sometimes on the pediatric ward. I'm a pediatric nurse. Jamie's the doctor – he's interning under your uncle."

"Oh – I see," said Hal.

Karen tapped Christy on the shoulder. "Hi, Christy…"

Christy had just bitten into a deviled egg; her mouth was full when she turned around. "Hmm…" She pointed to the other half and swallowed. "Ha-ha – want some…?"

"No thanks," said Hal, laughing, unable to take his eyes off her.

"Christy," said Jamie, "meet Hal Walker from across the Hudson, and nephew of Carl."

"Hi, are you really *from* New York?" said Christy. "I only know people who move there."

"I'm of the *moved* variety – I'm working there," said Hal. "I'm originally, well – my home, I'd guess you'd say, is Vermont."

"Lucky you," said Christy. "I've been there a couple of times – skiing at Stowe and once at Mad River Glen."

"Really – which do you prefer?" asked Hal.

"Stowe by far – more trails," said Christy.

"Have you tried Nose Dive?" asked Hal.

"Ha-ha – once," said Christy, "almost killed myself."

"It's that third turn – ya have to stay way up…" said Hal, extending his arm in an arc that almost touched Christy's hair.

Jamie and Karen smiled at each other, their job was over. Christy and Hal barely noticed them walking away.

Hal reached for some popcorn and started eating it. "Oh, I'm sorry, would you like some?" He started to pass the bowl and dropped his handful of popcorn in the process.

"Whoops," laughed Christy.

"Oh boy – where are the pigeons when you need'em," said Hal, as he picked up the spilled popcorn.

"They're busy in Central Park," smiled Christy.

Hal straightened himself up and took a drink of his beer. "Yeah – um – do you work in New York too?"

"Only part time – social work, three days a week."

"That's nice," replied Hal, "you can explore the city the rest of the time."

"Ha-ha – don't I wish. Only problem is I can't afford to live there. I have to commute from home."

"Oh," said Hal, "that's – ah "

"Very boring," chimed in Christy, "but luckily I have some friends who have real jobs and apartments. Lots of times I spend the night with them."

"That's great," said Hal, "I mean – a lot easier than..."

"Hey –," called Carl, "we need two more for badminton!"

"You game?" asked Hal, looking at Christy.

"Sure!"

"Whew," said Carl, wiping his brow, "you two could be the next club champions."

"Runner-up will do," laughed Hal and Christy, simultaneously.

They heard a bell clanging. Hen was down on the lawn ringing it. "Okay everybody – come and get it – time to eat!"

"That's my call to duty," said Carl. "I'm the kitchen boy."

"Do you need some help?" asked Christy.

"No thanks – just have a hearty appetite."

Christy turned to Hal. "Your Aunt and Uncle are so nice, do you see them often?"

"Not really, this is my first time out here."

"Oh," said Christy.

"Yeah – work and everything..." Hal hesitated a second. "But sometime when you're at your friend's in the city, maybe we could get together." Christy's sudden grin encouraged him. "I know this great pub on Madison…"

"Oh sure – Michael's!

"Oh – you've been there?

She nods.

"Do you want to meet there Wednesday… about six?"

"Yeah," laughed Christy with delight. "I'll check with my friend – see if I can stay at her place."

~~~~~~~~

Shortly after Trudy had returned from Falmouth, Hal telephoned her. He said how nice Carl and Hen had been, and mentioned Christy briefly, describing her as a really nice girl who liked to ski in Vermont, and could play a mean game of badminton. After that, he said very little to Trudy about Christy, or what he was doing socially. Their phone calls centered around work, and the summer heat in New York.

Hal didn't know it, but that's just what Trudy had hoped for, a separate social life for Hal – away from Vermont. She didn't like the financial "arrangement" he'd made with Marie, and hoped that he would stay away from Bellows Falls. Even though her friends in Falmouth had reassured her that Hal was capable of handling Marie's possessiveness, Trudy worried that Hal might spend the rest of his life dancing to her tune.

All in all, the trip to Falmouth had been fun. Margo and Thadd couldn't have been nicer. Their understanding, and almost casual thoughts on "this situation of Hal's child" – as they referred to it – helped Trudy put things in perspective, but she also knew that they might think differently if it were their son who was going to be pulled in two different directions. And when Margo suggested to Trudy that perhaps she hadn't given herself enough time to mourn Harold's death, Trudy had purposely let that topic drop. She knew that her frightful suspicions about the cause of Harold's death, as well as her obvious concern over the baby's identity, had precluded any so-called *normal mourning* period. And now, six months after his death, her sense of anxiety was even worse. Frankly, she wished that Hal had not approached Marie with his grand plan. In time, she would have confronted her – mother to mother. They could have had a frank, and straightforward discussion. They could have shared their sadness, and maybe… even the joy of Hal's son. But no, from what Hal told her, Marie would go to her grave hating the Walkers.

~~~~~~~~

When Marie wanted to sell a piece of silver – usually a small bowl or serving spoon – she took it to an antique dealer in Springfield. The transactions were in cash, and no questions asked. Occasionally she'd offer the information that her mother in Canada had recently died, but usually she simply took the money, and went directly to the bank in Bellows Falls. With each entry in the passbook, she felt a growing sense of pleasure.

Repairs on the house were progressing nicely – without the loan from Sam Aldrich. The porch, however, cost more than she'd anticipated; a good deal of it was rotten and needed to be replaced. The money Hal had given her was gone, and with only fifty dollars a month coming in she'd have to sell a lot more silver, or get Hal to increase his payments. It was the middle of August. Maybe she should write Hal and ask if he could add twenty-five dollars to the September deposit. Her reasons for the increase? Paulie is growing fast – he needs more food? No, she thought, not urgent enough. Sickness? Yes, that's it. She can say that she's had to take Paulie to the doctor's a couple of times – nothing too serious, but the appointments do cost money. Marie smiled at Paulie, who was crawling up and down the porch steps.

"Your father's a softy, but I don't want you to be that way. You learn to get what you want, and keep it."

~~~~~~~~~

Christy had arranged to spend two nights in a row at her friend's apartment. She would see Hal at Michael's on Wednesday after work, and then Thursday evening she'd spend making a special picnic lunch – for Friday – in Central park. She planned to ask him on Wednesday, hoping that he would be able to take some time off for lunch.

"Over here!" called Christy, waving to Hal.

Hal had taken off his seersucker jacket and loosened his tie. He saw that Christy had spread the picnic out on a blanket. "And I thought that I could be gallant and spread out my jacket for you to sit on." He smiled and sat down "This is nicer."

"Hmm," said Christy. "Here – have a deviled egg." She held one up for Hal.

"Oh boy – real food, and I'm starving."

"Careful, don't get it on your necktie."

"Yeah – eggs 'n banking don't mix," laughed Hal. He peered into the picnic basket.

"Yes, there's more," said Christy, spreading out the potato salad, ham, and butter rolls. She looked at her wristwatch. "I know you have to get back to work, but I'm dying to ask you this now."

"I'm all ears," said Hal.

"Well, you know my parents have a place in Quissett on the Cape?"

Hal smiled and took a roll. "Yes…"

"Well next weekend there's a mini regatta – small Cat boats." Christy handed a plate of salad to Hal. I'd love to enter it and have you be my crew! My parents don't have any room, but they said you could stay in the Harbor House – it's kind of a special guest inn, my mom says, for Quissett "overflows".

"I'm not much of a sailor," said Hal, "but sure, I'm game."

It was almost with relief that Hal read Marie's request for more money. He'd had such a good time in Quissett, sailing with Christy and being with her family that he was starting to feel disloyal to his mother. And now, as his fondness for Christy was growing, and becoming apparent to everyone, he felt quilty. When and how was he going to tell Christy about Paulie?

Instead of another weekend in Quissett, he should go to Brownsville, and Bellows Falls.

Hal hoped Christy would answer the phone, not her mother. He didn't want another invitation to the Enders' just yet.

"Hello? Mrs. En-"

"Hello – oh, hi Hal," laughed Christy. "You really want to speak to my mom?"

"No, I mean – you sounded different," said Hal, suddenly feeling nervous. "I guess it's the noise on the street."

"You're lucky to have some noise. It's quiet and boring out here," said Christy. "Englewood is definitely not the place to be in the summer."

Hal relaxed. "Okay, I've got an idea. How'd you like a weekend in Vermont, say Labor Day weekend? There's plenty of room in my mom's house, and…"

"Sure – I'd love it! But, is it okay? Maybe your mom's busy."

"Nah – I mean she'd love it if we come. I'll call her

269

tonight." Hal hesitated a minute. "Your parents won't mind...? If you're not in Quissett that weekend?"

"Of course not, silly. They'll understand – you have to spend time with your mom too!" Would we leave that Friday when you finish work?"

"Yeah, is that okay? I could pick you up around five-thirty – six o'clock."

"Great – I'll plan to be at Lizzie's apartment, so you don't have to drive out here. And can we go to Bellows Falls? Is it close enough? I'd love to see where you used to live."

"Yeah, sure – we can do that." Hal almost gulped with relief. "But don't forget, we're gonna see each other between now an' Labor Day – this coming Wednesday at Michael's?"

"Of course," said Christy, with a smile in her voice.

As soon as he got off the phone with Christy, Hal called his mother – hoping that nine o'clock wasn't too late.

Trudy *was* surprised to hear the phone ring but she wasn't asleep. Cinders had taken care of that. An evening run in the field had turned into a two-hour "hunt" for rodents. As soon as Cinders got the scent of any other creature – be it fowl, feline, or a silly little mouse – she took off like a shot, returning in her own sweet time. Tonight, however, she announced her return with several loud barks. It might have been more, but

Trudy let her in the kitchen before her barking woke up Lester and Louise in their house across the street. She was just going back to bed when the phone rang. "Hello?" she asked, wondering who'd be calling her this late.

"Hi, Mom," said Hal.

"Well, 'hi' yourself – what's wrong?" said Trudy.

"Nothing," said Hal, "sorry to call so late – it's just that I'm usually so busy during the day and, well – I've got some good news."

"You got a raise!" said Trudy.

"Nooo – not yet," said Hal. "I'm coming up for a visit over Labor Day weekend."

"That's wonderful," said Trudy, "but I thought you'd be doing something with your friend... Christy, is it?" Trudy knew her name perfectly well.

"I am," said Hal. "I've invited her to Brownsville. She loves Vermont. You don't mind, do you?"

"Good heavens no – I'm delighted," said Trudy. "I'll air out the guest room. I hope she likes dogs – Cinders still has no manners."

"Don't worry about that, the Enders have a bunch of dogs – boxers – and they slobber on *everything*," said Hal. "And Mom, don't go to any trouble – Christy's really nice."

"I'm sure she is, Hal – I'm looking forward to meeting her," said Trudy, smiling to herself. This girl must be pretty special. She hadn't heard this much enthusiasm in

Hal's voice for some time. "You gonna drive up Friday or Saturday?"

"Probably Friday night – it'll be late – around midnight – that okay?"

"Sure – Cinders can greet you," said Trudy.

"Great. It's settled, see you in a couple of weeks," said Hal.

FIFTEEN

Marie read Hal's letter with mixed feelings. He was going to increase the monthly deposits to seventy-five dollars, and he was coming to Bellows Falls on the Sunday of Labor Day weekend. Could he stop by for a visit? He'd call to arrange a time when he got to his mother's house.

Marie had assumed that Hal would tell his mother that he was Paulie's father. But it did not please Marie to know that he'd be telephoning her from Trudy's house. Sooner or later Trudy would be influencing Hal's decisions, and the more people advising him, the weaker her position would become. Marie made herself a cup of tea, and thought it through. Hal came up with the idea for the bank account; he needs to do this for his own salvation – not his mother's. However, it's still his money – he makes the deposits. So, regardless of Trudy, Marie knew that she had to be nice to Hal. After all, her objective is *cash* – enough of it to repair this house. Yes, she thought, satisfied with her logic, I must stick to my goals – plan ahead, and let nothing get in the way.

When Marie walked to the sink with her teacup, Paulie came crawling toward her from the corner of the kitchen where she'd plopped him down with some toys. It was becoming increasingly difficult to keep him in the playpen. Pretty soon she'd need to fence in the backyard – but even that, she thought, if you're anything like your daddy – won't be enough. You'll climb over it! Marie picked up Paulie and nuzzled him.

"I guess it's time to decide what sickness you have that causes so many doctor appointments," she said. As if on cue, Paulie coughed up a piece of his Zwieback cracker. "Why, thank you, Paulie – you always know the right thing to do." She put him back on the floor and filled his bottle with some apple juice. "We'll tell your father that you had a cold followed by a nasty cough, and coughing is something to keep an eye on."

~~~~~~~~

Trudy went to sleep happier than she'd been for some time. Hearing Hal's cheery voice on the phone was just the right tonic, and, she could hardly wait to meet Christy. She sighed with contentment.

A violent retching sound woke Trudy from a sound sleep. She turned on the bedside table light – it was two in the morning.

"What – the...?" She sat up and listened. More retching – it was Cinders. "Oh no, what's she been into?" Trudy swung her legs over the side of the bed, and put on her bathrobe. "Hold on, here I come," she called out to Cinders.

Halfway down the back stairs Trudy smelled the trouble; she almost had to cover her nose and mouth. Turning on the kitchen light, she saw pools of blood and green slime on the floor. "Oh my…" She stepped around the puddles, and grabbed the paper towels off the kitchen counter, and got a plastic tub from under the sink. She murmured to Cinders. "It's okay – you'll be okay…I'll just clean this up and when you're through…"

Cinders threw up one more time, and then collapsed onto the floor. Trudy felt a knot of panic in her own stomach. It was two in the morning, and this dog was turning inside out. She tried to think what she used to do when Hal was sick to his stomach: let him get it all out, then rest, and ginger ale – tiny sips. Maybe not ginger ale for a dog, but…she watched Cinders panting – as if she were short of breath. Water – maybe a little bit of water. Trudy tore off a few pieces of paper towel, and ran cold water over them. Then, ever so gently, she wiped Cinders' mouth and face. The dog barely reacted. The stench was getting bad, and the mess on the floor was beginning to seep under the refrigerator. Trudy gave up on the paper towels as a cleaning tool. She went behind the back stairs, and grabbed an old bedspread, and pieces of torn sheets intended for rags. She slid the sheet under the front of the refrigerator, and started mopping with the bedspread. Once most of it was contained, she carried the bedspread to the garage, and finished cleaning the floor with paper towels and soapy water. She hoped the sheet would prevent the mess from oozing too far under the refrigerator. In the morning, she'd ask Lester to help her move it. During this frantic cleaning, Cinders had not moved; now she was beginning to shake *and* pant. Trudy was frightened. Cinders was shivering because she was dehydrated, and cold – who wouldn't be, lying on this floor. She rushed back to the alcove next to the stairs and pulled two terrycloth bath towels from the laundry basket. She draped one of them on top of Cinders, and folded the other to make a pillow for her head. Cinders tried to lift her chin but the best she could do was roll her head to one side of the makeshift pillow, and look at Trudy.

"Oh, Cinders…" said Trudy, gently patting her head, "what's wrong – what did you get into?" Cinders shut her eyes. The shaking seemed to have slowed down but the panting continued. Trudy put the water dish closer to Cinders' mouth, hoping that she might be able to take a drink. "I'll leave it there," she said to Cinders, "in case you get thirsty."

By now Trudy was wide-awake, and worried enough that she knew sleep would be impossible. She made a cup of chamomile tea, and took it to her chair in the living room. She'd stay there until Cinders fell asleep. Then, she thought, it would be safe to go upstairs.

In the semi-state of sleep and dreaming, Trudy felt

something warm on her face; she remained still and content, thinking it was Cinders, but the consistent chatter of the birds, and the early morning sun pulled her out of her reverie. She'd fallen asleep in the chair, and the sun streaming into the living room was providing the warmth. She sat right up.

"Cinders!" she shouted. Trudy got up, and ran toward the kitchen. The stench was still there – only stronger. She stopped on the threshold, and unconsciously covered her mouth against the smell. Cinders lay stretched out on the floor – stiff. No more shaking or panting: she'd stopped breathing. Tears rolled down Trudy's cheeks. Why didn't she stay with Cinders through the night when she was ill. I should have called Midge – or taken her to the vet, she thought – or something! She looked at the kitchen clock on the wall. Six o'clock. Well…she sighed, by the time I get this cleaned up the vet might be open, and then…I guess I'd better call Midge.

By seven o'clock, Trudy had Cinders wrapped in a sheet and the kitchen floor more or less clean. Then she went upstairs, and got dressed. An old pair of blue jeans and a shirt would do. Just as she was preparing to carry Cinders out to her car, she looked out the back hallway window. Lester was in the field next to the driveway, hacking away at a scrappy hedgerow between the field and the road.

"I'll ask him to carry you," she said softly to Cinders.

"You're a big dog." She wiped another tear away. "I was really beginning to like you – we could have had lots of fun together."

Lester stopped cutting when he saw Trudy walking toward him. "You're up 'n about kinda early, aren't ya?" As she came closer Lester noticed Trudy's tearful face. He dropped the hedge cutters and ran up to her. "What…?"

"It's Cinders – she's dead," said Trudy. "She's in the kitchen – I need help."

Lester took her gently by the arm, and they walked back to the house. "I'll get her. We can take her to Doc Thompson's in Windsor."

"Should I call him? I mean – let him know we're coming?" said Trudy.

"Naw," said Lester, "this time o' day he's usually still there. If he ain't, Moira will take care o' things."

As soon as they opened the kitchen door, Lester smelled the strong odor. He reached down to pick up Cinders. "I'll carry her over to my truck – best to put her in the back, for the drive." Standing in the doorway with Cinders in his arms, he nodded toward the kitchen windows. "You might want to open them, and – ah…I'll have Louise bring over some disinfectant when we're gone."

Trudy stared numbly at the floor, and the wastebasket filled with foul paper towels. "Yes, thank you," she said weakly. "I – I didn't notice, guess I was getting used to it…" She opened the window above the kitchen sink, and moved the wastebasket toward the door.

While Lester went to get his truck, Trudy thought of calling Midge, but realized that it was only 7:15. *She'd kill me if I woke her up with this kind of news. I'll do it later.* Then Trudy wondered if Midge would want Cinders buried next to her other pets in the special "Pet Plot" she had on her property. *Yes, I suppose she will.* Trudy sighed and took the wastebasket outside, placing it alongside the large trash-barrel next to the garage.

Lester got out of his truck to open the passenger door for Trudy. "Just a sec," said Trudy, "I forgot my pocketbook."

Lester walked over to the trash barrels, and inspected the saturated towels. *Hmpf,* he thought, *that's a familiar smell…*

"Okay, I'm all set," said Trudy, looking into the bed of the pick-up truck before getting in the cab. She saw that Lester had placed a burlap bag around the soggy sheet in which she had wrapped Cinders. "That's better," she said, and settled herself in the passenger seat. "On our way, can you stop at Cullins' Market? I want to get a big jug of Clorox; that'll help clean things up."

"Yes, it will. That 'n Louise's special concoction." He glanced at Trudy, checking on her condition before saying anything about the dog. *She seemed over her case of the nerves.* "D'ya know the where'bouts of Cinders last night – 'fore she got sick?"

"Outside someplace," said Trudy with a shrug. "She roams – well, *roamed* – all around, chasing birds – mice – God knows what-all. Last night she didn't come back 'til nine, started barking so much I had to let her in. Hope she didn't wake up you 'n Louise."

"No – no – didn't hear a thing," said Lester. "I was asking 'cause…well, I think she got into some o' them nightshade berries – along with the stalks – either that, or she ate some animal that was just fresh with 'em."

Trudy froze, and stared straight ahead. She barely moved a muscle.

"Don't mean to alarm ya," said Lester, a little alarmed at her reaction. "It's just that Lucifer – ya know, my cat – he threw up sumpin' awful yesterday. Some o' them berries were still whole, an'…well, that odor – ain't nothin' like it."

"But Lucifer isn't dead…" said Trudy.

"No…that's right. She ain't. 'Cause she's used to regurgitating – does it all the time with birds 'n stuff." He chuckled. "Got eyes bigger 'n her stomach. I'm thinkin' your Cinders was after some critter hidin' in the bushes, an' she ate clear through the vines to get at it."

"But where? I thought we cut all of it – around my yard anyway," said Trudy.

"We did, but some more cropped up in the ditch across from my house. That's what I was cuttin' this morning. Lucifer's always lookin' for mice in there." Lester saw that this information wasn't helping Trudy.

"But that dog – roaming the way she did – could'a been into anything – I'm jus' guessin'."

"Yes – yes – of course," said Trudy in a matter-of-fact tone of voice. "The vet will tell us."
They were approaching Cullins' Market. "Don't forget to stop."

Lester pulled up in front to let Trudy get out. "I'll go down there 'n turn around." He pointed to the small parking area behind the store.

Trudy tried to take a few deep breaths as she walked into the store. Every muscle in her body was tight. Her jaw was clenched so tightly that it hurt. *Calm down! You're over-reacting – and exhausted – so just stop it.* She picked up a jug of Clorox off the back shelf, and went to the cash register. A large basket of apples was on the counter. *That's it – of course – you haven't eaten anything.* She asked the clerk to put six apples in a bag. Back in the truck she offered one to Lester. He declined but told Trudy to dig right in – "ya know what they say about apples…"

Trudy polished one of the Macintosh apples on the sleeve of her sweater and started eating. She reminded herself to slow down, or she'd choke.

The veterinarian, Herbert Thompson, was a man of few words. His wife, Moira, claimed that he said more to his animals than he ever did to her.

When Lester told Doc Thompson that they had a

dead dog in the back of his pick-up truck, the vet pointed to a door on the side of his office. "Get the dog, and follow me." Lester picked up Cinders, and did as he was told. Trudy followed Lester into a small, crisp and clean examining room. They both stood to the side as Doc Thompson removed the burlap, and then the sheet from Cinders. He smelled both of them. "How long she vomit 'fore she couldn't breathe?" asked the vet.

"Um... I – I'm not sure," said Trudy, "I'd been sleeping – it woke me up – the noise."

"Yup," said Herbert. "And then she was shaking?"

"Yes," said Trudy, "I didn't know what to do – I put a blanket on her, actually an old bedspread," she added.

Without another word, Herbert bundled up the soiled material, putting it carefully in a receptacle in the corner of the examining room. Then, he took a large clean white cloth that looked as if it had been part of an old sheet and gently covered Cinders. He tucked it under her belly and then patted her. "It was poison – deadly nightshade. Two days ago – I was up to the Johnston Farm – one of their calves got into it. Died three hours later."

Lester nodded in agreement. "It's awful stuff – seems the young ones get into it more, and then they don't regurgitate in time. My cat, by God – she gets rid of it real fast."

Trudy was trying to maintain her composure. Her mind was spinning, her head ached, and her mouth was so dry she could hardly speak. She wanted to escape.

"I understand," she said, addressing the vet abruptly. "You don't mind if I leave Cinders here for awhile. I'll call her owner – the person who loaned Cinders to me. She'll want to come and get her." Trudy didn't wait for an answer. She was out the door before Herbert Thompson replied.

"Just let me know if she wants the dog cremated or if she's gonna pick her up whole," said Herbert – more to Lester than Trudy.

Lester nodded in the affirmative, and followed Trudy to his truck. On the ride back to Brownsville, Lester interpreted Trudy's silence as fatigue and hunger. "You're lookin' some peaked – how 'bout if Louise brings over some muffins, they're blueberry – awful good, and bacon…on the side…?"

"No – no," said Trudy, too quickly. She tried to amend it. "I – I think I just need to sleep. I'll be okay in a couple of hours." Trudy knew that sleeping was out of the question right now, but the last thing she needed was Louise hovering around trying to be helpful. She forced a smile. "That's very thoughtful – but really, I'll be fine."

"Whatever you say," said Lester, pulling into Trudy's driveway. "If ya do need anything, I'll be home most of the day."

Trudy stepped out of the truck, and shut the door. She wanted to run into the house, but paused long enough to be polite. "Thanks again for helping me. I'm not sure I would've been able to take her to the vet's alone."

Lester nodded his head in understanding, and started to back down the driveway when he saw the Clorox. He stopped, and got out with the jug.

"You'll be wanting this," he said, handing it to Trudy.

"Oh yes…" said Trudy, as if she'd never seen it before. And then she remembered the apples. "Golly – I *am* tired – the apples."

Lester reached in the cab of the truck, and grabbed the bag from the seat. "Well, that's a better excuse 'n I've got, I didn't even *see* 'em."

Once in the kitchen, Trudy's mind went on automatic: Call Midge, shower, a pot of coffee, and then she'd sit down, and work this thing through once again.

It wasn't until she'd finished talking to Midge that Trudy realized there was no odor in the kitchen. The floor was clean – even around the refrigerator. Touched by Louise's kindness, she felt all teary again. Oh, get hold of yourself! Trudy muttered, and resolved to go over and thank Louise later in the day.

The aroma of fresh coffee brewing, and the hot shower she'd just taken was a sufficient pick-me-up for her. As always, when seeking order – with her thoughts or household chores – she started another list, prioritizing her concerns. After jotting down a few tentative thoughts about deadly nightshade, Trudy crumpled up the paper, and threw it on the floor. Then, making a concerted effort to think rationally, she spoke softly, and slowly to herself. *Face it, you think Marie poisoned Harold. You just don't know how. Could she have done it with those nightshade berries? Well, find the answer. Call your brother, the doctor, and ask him: is it possible that Marie Furneau killed Harold?* Trudy poured more coffee, cut a large piece of raisin bread, and put in the toaster. *First thing he's going to ask is, what took you so long to come up with this idea.? And that's gonna open up a whole can o' worms. First the baby, then Hal's role, and my wish to protect him... What a mess. Why am I doing this? Hal's perfectly happy. He's coming up here in a couple of weeks, with a new girlfriend... No,* thought Trudy, *stop making excuses. Hal came face to face with his responsibility; you can do the same.* However, she thought, owning up to fatherhood, and accusing someone of murder were hardly on the same plane, but that didn't matter – it was a frightening possibility that she could no longer ignore.

The raisins in the bread were burning in the toaster. Trudy tried to grab the piece of bread with a fork; the toaster sparked – *then* she unplugged it. Stupid, she muttered. She slathered raspberry jam on the partially burned toast, took a big bite, and thought quietly for a second. *You should explain everything to Carl –*

including the bank account. And simply ask him not to tell Hal.

The telephone starting ringing. Trudy looked at the kitchen clock. It was past nine – long past the morning round of gossip, so she listened in case it was her ring. It was. She put her coffee down, and picked up the phone that she'd recently installed in the kitchen. "Hello," she said flatly.

"Hello…" answered an unfamiliar male voice. "Is this Trudy Walker?"

"Yes," replied Trudy with a cool formality, "with whom am I speaking?"

"This is Walter, Trudy, Walter Luden – Cynthia's husband – *late* husband, that is."

"Of course," said Trudy, wondering what in the world he wanted. "How are you, Walter?"

"I'm fine, thank you, gettin' along just fine. I'm callin' 'bout Cynthia's stuff, it's – a…"

This is ridiculous, thought Trudy. "If you don't want it, I'm sure Marie would be happy to have it all back."

"It's not that…" said Walter, hesitantly.

Trudy was losing her patience. "If you're worried about Marie, don't be – just leave the stuff on her porch."

Walter tried to explain. "I went through Cynthia's desk yesterday – found papers 'n things – personal papers of Margarite's. You remember when she took all that stuff from Margarite's house?"

Trudy remembered all too well. "Yes, I do, Walter."

"Well – Cynthia put pret'near all the contents of Margarite's desk in a box, and now it's here, and I'm not sure what to do with it. In a couple of weeks, I'll be moving to Montpelier."

Trudy was tempted to tell him to burn everything. She caught herself. "Perhaps you could – "

"Some of the papers look like they relate to Margarite's house. I didn't know but you might want to see them."

That got Trudy's attention. Maybe Walter's not such a dummy. She softened her response. "That's very considerate of you. You're going to Montpelier in a couple of weeks?"

"Yes, on a Sunday – day before Labor Day. I'll be leaving in the morning; people who bought the house are coming that afternoon."

Well – well, no flies on Walter, thought Trudy. "Fine," she said, "Sunday. Call me before you leave Walpole," she added, thinking that with some advance notice, she could get Hal and his friend Christy out of the house for a while. No need to involve them.

"I'll be sure to do that," replied Walter, courteously.

This conversation sent her mind racing: Margarite's garden, the grape arbor, Marie... Then her house on Atkinson Street came to mind: Marie serving tea, the clogged kitchen sink. Trudy picked up her list, and started writing down these thoughts. A clear, logical presentation – that's what she needed for Carl. If he agrees with her, that Marie could have poisoned Harold *and* Margarite with nightshade berries, they would have a starting point.

Trudy put the list aside, and sliced more raisin bread. She knew that this sudden bravado was only temporary, typical of the way she solved problems – bulling ahead. Once a decision had been made, nagging doubts would be turned into positive action. She adjusted the toaster to a lighter temperature so the raisins wouldn't burn, and reheated the coffee. Trudy liked having a plan of action. She now realized that the lack of one – burying her doubts about Marie – had been keeping her off balance. It took poor dear Cinders' death to get her to focus. The toast popped up – nicely done. She buttered it, and thought about Cinders. She'd collect the few toys – a tennis ball, an old slipper, and her favorite throwing stick. When she and Midge buried Cinders later today, these things could be with her.

The head nurse in Carl's office told Trudy that Carl was making his hospital rounds. He'd be back in the office at eleven, and his first patient of the day was scheduled for eleven–thirty.

"Very well," said Trudy, "I'll call him at eleven-ten." Ordinarily she didn't call Carl during the day – least of all in his office, but this couldn't wait. She needed some answers.

To keep busy for the next forty-five minutes, Trudy weeded the flowerbed in front of the living room window, grateful that it was small enough to keep tidy with minimum effort, yet still provide her with a nice variety of flowers. She never could understand how Margarite kept up with her multiple gardens. She *didn't* – that's how, laughed Trudy, remembering that Margarite didn't require a picture-perfect garden – she *liked* being in that jungle, and might still be there...she thought sadly.

Trudy was in the garage collecting Cinders toys when the phone rang. Darn, she thought, just when I want to use it. After a few rings she realized it was *her* ring. She dropped the toys back into the peach basket and ran to the kitchen phone.

"Hello," she said, out of breath.

"Tru...? It's me – Carl. You okay...? Marylynn said you called."

"Yes, I'm okay, and yes, I called." Trudy grabbed her list and sat at the kitchen counter. "Carl, I have a problem. It...well – I'll come right out with it. I believe that Marie Furneau poisoned Harold, *and* Margarite Pierson with nightshade berries. Is that possible?"

Carl got up from his desk, and made sure that the door to the waiting room was firmly shut. "Are you asking if it's possible to *believe* that such a thing occurred...or if it's possible for a solution of nightshade berries to kill a human being?"

Trudy had to smile. Carl – ever the analyst – no wonder he's a doctor. "I *believe* she did it – that's not my problem. What I don't know is the *how* part – if it's possible..." Trudy rushed on before Carl could respond. "Remember...I think it was in June – I was asking you about nightshade...? You said in Victorian times – or in novels – people did each other in that way – too much belladonna...or was that the stuff for eyes?"

"Both," said Carl quickly, taking advantage of his sister's slight pause in the conversation. "But back up a bit. *Why* would Marie want to kill Harold and Margarite? There's a motive for everything."

"Because of the fire – Marie's daughter Jenette died in it."

"Oh my ," said Carl, "that's right – I forgot about that. Sure, revenge – the oldest motive of all."

"There's more," said Trudy. "Jenette had a baby – Hal's the father."

Carl took a deep breath. "Oh, I see. And the child is now with Marie?"

"Yes," said Trudy.

"And Hal..." asked Carl, "does he think Marie-"

"No, not at all," Trudy said before Carl could finish his thought. "If anything, he's hoping to ingratiate himself with Marie so he can see more of Paulie – that's the baby – a boy – named after Jenette's father. He's even set up a bank account for the child in

Bellows Falls."

Carl whistled softly through his teeth. He took another deep breath. "Tru, do you have any concrete evidence? Did you ever *see* Marie doing anything with the berries? I'm not trying to trivialize this, but normally people have to ingest the stuff before dying. And what about autopsies – reports from a medical examiner...? What did they say?"

Trudy looked at the clock. It was eleven-fifteen; she knew Carl would have to get off the phone in a minute, and start preparing for his first patient. She tried to be brief. "I don't think there was an autopsy for Margarite. She had a history of heart trouble, and she died in the presence of a doctor. For Harold, the autopsy report indicated heart failure. Don't you remember? After the funeral, that's all people could talk about, *poor Harold, the fire made his heart give out.* Well, he'd *never* had heart problems. The only thing Doctor Barnes mentioned was the curious build-up of belladonna in Harold's system, but all he could come up with was 'cough syrup' – he wondered what kind Harold had been using!"

"Yes, I see," said Carl calmly. "Look, I can see how this is eating at you. Can I call you tonight?"

"Yes – yes – I know you're busy now, I can tell you more tonight." Trudy could hear the "doctor" tone in her brother's voice. She started to hang up. "Wait – Carl, don't say anything – to anyone, except Hen of course, about my suspicions – or Hal being the father."

"You know I wouldn't – bye, Tru," said Carl.

The full impact of what Trudy told Carl didn't hit him until that evening when he told Hen about Trudy's revelation. Hen's reaction was immediate – and sympathetic.

"Poor Trudy – poor Hal, no wonder she kept all of it to herself," said Hen, shaking her head in disbelief. "And that woman is taking care of a baby? What if she decides to…?"

"Oh, come now, don't go jumping to conclusions," said Carl, pouring himself a stiff bourbon.

"Trudy's not a skittish schoolgirl. She didn't just dream this up," Hen stated firmly. She noticed Carl's skeptical expression. "And no, it's not a result of grieving or shock over Harold's death. I know your sister as well, or better, than you do. Trudy wrestles with problems, then faces things straight on."

Carl took his drink outside to their flagstone terrace. He sat down wearily. "I know – I know. It's just that – well, it's all so improbable…"

"And, like your sister, you're concerned about Hal." Hen followed him to the terrace with a plate of Triscuits and cheese. She put it on a small wrought iron and glass top table.

"Listen," said Hen," it seems that Hal, from what Trudy said, has owned up to his part in this – fatherhood, for heaven's sake. He can certainly handle the truth about his own father's death. Trudy wouldn't be accusing…"

Carl raised an eyebrow.

"All right," said Hen, "… *suspecting* the baby's grandmother of something as awful as murder, unless she really believes it. She wouldn't do that to Hal. After all, you know how much she and Harold looked forward to his career in banking."

"Hmm," said Carl, "and I've never been convinced that that's what *Hal* wanted."

"Well," continued Hen, "be that as it may – Trudy wants the best for him. She would *never* stir things up without a very good reason." Hen took a drink of her gin and tonic and leaned back in the chair, satisfied with her case.

Carl took the challenge. "All right, I'll research the properties of nightshade – the quantities necessary for a lethal dose. But," he said in a very precise tone of voice, "there is one thing you and Trudy are forgetting: the body – tangible evidence – there is none. Harold was cremated. And unless that friend of theirs – Margarite…"

"Pierson," said Hen.

"Hm – Margarite Pierson," said Carl. "Unless she was buried, *not* cremated, we are out of luck. Even then, we'd have to present some darn good evidence to have her body exhumed."

Hen was almost speechless. "You mean she killed *two*

people…? You didn't tell me that – oh-my-heavens – what are we going to do?"

"To begin with," said Carl, "we can't go around saying Marie Furneau *killed* anybody. We simply don't know." He shook the ice in his empty glass. "I'm mixing another one. Can I freshen yours?"

Hen handed Carl her near empty glass. "Yes, thanks – double. Honest to God, this is awful," she said, crossing her arms like pouting child.

"I'm going to call Trudy in a few minutes," said Carl, returning with the drinks. "I'll tell her the same thing I told you: we need a body. Without a body, or bodies – *corpus delicti*, any determination I make about the exact dosage required for poisoning by nightshade is irrelevant. We need proof."

Hen was quieter. She got up and started pruning the potted geranium. "Hmm, I suppose we should concentrate on Hal now, and his son. Good grief – what's he going to do with a child?" She put the dead blossoms in a little pile on the corner of the terrace, and turned to Carl with an impish grin.

"Uh-oh! What are you thinking…?" asked Carl.

"Oh, nothing…I was just wondering about Christy Enders – she and Hal are together all the time…"

"Uh-oh! – I know what you're thinking; let's not add marriage to the mix." Carl shook his head in mild disbelief. "I'm gonna call Trudy. You…" he said, pointing to Hen's mouth, "keep it zipped."

"At least tell her that we'll all help her with the baby…if it comes to that," said Hen.

"Yes, *if* it comes to that. First things first." Carl smiled at his wife's eagerness to join the battle, as it were. He often thought that she was the one who made their marriage work, juggling her practice in pediatrics to accommodate *his* erratic schedule, plus take on other people's causes. *Trudy,* he thought, *you could have no better ally.*

SIXTEEN

Trudy felt better. Reviewing the order of suspicious events: finding berries in the kitchen sink drain after Harold's funeral, Margarite's last cryptic words about tea, and then Cynthia's sudden heart attack, had helped. And Cinder's death, while not suspicious, certainly brought things to a head. It didn't matter that Carl had spelled out the legal facts of the matter: no body – no evidence. Somehow she'd find the answers. For starters, she'd ask Walter if Cynthia had requested cremation for Margarite. As she recalled, all deceased members of the Pierson family were buried – intact – in the family plot in Bellows Falls. Why the exception for Margarite? Having this little clue to go on, gave Trudy some hope, and belief in herself – she wasn't crazy. Carl could do the forensic work; she'd be the detective!

This much resolved, Trudy felt she could focus on Hal's upcoming visit...with his girlfriend! She started planning each meal as well as a few activities. The meals would be Hal's favorites: a chicken and rice casserole – in case they're hungry when they arrive late Friday night.

Lamb chops and asparagus Saturday. Then a small roast beef with peas and roast potatoes on Sunday night. She'd make lots of chocolate chip cookies, and ask the bakery in Windsor to save a lemon meringue pie for her to pick up Friday afternoon. Hal had cautioned her against planning too many activities, but Trudy thought tennis, followed by lunch at the club, would be all right. After all, it wasn't every day she had a chance to show off Hal *and* his girlfriend. No doubt the Enders saw to it that Hal met plenty of *their* friends in Quissett. Trudy did wonder if Hal had mentioned Paulie to Christy. Somehow she thought not, and decided to leave the subject alone. Best to keep everything light. Sooner or later, if anything comes of this friendship, he'd *have* to tell her. On Sunday, she was going to suggest that Hal take Christy for a hike up Mount Ascutney; they could pack a picnic lunch. That way she could avoid any awkward introductions between Walter Luden, and Hal and Christy. A hike would take most of the afternoon, and she wanted plenty of uninterrupted time to discuss things with Walter.

As the Labor Day weekend approached, Hal became more and more anxious about telling Christy that he had a son. He'd go back and forth. Should he bring it up during the drive to Brownsville on Friday night? Or wait until they were on their way to Marie's on Sunday? Maybe say nothing; postpone the visit to Marie – come up some other weekend – alone.

Thursday, the night before their departure, he still hadn't made up his mind. He called Christy to say that he might not be able to pick her up until five-thirty or six the next day, and they wouldn't get to Vermont until midnight. After she laughed, saying that that would make waking up in a new place all the more fun, he began to think that maybe it wouldn't be so hard to tell her about Paulie – that she wouldn't be shocked. Who knows, he thought – she might even want to meet him.

Christy was waiting outside her friend's apartment in Greenwich Village when he drove up at 5:45. She was sitting on the stoop next to a small suitcase. When Christy saw his car coming down the street, she stood up and brushed off her skirt. It was a blue and green madras pattern and fell just below her knees. With it, she wore a white short-sleeve blouse with a Peter Pan collar. A navy blue cable knit sweater was tied around her waist. Christy smiled and gave him a big wave. In that instant, Hal felt himself freeze. A different girl, but same wave. A vision of Jenette flashed in front his eyes. He couldn't move. Christy ran up to the car.

"Hey – you going to open the door?..." she asked merrily.

His heart was pounding. He tried to smile. He kept hearing Jenette's voice, but it was Christy's.

She ran around to his side of the car. "Are you okay? Looks like you've seen a ghost," said Christy, poking her head in the car window.

Hal blinked his eyes – hard, and shook his head. "Yeah – whew – I guess it's the heat, or too much work – ha-ha." He opened the car door, stepped out, and gave her a kiss. Then, taking her by the arm, he formally escorted her to the passenger's side. "Let me – madmoiselle," he said, while opening the door with a grand flourish.

"Thank you, kind sir," replied Christy, gracefully getting in and smoothing her skirt.

For the first twenty minutes or so, Hal was quiet, feigning concentration on the rush hour traffic – greater this evening because of the holiday weekend. The recollection of Jenette had thrown him for a loop. He needed a few minutes to calm down. By the time they were on the West Side Drive, he seemed to have things back in perspective.

Christy chatted amiably about her job prospects: Dwight School for girls in Englewood might have an opening – only part-time, fourth grade gym and social studies. "But – that's better than nothing," she said, shrugging her shoulders.

"Better than...what?" asked Hal.

"No job," laughed Christy. "I was talking about teaching...?" She reached in her pocketbook and took out a Hershey bar. "Here – eat this – it'll give you energy.

It's got almonds. They're good for you too. My dad always keeps a bunch of 'em handy." She unwrapped the chocolate bar halfway and handed it to Hal.

Hal took a big bite. Still chewing, he thanked her. "Hmm – thanks – I love these."

By the time they reached the Taconic Parkway, Hal was thinking how much he liked Christy. Every time he looked at her, he wanted to smile. When they got to Manchester, Vermont, he suggested that they grab a bite to eat. Then, remembering his mom's chicken casseroles, he told Christy that maybe they wouldn't need to stop; his mom would probably leave something in the oven for them to have when they got to Brownsville.

"Boy, that didn't come out right, did it?" said Hal. "Sounds like I'm too cheap to pay for a whole meal."

"No – no," said Christy, "we're hungry *now* so we should eat – we just won't have dessert. That'll save lots of room for another meal!"

During the meal everything started to fall into place. Hal talked about Brownsville, his mom's house, and what they might do over the weekend. On Saturday, tennis or hiking would be a possibility, or maybe they could go up to Dartmouth.

"Actually…" said Hal looking slightly apologetic, "I just remembered – my mom wants us to have lunch with her at the tennis club, but," he added quickly, "that won't take all day."

"That sounds like fun," said Christy. "Gosh, all the things my parents dragged you to... And besides, we have Sunday – remember?"

Hal had just finished his bowl of corn chowder. He picked up a piece of corn bread, buttered it, then put it back on the plate.

Christy was smiling at him. "Saving room for the casserole...?"

Hal looked at his empty hand. "Oh, well – um... no," he said softly, "it's, ah...about Sunday." He decided to say it all at once. "On Sunday, I have to go back to Bellows Falls. I have to see someone – two people actually." He paused and looked directly at Christy.

"Christy, I have a son – a baby – baby boy." He laughed nervously and squeezed his forehead. "Yeah – son...a boy, his name is Paulie." Christy smiled ever so slightly while Hal continued.

"He's young – less than a year – he lives with his grandmother..." Hal looked down at his hands. "The mother – Paulie's mother...died...she died."

Hal had spent himself. He looked up at Christy. "That's it," he said sadly, opening his hands in a futile gesture.

"Wow..." said Christy, as she put her elbows on the table and rested her chin on her hands. She looked at Hal with an expression he couldn't read.

"Yeah – I don't blame you for being mad; I should

have told you ages ago, before…well before we got to like each other."

"I'm not mad…." said Christy, "I'm – ah – I guess I'm touched, and – and impressed…"

Hal shook his head, aware of Christy's weakness for the downtrodden. "You don't have to say those things; I know it's a lot to swallow – my being a father."

"Hal…" said Christy. "*You* don't understand. When I'm volunteering at Social Services, most of the children I see *do not know their fathers* – and never will." She sat back against the chair and crossed her arms. "I admire you for being honorable." Then she leaned forward and gave him a big smile. "Can I go with you to Bellows Falls? I'd love to see him; Paulie…is that what you said?" Christy thought that maybe she'd gone too far. "Of course – I understand – you probably want to go alone…"

"Oh, no!" said Hal, trying to resist the urge to reach over the table and hug Christy for as long as he could. "I'd love it! But…"

The waitress came with the check. Hal looked at his watch. "Maybe we'd better get going."

For the rest of the drive to Brownsville, Hal related the whole story, omitting nothing. Christy listened quietly, occasionally wiping a tear from her cheek.

Only when Hal finished did he notice her tears. "Oh boy – I didn't mean to make you…"

Christy took a Kleenex from her pocketbook and

wiped her eyes. "That's the saddest, and the sweetest thing I've ever heard." She moved next to him, resting her head on his shoulder. "Hal – you are amazing, and I can't wait to meet Paulie."

"Thanks," said Hal, his heart swelling. Yeah – he thought quietly, I guess this *is* love.

~~~~~~~~~

Trudy knew the easiest way to get Hal up in the morning was to fry some bacon. Given the late hour of their arrival, she waited until 8:30, and sure enough, by 8:45 she heard water running in the upstairs bathroom. She put some dishes on the kitchen counter, along with orange juice, fresh fruit, and cereal – just in case Christy wasn't a hearty breakfast eater. She was turning the pieces of bacon when a pleasant voice entered the kitchen.

"Golly, I hope I'm not the last one up," said Christy, extending her hand as Trudy turned around.

"Goodness no, and welcome!" said Trudy, shaking Christy's hand. "Hal's still asleep." She turned off the stove and pointed to the stools in front of the counter. "Sit – sit – have some juice." She smiled broadly at Christy. "It's so nice to have you here."

"Thank you, Mrs. Walker; I'm glad to *be* here." Christy put a small gift box on the counter. "This is for you. My mom helped me pick it out."

Trudy picked it up, smiled, and shook it, trying to guess the contents. "Ooh – may I open it? I love presents."

"Sure," said Christy, as Trudy opened the little box.

"This is lovely," exclaimed Trudy, holding up a small cut-glass vase. "How did you know…?"

"Hal told me that you liked to arrange flowers in the house," said Christy.

"Did I just hear my name?" asked Hal, coming down the front stairs.

"You sure did," said Trudy, holding the vase and giving him a peck on the cheek. "Welcome, sleepy-head."

Hal looked at the wall clock. "Wow – almost nine." He smiled at Christy. "I guess you've already met my mom…"

"Yes indeed," said Trudy, speaking for Christy. "Not only have we met, but Christy's given me a beautiful gift." She showed the vase to Hal. "How'd you remember that your old ma liked flowers in the house?"

Hal went to the stove and picked a piece of bacon out of the frying pan. "Remember…? How could I forget – every holiday – flowers everywhere!" He laughed and looked at Christy. "Wait'll you see what it's like around here on Thanksgiving."

"Don't listen to a word he says…" replied Trudy. She gave Hal a tap on the wrist, pushing him away from the stove. "Hey, that's not all for you."

"Oops – oh yeah," said Hal sheepishly as he put the rest of the bacon on a platter.

When they finished breakfast, Christy suggested that she and Hal wash the dishes.

Trudy accepted the offer. "Just make sure Hal dries everything, sometimes…"

"Yes, Mom," said Hal, "I know…"

"I'll be out in the garden," said Trudy. "Come look at my new roses when you've finished.

Hal stood on the stone steps in front of the house. He was expecting Cinders to come running across the field. When he didn't see her last night, he assumed that his mom had trained her to stay overnight in the small barn – now kennel – on the edge of the pasture. He gave a loud whistle and started walking toward his mom in the garden.

"Hey – where's the mutt?" he asked.

Trudy stopped her weeding, and leaned on the hoe. "She's gone – she died last week."

"Really…that's too bad," said Hal. "How…?"

"Poison. There are a lot of plants around here, and well, Cinders was into everything." Trudy wanted to be matter-of-fact and brief about it. "The vet said that it's not uncommon for puppies to get into the stuff."

"What sort of plants?" asked Hal.

"One variety is something called nightshade – the berries are poisonous. Lester says farm animals get into them."

"And humans…are they susceptible?"

Trudy shrugged. "Umm – I don't know. It's an

306

unfortunate country occurrence."

"Oh," said Hal, disappointed not to have Cinders around. "I'm sorry. Are you going to get another one?"

"No, not for a while anyway," said Trudy, grateful to see Christy coming across the lawn.

"Need some help weeding?" asked Christy.

"Nope, I'm all set, thanks," said Trudy, looking at her watch. "Why don't we put on our tennis clothes and head on over to the club. I reserved a court for eleven o'clock. We'll play mixed doubles. George Bacon, an old friend, said he'd be my partner."

After their tennis match, they had lunch on a terrace next to the clubhouse.

"At least we old folks gave you a run for your money," said Trudy.

"Yeah – 'run' is the operative word," said Hal. "You guys can place your shots."

"I second that," said Christy. "You kept us busy."

"Ha-ha, that's my only defense; these ole knees *won't* run," said George.

"Well, I think we deserve a gin 'n tonic for the two games we *did* win," said Trudy, signaling the waiter. "How 'bout you two," she asked, looking at Hal and Christy.

"Cold beer – Budweiser – for me," said Hal.

"Me too," chimed in Christy.

After dessert, George excused himself. "The garden is calling me: the weeds are taking over..." He rose from the table and took the check. "Allow me," he said, bowing graciously in Trudy's direction. Turning to Hal and Christy, he said, "Delighted to meet you. I'll expect a rematch – soon!" He laughed and strode off.

"Nice guy," said Hal.

"Yes," said Trudy. "Your father and I used to play tennis with George and his wife when we came to Brownsville, visiting your grandfather. Patsy died three years ago – cancer."

"That's too bad," said Christy.

"Hmm – well, that happens sometimes," said Trudy, clearly not interested in pursuing the topic. She ate the last of her orange sherbert and vanilla wafer. "What have you got in mind for this afternoon?"

Hal was a little surprised at his mother's off-hand manner, but let it pass. "There's still time to climb the mountain, or...we could go up to Hanover," he said to Christy. "I'll show you my old frat house."

"That's a good idea," said Trudy, before Christy could respond. "Then you can have all day tomorrow to hike up the mountain."

"Yeah..." said Hal vaguely, "that's a possibility." He looked at Christy, who seemed to understand that he didn't want to bring up Bellows Falls right now.

"I'd like to see Dartmouth," said Christy.

"Wonderful!" Said Trudy, with such exaggerated enthusiasm that Hal wondered what was going on with his mom.

As soon as Hal and Christy left for Hanover, Trudy decided to allow herself a brief nap. Then she'd call Walter; the last thing she needed was ole Walter showing up unannounced. Hal would want to know what *sort* of legal papers – if they pertained to Marie. *Oh no, no, no – not a good idea.* She shuddered at the thought.

Trudy tried, but sleep didn't come. She reached for her address book and called Walter.

The phone rang and rang. "C'mon, Walter – be home, answer the phone..."

Finally: "This is Walter Luden speaking..."

"Yes, hello, Walter, this is Trudy Walker..."

"Hello there – how are you?" answered Walter. "I was just thinking about when I'd be stopping by your place, but the last time we came to your house I wasn't driving, so I won't be able to find you. That's no good is it?"

"No," said Trudy, "Take Route 5 to Windsor, then follow the signs to Brownsville. Now, let's decide on a time."

"I was thinking about eleven o'clock in the morning."

"No," said Trudy abruptly. "I have company; they'll be leaving about then. Noon is better."

"Well...I gotta get to Montpelier by four," said Walter.

"You'll have plenty of time," said Trudy patiently, "our business won't take more than twenty minutes."

"I guess," said Walter, "if you say so..."

"Yes, I can assure you; you'll be in Montpelier well before four. We'll even have time for a cup of tea."

"Tha'd be nice," said Walter, "see ya then. Bye."

God, muttered Trudy, why doesn't he look at a road map?

After a nice long shower, Trudy went to her clothes closet and spent a few minutes deciding what to wear. Tonight, of course, with Hal and Christy here, she would do more than change her blouse or sweater. She chose a lime-green linen dress to wear, a straight shift with short cap sleeves trimmed in white, and a round collar also bound in white. The hemline fell just below her knees. She wore low-heeled Capezio shoes of the same color. For jewelry, Trudy decided to wear the gold twist earrings Harold had given her when Hal was born. And then, feeling particularly sentimental, she put on the scarab bracelet that *Hal* gave her one Christmas years ago. After the summer's sun, her silver-blond hair had more of a blond color, and the natural soft wave let it fall easily at a length just below her chin. Trudy brushed it straight back in the page-boy style. For makeup, she always used the minimum: lipstick – pinkish color, and face powder – from a compact. Every now and then, looking at the increasing number of lines around her eyes and mouth, she wondered about improving her makeup selection, but that's as far as it went – she had yet to make any changes.

After applying a dab of perfume – Chanel No. 5 – Trudy stood in front of her full-length mirror. She approved: the dress was smart and...she thought, thanks to tennis, the ole legs were still in pretty good shape.

Just as she got to the kitchen the phone rang, her ring. "This better not be Walter..."
She yanked the phone from the receiver. "Hello," she said abruptly.

"Trudy...?" asked Carl.

"Carl – oh, sorry, I thought..."

"That I was someone else...?" replied Carl, laughing. "Who were you expecting...?"

"Walter Luden – Cynthia's husband; she is – *was* Margarite's sister. It's a long story." Trudy opened the refrigerator with her free hand and took out the lamb chops, put them on the counter, then reached for the frozen peas. They slipped and fell on the floor. "Nuts," she said, picking up the peas and placing them firmly on the kitchen counter.

"Me or Walter...?" said Carl, smiling to himself.

"Neither. I'm trying to get supper ready. Hal's here – with his girlfriend; at least I hope Christy's the one – she's great."

"You bet she is," said Carl. "Why do you think Hen invited her to our July Fourth party?"

"Well, please thank her on my behalf. Hal's too – I guess," laughed Trudy. "Now, I've completely forgotten my train of thought," said Trudy. "What did you tell me...?"

Carl laughed. "I was about to, I've done some more research on deadly nightshade. Most of it corroborates what I've already told you: it can kill humans, the quantity needed varies."

"On the size of the individual, I suppose...?" said Trudy.

"Yes, and I can explain more about that, but there's something else you should be aware of. Hen was discussing psychotic behavior with some of her colleagues. Different aspects of revenge can be troublesome...the manner in which people seek it can be..."

Oh great, thought Trudy, what's this got to do with poison? She heard a car door shut and looked out the window next to the back stairs. "Carl, I'm sorry to interrupt, but Hal and Christy just drove up. Can I call you tomorrow?"

"Yes," said Carl, "before two; I have a tennis match at two-thirty."

Trudy thought quickly about tomorrow's schedule; getting the kids out of the house and Walter's arrival. "Yup, I'll call at one o'clock."

"That'll be fine," said Carl. "This is important. Don't forget."

"No, of course I won't, and thanks for calling. Bye."

Forget? What is he thinking – I'm the one who brought

it up!

As soon as Hal and Christy walked through the door, Trudy's grumpy mood vanished. Their smiling, happy faces brightened everything. And Hal's compliment didn't hurt.

"Wow! Mom, you look great – new dress…?"

"Why, thank you," said Trudy, smiling at Hal's exuberance. She'd worn the dress dozens of times before. "How were things at Dartmouth?"

"What a beautiful campus," exclaimed Christy. "I can't believe that I'd never seen it before."

"Guess you were too busy going to all the *Harvard* football games," said Hal, giving her a playful poke in the ribs.

Christy laughed back at him, then turned to Trudy. "What can we do to help with supper?"

"Nothing," replied Trudy. "I'm just going to put in some potatoes and make a salad. The chops can cook while we're having drinks."

"Okay, I'll go up and take a shower and change," said Christy.

Trudy assessed Hal's appearance. "Wouldn't hurt you to put on a fresh shirt…and then you can set the table."

Hal gave a mock salute. "Yes, ma'am. Geez – and I thought things might have changed."

"Only your shirts, dear," said Trudy.

"I'll set the table now, while Christy's showering," said Hal, taking out the kitchen forks and knives.

"No-no," said Trudy, "I want to use the silver tonight, top drawer of the sideboard – in the dining room, and linen placemats; they're in the bottom drawer." She handed him some freshly washed grapes. "Here – put these in the silver bowl."

"Where?" asked Hal.

"In the center of the table," said Trudy laughing, "it's called a *centerpiece*."

"Oh, don't we get to eat any of them?" asked Hal.

"Hmm – *after* dinner," said Trudy, shooing him out of the kitchen. "Now hurry up, I'm getting thirsty."

During cocktails, Trudy asked Christy where she was going to college. It surprised her to learn that not only was Christy a recent graduate, but that she had been volunteering as a social worker in New York.

"I hope you're not offended, but you look – well…so young," said Trudy, looking at Christy sitting there, as fresh as a daisy, in a blue and white cotton Lanz dress.

Christy tossed her head back, laughing. "Oh no – not at all. My mom says it's in the Hamilton genes – that's her family." She shrugged. "I guess I'm stuck with it."

"Not a bad thing to be stuck with," said Trudy, handing Christy a small silver bowl of nuts. "Now, tell me, this social work you do… it must be – ah – challenging. I mean New York's a big place, a lot of needy families."

"Yes, but I work with a trained social worker in

specific neighborhoods. Mostly it's troubled families: sick little kids – getting them to doctors. It's really sad; some of them have no guidance whatsoever. The parents just don't know what to do…"

"Yes – I can imagine…" she said, smiling at Christy, but noticing at the same time a quick exchange between Hal and Christy, kind of a private look. Odd, she thought, getting up from her chair. "I'd better start those lamb chops or we'll never eat. You two relax."

In the kitchen Trudy thought more about the odd exchange, particularly Hal's expression: a slight flush and then determination. What-in-the-world…? Oh my God, she thought, Christy's probably *expecting*. Quickly she put the chops under the broiler and mixed herself another drink. Of course – that's why they came up here; they're going to tell me at dinner. Her mind flashed to Marie. Oh boy – what am I going to do? I can't stir things up now. She shook her head wryly. Really Hal – didn't you learn *anything* at Dartmouth Then she remembered her own hastily arranged wedding and laughed: like father – like son.

Hal wasted no time digging into the lamb chops. "Hmm – boy," he said with a mouthful, "these are delicious – I don't eat like this anymore."

"They sure are," said Christy, "how do you get them so juicy?"

315

"Practice," said Trudy. "They were Harold's favorite, and now," she smiled, "I guess Hal likes them."

Hal chewed every last bit of meat off the lamb chop; it was the kind of chop referred to as loin or kidney, and he always liked to dig out the marrow from the back of the bone.

After wiping his mouth with a linen napkin and placing it carefully in his lap, Hal cleared his throat. "Mom, I've made some plans for tomorrow…"

Here it comes, thought Trudy, but she played dumb. "Oh good, you've decided on climbing up Ascutney?"

"Ah…no," said Hal, "I've made arrangements to visit Marie."

The water glass almost slipped out of Trudy's hand. All she could do was stare at Hal. "Um – a…" she glanced at Christy.

"Christy knows all about Paulie," said Hal. "I told her yesterday, last night actually – driving up here."

"Yes, I asked Hal if he minded my going along with him," chimed in Christy. "I'd like to meet his son."

Trudy was trying to keep her emotions in check. What-in-blazes was Hal thinking! "And Marie…does she know that you'll be bringing Christy? Won't it be – a – uncomfortable?"

"I don't think so," said Hal, "I mentioned it to Marie."

"Oh, I see," said Trudy. "And I take it you've already planned the time of this visit."

"Yes," said Hal, "I called her this morning, um – from upstairs."

"I see," said Trudy as she helped herself to salad and passed it to Christy. "And what time might that be?" Trudy didn't know whether she was more annoyed that he made all these plans without telling her, or that he called Marie from *her* house.

"One o'clock," said Hal. "Marie said that was a convenient time for her."

Under the best of circumstances, Trudy did not like surprises. She particularly disliked it when someone else put a kink in *her* plans. Hal was coming very close to doing that. "In that case, you should leave here at eleven."

"Nah," said Hal, "it doesn't take long to get to Bellows Falls."

Christy picked up on Trudy's mood. "Eleven makes sense, Hal. I'd like to see the town, and your old house."

"And you'll want a bite to eat," said Trudy. "You can take Christy to the hotel. They serve a nice Sunday lunch."

With that much established, Trudy was able to serve the lemon meringue pie for dessert and keep the conversation light. After dinner, however, she let Hal and Christy do the dishes while she pleaded fatigue and went upstairs. She needed some time alone to digest Hal's plans. Lucky for him, she thought, that Christy's here. Otherwise I'd give him a piece of my mind. The very idea – letting Marie call the shots while *he's* the one

317

supporting Paulie! Her head ached. Calm down, she thought. Tomorrow, as soon as you get rid of Walter, you can call Carl.

All of a sudden, she felt depressed and lonely. Hal had Christy; he didn't need or *want* her advice anymore. Harold was gone, and she was on a wild goose chase – a pointless one, according to Carl. But damn it, she muttered, it's *not* pointless. For God's sake, my husband's dead, and I think Marie killed him!

Trudy put on her nightgown, brushed her teeth and climbed into bed; the only comforting place she could think of. An Agatha Christie mystery was on the bedside table. Trudy picked it up. Okay, Agatha, how would you solve my dilemma?

Breakfast went smoothly. Hal showed off his cooking skills with his one – and only – signature dish: pancakes. Christy poured the orange juice and set the table.

Trudy drove to the General Store for the Sunday paper. She felt somewhat refreshed but intended to keep *her* agenda: get them out of the house by eleven, call Carl, and then meet with Walter.

As soon as Hal and Christy drove off, Trudy picked up the phone and called Carl. Perfect timing, she thought; everybody's in church, no bored eavesdroppers on the line.

Carl picked up his phone on the first ring. "Good morning, Tru...did ya sleep well?"

"No, this whole thing is driving me crazy, and to make matters worse, Hal and Christy are on their way to Marie's."

"Now?" asked Carl.

"Yes, *now*. It's absurd, I know, but not a damn thing I can do about it. Hal's even told Christy that he's Paulie's father!"

"Well, he is," said Carl with annoying logic. "And it's probably good that Hal keeps in touch.

"Oh sure, he's keeping in touch all right. He's giving Marie all of his hard-earned cash, and then lets *her* call the shots. God knows what she's doing with the money."

"Trudy..." said Carl, "that's all right. As a matter of fact, it can work to his advantage."

"Oh...? Do tell," said Trudy.

"Let's put that aside for a minute," said Carl. "Here's the situation. We've got two things to think about: a suspicious death for which we have no evidence, and – "

"Yes, but you told me that nightshade berries *could* kill a person. She used them on Harold, I know it!" said Trudy.

"How? Did she serve them for dessert? And where were you – why didn't you eat them?"

"She could've slipped him a mickey – in his bourbon," replied Trudy.

"*Slipped him a mickey* – really, where do you come up with these things?" said Carl. "Granted, any poison is going to work faster in liquid form, but no, Harold liked

319

his bourbon too much. He would've detected the different taste."

"How about *tea?*" suggested Trudy, ignoring her brother's sarcasm. "Marie was always serving different varieties of tea."

"Hmm, I suppose that could have worked, but *listen* to me: that's a moot point. We have no body – no proof. The only thing we know is that Marie is a bitter, grief-stricken grandmother."

"And I'm not?" asked Trudy.

"Not in the same way. No," said Carl. "You're not looking for a way to strike back. Marie wants to hurt the people she holds responsible for her daughter's death."

"And she held Harold responsible!" said Trudy. "I rest my case."

Carl took a deep breath and continued. "As I've been trying to tell you, yesterday I spoke with some people in the psychiatry department…"

"And you think I'm crazy," said Trudy.

"Trudy! Please let me finish," said Carl. "I asked them about grief and revenge – what could develop."

"And…?" said Trudy.

"Basically, Marie could become psychotic, if she isn't already. And…the whole point of this phone call is to suggest that you and Hal – all of us, figure out a way to determine if she *is crazy*, to put it bluntly."

"And if she is certifiable, if we have *proof*," said Trudy, "what then?"

"We figure out a way to give Hal custody of the child," said Carl.

"Okay, and I'm suppose to stand by and watch this poor grief-stricken granny get away with murder."

"Trudy…" said Carl, "first things first. Hal is doing the right thing by keeping in touch with…"

"Yes, Carl," said Trudy, annoyed with his calm 'doctor' voice, "I do understand that the important thing now is to protect the child." Trudy felt deflated. "Walter Luden is due here at noon. I'll call you if he has any interesting tidbits about Marie. Presumably he's bringing stuff that was in Margarite's desk. His wife was Margarite's sister. I guess Marie had it out for her too."

"What do you mean?" asked Carl.

"Oh, nothing," said Trudy, "it just angered Marie when Cynthia started clearing out Margarite's china. I'm sure Marie was counting on a fancy tea service for her inn guests."

"Oh, well, call me anyway," said Carl. "I'd like to know what sort of stuff he gives you."

Trudy hung up, and reached for the Sunday paper, but changed her mind. A brisk walk would do more to clear her mind than dreary news. No sooner had she walked out the door, than Walter pulled in the driveway.

"Not quite noon," he said, stepping out of his car, "but figured you wouldn't mind."

"It's eleven-thirty," said Trudy. "I was going for a walk." She headed back to the house. "C'mon in, you might as well show me what you have."

Walter grabbed a small cardboard box from the back seat of his car. "This won't take long...it's just that I'm on my way – "

"I know," said Trudy, "to Montpelier."

In the kitchen she pointed to the kitchen counter. "Put the box there. You can show me the stuff while I warm up some coffee." She pointed to the pot. "Like some? It's from breakfast, but still good."

"Thad'be nice, thank you," said Walter.

Trudy had just poured two cups, when the phone rang. She handed one to Walter. "Excuse me a minute," she said to Walter, and went into the living room to answer it.

"Hello," she said, hoping it wasn't Carl.

"Hi, Trudy, George here. How about another round of doubles: you and me take on the young people again?"

"Why George, that sounds lovely; but the kids have gone off for the day."

"How 'bout if I get the Talbots; just saw Hank when I got the paper. I'll give him a ring. How soon can you be ready?"

Trudy looked into the kitchen at Walter. "I'll need about twenty minutes to get over there."

"Great," said George, "see you shortly."

Walter put his coffee cup down and got up when Trudy came back to the kitchen. "Guess you have to go someplace..."

"Yes, something unexpected has come up," said Trudy. She tapped the top of the box. "What I can do is look through all of this, and if I have any questions I'll call you." She reached for her note pad next to the kitchen phone. "What's your number in Montpelier?"

"It's my sister's: 2640," said Walter.

Trudy jotted it down. "Thanks. I'm sorry to be rushing but I'm sure you understand."

Walter said a polite goodbye and left. Trudy knew she'd been rude. So what, she muttered, taking the box with her as she went upstairs to change for tennis.

SEVENTEEN

Marie was agitated. Being pleasant to Hal was one thing. She had a good reason: money. And so far he was cooperating; she expected to have the check for $75.00 that very afternoon. It was future checks she worried about. Who was this Christy? How much influence would she have over Hal? A lot, if they got married.

She went outside and sat on the side lawn with Paulie. In seconds, he was crawling in between the flowerbeds. "Hey – come here, you little monkey." Paulie giggled and kept going. "I think we'd better wait inside for our visitors; be easier to keep an eye on you." Marie picked him up and took him into the kitchen. After putting Paulie in the high chair, she looked him in the eye and spoke as if he were an adult. "I don't want you smiling at that girlfriend of your father's." She made a peanut butter sandwich, cutting it in four small squares and put it on the tray of the high chair. Paulie responded with a big grin and grabbed one with his pudgy hand. "Hal has no business bringing her here." But, it was more than that. Marie's stomach was in knots; to be reminded of Jenette in this way – Hal with a new girlfriend – was cruel. Why did she consent to this? *Never again, Hal has no right – no right to have a say in Paulie's life, or...*hot tears burned her eyes...*to be happy."*

On the way to tennis, Trudy realized that the last thing she wanted that evening was a conversation revolving around Hal and Christy's visit to Bellows Falls. If George was free, she'd invite him and the Talbots for dinner, make a little party of it. She could stretch the roast beef with lots of potatoes. She had plenty of peas in the freezer, and enough tomatoes and lettuce for a big salad. Yes, we'll have a pleasant evening, and I won't be tempted to say anything nasty about Marie.

Instead of going to the hotel for lunch, Hal took Christy to a diner on Route 5. "In high school, I used to come here a lot with my friends," said Hal as he took a big bite of a hot dog. "Waddaya think?"

"The hot dog?" asked Christy, putting mustard on hers. "Or this place?"

"Both," laughed Hal.

"Hot dog: A plus," replied Christy. "Diner: B minus."

"Okay," said Hal, "next time I'll take you to the hotel's fancy restaurant." He wiped his mouth with a napkin and put his hands on the table, preparing to leave. "But now, before we do anything else, I want to take you to the paper mill."

Christy hurried to finish her hot dog. "I thought you said it burned to the ground..."

"Yeah, it did, but a lot of the brick is left, the frame...you can still see how big it was. I can still picture..." Hal looked down at his hands, self-conscious of his feelings for the mill.

Christy got up from the booth. "Let's go. I've never seen a paper mill."

Hal was sorry that he drove down to the mill. The remains were less impressive than he'd remembered. It was a shell of scorched brick and timber. When they got out of the car, he felt foolish. "I guess it would take a pretty wild imagination to picture it as it once was, but every now and then I fantasize about rebuilding it."

"Why not?" said Christy, "everybody needs to dream."

"Yeah," said Hal, "I guess so." He opened the car door for Christy. "We've got time, we'll swing by my old house before going to Marie's. Don't think we can go in; people are living there, but you can get an idea."

Try as she might, Marie could not get Paulie to take a nap. She finally gave up and put him in the playpen while she prepared for Hal's arrival. She thought about sitting outside again but decided against it. Too easy for one of them to pick up Paulie if he was crawling on the grass. They'd sit in the parlor and Paulie would darn well stay in the playpen – in the kitchen.

Hal had always, from the time he was a little boy, worn his heart on his sleeve. He could no more conceal sadness, or joy, than fly to the moon. When he and Christy walked up to the front porch, and Marie saw the happiness in Hal's eyes, it was all she could do to open the front door. However, she remembered her plan. Everything would be all right if she stuck to that.

When the introductions were over, Marie showed them into the parlor. Christy sat next to Hal on the Victorian loveseat, a small sofa for two people. "What a charming room," said Christy, pointing to the other Victorian pieces of furniture and china figurines. "Are these all heirlooms?"

"Yes," said Marie, with no further explanation.

Hal sat awkwardly, craning his neck for a glimpse of Paulie. "Umm – is Paulie around, ah – in the kitchen...?" He smiled at Christy. "Last time I gave him Zwieback cracker."

"He's sleeping; I *don't* want to wake him," said Marie.

"That's for sure," said Christy, trying to be light-hearted, "never wake a sleeping baby."

"Stay here, I'll get tea," said Marie.

"Thank you," said Christy.

"None for me, thanks," said Hal.

"I know," said Marie, "you don't like it." She turned her back on them and went to the kitchen, staying there for what seemed to Hal and Christy an uncommonly long time.

Finally, Hal got up and whispered to Christy. "I'll go see what's keeping her."

Marie was standing at the stove, intent on what she was cooking. She didn't hear Hal approaching. "Need any help?" asked Hal.

Marie jumped, dropping a spoon. "What – what is it?" she said, glowering at him. He leaned down to pick up the spoon that had skittered across the floor in front of him. "Leave it alone," said Marie. It was too late; Hal already had it in his hand. She grabbed it from him. "I'll take it," she said. "Here, take these cookies and go sit down."

Hal saw that Paulie was sitting up in his playpen. "He's awake…"

"Yes, leave him alone," said Marie. "He's just getting over a cold – makes him fussy."

"Oh, I'm sorry," said Hal, anxious to appease Marie. "I got your letter; I can give you a check now."

"Please do," said Marie.

Hal reached in his pants pocket for his checkbook. "Oops, I guess it's in the car; I'll go get it." He went into the parlor and gave the cookies to Christy. "Back in a sec; gotta get my checkbook."

Marie set the tea service on a tea trolley and wheeled it into the parlor. "This is good China tea. Hope you don't want milk; I don't have any."

"That's fine," said Christy, although she did prefer milk in her tea and thought it odd; a baby in the house and *no milk*? She took a sip. *Different, but,* she thought, *I'd better drink it before she snaps my head off.*

Hal burst back in with his checkbook in hand. "Sorry – took so long, couldn't find it…" he laughed, "it was in the glove compartment, underneath everything." He sat at Margarite's desk. "Mind if I sit here?" He smiled at Marie. "I'll make it out to you – for seventy-five dollars…"

Marie was horrified. How dare he talk about this in front *her,* and *nooo,* she did not want him sitting at that desk. "We can go in the kitchen and talk about this," she said, standing up and turning her back on both of them.

Hal looked at Christy. She shrugged.

Boy-oh-boy, Christy thought, that grouch is taking care of a baby…? I guess it's a good thing that Hal will be visiting from time to time. Christy ate one of the sugar cookies and drank more tea. Actually, she thought, it's pretty good *without* milk.

~~~~~~~~

When Trudy issued the dinner invitation to her assembled tennis partners, they all looked at one another and laughed. "Did I say something funny?" she asked.

"No – not at all," said George. "It's just that we were going to invite you and your son and his gal to join us for dinner here – at the club."

"Yes," chimed in Nan, "it's a big Labor Day

330

buffet…and no one has to cook!"

"Well, now that you put it that way, sure," said Trudy. "I accept. I'm sure the kids will like it too."

~~~~~~~~

"Hi! Yoo-hoo – anybody home…?" said Trudy, coming in the kitchen.

Hal was coming down the front stairs. "Hi," he said, noticing her tennis outfit. "Oh – you played?"

"Yes, George called, wanting a rematch with you and Christy. Obviously that was out, so we played with the Talbots, and…" she said happily, "we're all invited to join them back at the club at six for a big Labor Day buffet!"

"That sounds great," said Hal, "but I think you'd better count us out."

"Ohh…?" said Trudy.

"Yeah, Christy feels kinda crummy, like she's coming down with something."

"Tired – or headachy?" asked Trudy.

"Kinda both, I guess," said Hal. "She says she probably caught a bug from one of the little kids at the social service place – where she works."

Trudy put her tennis racket away. "That could be. Why don't you take her some ginger ale and saltines. You don't mind if I go over…?"

"Not at all, I – we'd both feel badly if you stayed home," said Hal. "I want to get an early start tomorrow; a good night's sleep might not be a bad idea."

"What about supper?" asked Trudy.

"I'll make some soup 'n sandwiches – don't think Christy's going to want much."

"Right-o," said Trudy. "I'm going to shower, and go back to the club in awhile. See you at breakfast."

Hal and Christy were on their way by eight o'clock the next morning. Trudy thought Christy looked a little pale, but none the worse for wear. Hal was all bouncy and eager to go. She waved goodbye to them, admitting to herself that it was nice to see Hal so happy, in spite of the fact that he was letting Marie walk all over him. After another cup of coffee, Trudy remembered the box of stuff Walter had left. A lot of junk, she thought, but I guess I'd better look at it.

Christy told Hal that she felt better, but hoped that he wouldn't mind if she slept while they were driving back to New York. All night she'd been short of breath and feverish.

"Please – go to it," said Hal, "but, you know what...? I left my checkbook someplace – either at mom's or Marie's." He looked at Christy apologetically. "Do you mind if I stop here and call? It'll just take a second."

"No, take your time," said Christy.

Hal pulled into a gas station, parking on the side by a phone booth.

"Hi mom – it's me."

"Well that was quick," said Trudy. "Everything okay?"

"Yeah – fine – it's just my checkbook. I think I might have left it there – on the kitchen counter…?"

Trudy scanned the counter. "Nope – it's not here. I'll check your bedroom."

"Nah – don't bother, it's probably somewhere in the car… I'll call you when we get to New York."

"Good enough," said Trudy. " I'll look around here… How's Christy?"

"Fine – just sleepy. Gotta go – My dime's running out."

Hal walked over to the car and spoke to Christy. "Mom said it's not there; I'll just give Marie a quick call."

"Fine," said Christy, groggily, "maybe more of her tea will perk me up."

EIGHTEEN

Bank statements, check stubs, more bank statements, Trudy mumbled as she sorted Margarite's papers. Really…why didn't she throw some of this out? Trudy put all of the bank statements in a pile on the floor. Next she pulled out a manila folder tied loosely with string and put it on the counter. She poured herself another cup of coffee, and then idly started looking through the folder. A thick legal-sized envelope caught her attention. Well, I be… LAST WILL AND TESTAMENT – Margarite M. Pierson. Trudy put down her coffee and started reading. *I, Margarite M. Pierson of Bellows Falls, Vermont…* blah, blah, blah… Trudy skipped over the standard wording. Okay, here we go: *I bequeath all articles of jewelry given to me by our mother to my sister, Cynthia Lucen.* Hmpf, somebody can't spell "Luden," thought Trudy. Then she noticed more misspelling. Honestly, she thought, whoever wrote this must be blind as a bat. She read on. *I give and bequeath the rest of my jewelry to my cear friend Trucy Walker.* "Well, that's news to me; thanks a bunch, Cynthia." She flipped through eight more pages. Margarite had assigned many of her belongings to friends. I wonder if any of this stuff was distributed – what kind of lawyer did Margarite have anyway? Then she remembered and laughed. Good grief, it was Whitcomb – Jeremiah Whitcomb, useless ole coot, and Margarite felt sorry for him. Oh well, none o' my business. She continued reading the will. After page twelve, the numbers stopped. Trudy paused. She couldn't make out the word, what in the world... "a-c-c-e-n-c-u-m?" Oh, I get it – that "C" is the letter "d": *addendum*. How odd that no one bothered to fix... Trudy gasped and almost dropped the document – as if it were on fire. "My old typewriter!" The broken "d"... I gave it to Marie when Hal went to college. Her hands were shaking; she saw that the remaining lines had been capitalized to avoid the errant "d." Yes, that's what I used to do, she thought, and finished reading. MARIE FURNEAU and HER GRANDSON, PAUL F. FURNEAU, MAY HAVE FULL USE OF MY HOUSE ON TWENTY-THREE BURT STREET AFTER MY DEATH UNTIL SHE HAS FOUND ANOTHER SUITABLE DOMICILE. AT SUCH TIME THE HOUSE IS TO GO TO MY SISTER, CYNTHIA LUDEN. Trudy's heart started pounding; she turned the page over and could see where it had been inserted and stapled to the rest of the will. No wonder she didn't want Sam Aldrich to see this. I've got to call Carl. She grabbed the will and ran into the living room. Sitting in her favorite chair next to the window, she took a deep breath and tried to collect her thoughts. *Why don't you calm down a little before asking Polly to dial his number in New Jersey?!?*

"Good morning, Carl, hope you're not in the middle of something."

"Hi, Tru, thought it might be you, missed your call yesterday," said Carl.

"Yes, sorry, I had a tennis game," said Trudy.

"I'll accept that," laughed Carl. "Did that fellow – the one with Margarite's stuff – ever stop by?"

"Yes, he did. And I've read Margarite's will."

"Nothing unusual there," said Carl, "most likely just boilerplate stuff?"

"Carl! Listen to me," said Trudy, flipping the pages of the will. "Marie added an addendum just a week before Margarite died – saying that *she* could live in the house!"

"Not unusual…" said Carl, "a lot of people change their wills as they get older."

"Carrrl…! You aren't listening. It was *Marie* – not Margarite, who put in the addendum. She faked it – with my typewriter!"

"*Your* typewriter?" said Carl. "How – *why* would Marie have your – "

"I gave it to her years ago; the letter 'd' was broken. She used it and fooled the lawyer."

Sometimes Carl had trouble with his sister's logic, but he could usually put it together. "Yes…that does put a different light on things," he replied, "but surely Margarite's lawyer would have noticed..."

"Her *lawyer*, for pete's sake, was Jeremiah Whitcomb! He's ancient and blind as a bat. He couldn't read his own name."

"I don't know if I'd go that far..." said Carl.

Trudy rolled her eyes and tried not to shout at Carl. "Forget about the foolish lawyer, and listen to me: Marie killed Cynthia the same way she killed Harold, and probably Margarite. And don't tell me I can't prove it." Trudy paused long enough to take a breath. "Cynthia's buried in the Pierson family plot. Thank God for Walter; he insisted on it, said that Cynthia didn't believe in cremation."

"Well, you'll have to get hold of this Walter fellow," said Carl, now fully concerned, "tell him what you've learned; he can get a court order to exhume the body for an autopsy."

"But what – what about Marie?" said Trudy.

"Do nothing," declared Carl. "We wait for the results of the autopsy. For God's sake, you don't want to raise her suspicions; the woman may be psychotic."

Trudy was pleased that she finally had a positive reaction from her brother. "Okay – okay – I understand. Let me try to reach Walter now."

"Good. With any luck, you – actually Walter – might be able to get that court order by tomorrow afternoon," said Carl. "And call Harold's friend Sam Aldrich;

possibly he could expedite the process."

"He's my friend, *too*," said Trudy, "but right now I need a good lawyer, not a banker. I'll call you later."

"Yes, please do," said Carl, "and ... um, did you tell me that Hal and Christy visited Marie?"

"Uh-huh – yesterday – I didn't see her, but Hal said Christy felt sick last night."

"How was she this morning? You saw her before they left?"

"A little pale, but she seemed okay. They were in a hurry to leave, and – um…"

"Yes…said Carl.

"Hal called about twenty minutes ago – looking for his checkbook. He said Christy was sleepy."

"Hmm," said Carl, "that sounds okay. But for now it's best if *everyone* stays away from Marie."

"Absolutely. But what about the baby…is he safe?"

"Yes. Marie wants *him*."

"All right, I'll call you back as soon as I talk to Walter."

Trudy went into the kitchen and refilled her coffee cup. Her hands were no longer shaking but she began feeling apprehensive and oddly fearful. She put the cup down. Oh no! Hal and Christy are going back to see Marie.

~~~~~~~~~

They were standing on the porch saying goodbye to Marie and Paulie. The telephone was ringing in the house.

339

"You probably want to answer that," said Hal.

"No, if it's important they'll call back," said Marie.

"Well," said Hal, "I guess we'd better get going – long drive ahead of us."

Christy forced a smile. "Yes, bye, and thanks for the tea."

Trudy slammed the phone down. She's not answering! And I don't know where they are! Trudy started pacing back 'n forth – between the living room and the kitchen.

Finally she stood still for a second. Hal said Christy was sleepy. Carl said that was okay – sleep. And certainly Hal will take Christy to Englewood before going to New York. Trudy picked up the phone again.

"Carl? Oh whew – I'm glad I caught you!"

"What's wrong? You sound awful,' said Carl.

"I think that Hal and Christy stopped at Marie's – he's looking for his checkbook. I tried calling. No answer."

"Could be she's not home," replied Carl. What time do you think Hal might have been there?"

"I don't know. This morning – nine – ten. Carl! What if – oh – I can't even think it! What can we do?"

"Right now, not much. I'll be at the hospital this afternoon. If, for some reason Hal calls again, you call me right away."

~~~~~~~~

340

"Sorry to put you through that," said Hal, as they drove away. "Marie seemed so friendly – compared to yesterday – I wanted to take advantage of it."

"Hmm," said Christy, not wanting to hurt Hal's feelings with her opinion of Marie.

" And did ya hear? The next time I see Paulie, he'll probably be walking."

"That's nice," said Christy. She reached over to the back seat for her coat. She felt chilly, and feverish – at the same time. She bunched up Hal's sweater for a pillow. "I'm going to try 'n sleep."

"Sure," said Hal. "You don't mind if I turn on the radio?"

"Ut-uh," said Christy.

For the next several hours, Christy slept. When Hal stopped for gas, he asked if she wanted lunch. She shook her head "no." Hal bought some candy bars and chocolate milk for himself. By the time they reached the Taconic Parkway Christy was red-hot and trembling. "Hey, you better have some water or something," said Hal. "I'll turn off at the next exit."

"No," rasped Christy, "I – I can't breathe – go to Englewood…"

Hal didn't remember how he got there, but within an hour, he was banging on the Enders' front door. Christy's mother opened it. "Goodness, what's the fuss? Why, Hal – what a surprise…"

"Mrs. Enders – it's Christy – she's sick!" said Hal, pointing to the car.

Helen Enders raced to her daughter. Christy was panting and ghostly pale.

"We thought it was a cold," said Hal helplessly.

"Go to the hospital – immediately," commanded Mrs. Enders. "I'll call Steven, and your uncle Carl. I think he's on duty as well. Drive right up to the emergency entrance."

Hal did as he was told.

When Carl heard that Hal was bringing Christy to the hospital he found Steven Enders and explained the probable cause of Christy's illness. Given the the brief amount of time from ingestion to treatment, both doctors felt that a thorough pumping of Christy's stomach would remedy the situation.

However, neither man was prepared for what they saw. Christy was in a cold sweat, shaking, and panting short staccato breaths. Carl felt for her pulse. "How long has she been like this?"

"All day," stammered Hal, "but it got worse a few hours after we left Bellows Falls."

"Bellows Falls...?!" shouted Christy's father. "She's been doing this all the way down from Vermont?"

Two nurses and an orderly placed Christy on a gurney as Doctor Enders told them where to go. "Number two O.R. A poisoning. Prepare for a stomach pump."

"Steven," said Carl, "I'll take care of her. You call

Helen."

Hal was almost on the verge of tears. "Poisoning? What do you mean? Christy thought maybe she caught something from the kids at the social services."

"I'll explain after I take care of Christy," said Carl. "Call your mother and tell her that you're here."

Trudy couldn't sit still. She had to do *something* – when would Hal get to Englewood? Maybe he's already there, and everything's fine. Hal just hasn't had a chance to call her. She'll call Hen. She'll know what's going on.

"Hen…? It's me again. Just want to check up on the kids…"

"Hi Trudy," said Hen, I was just going to call you. Helen Enders called me. Hal has taken Christy to the hospital. She wasn't feeling…"

"Oh no!"

"I'm sure she'll be fine," said Hen. Carl said…"

" Carl's there too? I have to call them – right away!"

"You might not be able to get them…" said Hen, to an empty phone line.

Hen was right. Trudy couldn't get through. She left messages at the hospital to have Carl or Hal call her. Now the only thing she could do was wait by the phone.

She almost jumped when it rang five minutes later.

"Mom!" shouted Hal, "Christy's been poisoned – we're in the hospital."

"I know," said Trudy, sadly.

"How'd you…"

"Hen told me."

"I mean how'd you know it was poison?"

Trudy sighed. "It was Marie. She killed your father and…"

"What are you saying?!"

"There's a lot to explain. I was trying to protect – "

"By not telling me the truth? Christy's having her stomach pumped, and god knows what else, and you're worried about protecting me? What does Carl know?"

"Everything."

"I see – everybody knows but me," said Hal, "thanks a lot."

Trudy wished that she was there with Hal. "Are Christy's parents there?"

"Yes – in Doctor Enders' office. You don't think they're going to sit in the waiting room with me?"

Trudy was quiet.

"I'd better get off the phone," said Hal, "I'll call you later."

"Doctor Barlow", said the nurse in the operating room, "her blood pressure is dropping."

"Turn off the stomach pump! She needs fluids," said Carl.

He looked at Christy. All color had gone from her face. He was going to lose her! "Fluids! Intravenous – fast!"

When they got the I.V. set up, and fluids racing into Christy's system, Carl told the nurses to watch her carefully. He would have to tell Christy's parents that her condition was critical. They would have to wait and see if the fluids would bring her blood pressure back up.

The Enders had just come into the waiting room expecting to hear that Christy was fine. "Steven – Helen," said Carl, walking up to them, "there's been a precipitous drop in Christy's blood pressure…"

Helen gasped.

"And you've got her on intravenous," said Steven calmly.

"Yes," replied Carl, "we'll know within the hour."

"I understand," said Steven, as he put his arm around his wife. "We'll be in my office."

Carl walked over to Hal. "You heard what I told the Enders?"

"Yes," said Hal, "but she's going to be all right?"

"We'll know in a while," said Carl. "I'm going back in with her."

Hal sat down in the chair, and stayed there, barely moving. He had been responsible for Jenette's death, and now…maybe Christy! And the whole time he never knew what was happening – that Marie was poisoning her? God almighty – what was wrong with him? And his mother – were they both blind, deaf, and dumb?

More than an hour had passed. Hal was glad that no

one else was in the small waiting area next to the operating room. He couldn't think straight – let alone talk to anyone.

Suddenly Carl came in. "She's going to be okay. I'll be back in a few minutes with her parents."

Hal stood up when Dr. and Mrs. Enders walked in behind Carl. His words were barely audible. "Christy...she's all right?"

"Yes," said Christy's father, "she's going to pull through."

"We... I didn't know..." said Hal.

"She's resting now. We'll call you tomorrow," said Christy's mother, "or maybe Christy will call when she comes home."

Carl took Hal's arm. "C'mon, I'll walk you to the car."

Hal nodded.

"Hen is expecting you," said Carl. "I'll be along shortly."

When he got home, Carl was relieved to see that Hen had continued to reassure Hal about Christy's good condition. That left him free to call Trudy.

"Oh, Carl, what have I done This is all my fault." Trudy was crying, first for Hal, *her* baby, then for herself.

"Trudy," said Carl, "stop thinking that. You've been the detective. God knows what else that woman would

346

be doing if you hadn't listened to your instincts." Hen gave Carl a "thumbs-up" signal, encouraging him to say more. "Thanks to you, Christy's okay...I mean – we sure wouldn't have suspected nightshade poisoning."

"Hmm – maybe," said Trudy, "and I did call Walter..."

"He agrees, I hope," said Carl.

"He wasn't happy about it – exhuming Cynthia's body," said Trudy, "but yes, he promised me that he'd sign the necessary form."

"How – if he's in Montpelier," said Carl.

"He'll drive to Bellows Falls first thing tomorrow morning. I'm going to meet him at the courthouse, about eleven," said Trudy. "His lawyer said, considering the unique circumstance, they'll probably be able to exhume the body in the afternoon."

"*Then* what are you going to do?" asked Carl.

"Come back here, I guess," said Trudy. "It'll be hard...waiting."

"Yes, it will be," said Carl. "Listen, I'll get the lab results on Christy first thing in the morning: seven at the latest. After that, Hal and I will drive up there, and meet you in Bellows Falls." Carl looked at Hal for confirmation of this new plan.

Hal was surprised, but pleased with Carl's sudden decision. He took the phone as Carl passed it to him.

"Hi, Mom, I'm sorry..." He started to choke up.

"Oh Hal, sweetie," said Trudy, "don't be ..." Her

heart ached for her son, and the turmoil surrounding him. Trudy reassured him – even though she didn't feel all that confident herself. "Don't worry – things'll work out. Have Carl call me before you leave Englewood."

NINETEEN

Marie put the last of the tea service away. There, she thought, you've *served* your purpose – for now anyway. She chuckled at her own pun.

It was such a nice day that Marie decided to go to the bank and deposit the check from Hal. Paulie needed some fresh air; a long walk would be good for both of them. She liked the paths in the cemetery, and thought it would be a good idea to visit Jenette and Paul. She hadn't been there for a while and had a lot to tell them. She picked a bunch of black-eyed Susans from the garden. "These were always your mama's favorite flower," she told Paulie. "They'll look pretty on her gravestone." Paulie reached out of the carriage and tried to grab the top off some zinnias. Marie laughed and pulled him back in. "I see, you want some for your grandpa too; all right, we'll pick the orange ones."

Marie saw a truck, and several men digging on the east side of the cemetery. "Wonder who died…" she said to Paulie, "let's go see." As they approached the gravesite, Marie became apprehensive. The workmen looked to be awfully close to the Pierson family plot. She put the brake on the baby carriage and walked up to one of the workmen. "What's happening?" she asked, pointing to the coffin sitting on the ground next to the gravestone marked Cynthia Pierson Luden.

"They wanna look inside," said one of the men, wiping his brow.

"Yeah," said another gravedigger, "the husband wants ta make sure she's really dead – ha-ha – 'fore he takes off – ha-ha."

Marie turned in a flash, almost tripping on loose stones that had scattered along the pathway. One of the men tried to help her. "No – leave me alone," shouted Marie as she grabbed the handle of the baby carriage and began pushing Paulie out of the cemetery as fast as she could. All of the flowers she had picked fell onto the pathway.

"Guess it was your good looks, Homer..." laughed the first workman.

~~~~~~~~

"Are you sure that you don't want to come with us?" Trudy asked Walter as they left the courthouse, heading for the cemetery.

"No. I mean, *yes*, I'm sure," replied Walter. "I'll come back when they're through with her...and bring lots of fresh flowers for the grave." He shook his head sadly. "Poor Cynthia, all she wanted was a few things from the house…"

"All right," said Trudy.

Carl and Hal walked up to Trudy as she waved goodbye to Walter. "Poor guy," said Carl, "he wasn't happy about any of this."

"No," said Trudy, "but he understands the reasons for it."

"Let's get a move on," said Hal. "It might seem ghoulish, but I want to be sure they're digging up the right person."

"Hal – really!" said Trudy. "The gravestones are clearly marked."

"I'll get the car and meet you there, said Carl." He checked his watch. "It's three-forty-five; we're supposed to be at the police station at four. Chief Wilson Wood wants us to accompany him when he questions Marie at her house, unless you don't *want* to be there."

"Of course we'll be there," said Trudy, "But what's he going to say? The autopsy's not 'til tomorrow. Remember – we need proof…?"

"Yes Trudy…you're right. But I think Chief Wood is interested in circumstances – how Marie came to live in the house, that sort of thing."

"*I* could explain that," said Trudy.

"It's called police procedure," said Hal. "Let's go."

The gravediggers were filling in the hole where Cynthia's casket had lain. "Geez-um – we'll be puttin' her back in here – don't know why we can't leave it open," said Homer.

"'Cause, you dub – it's a hole," said his buddy, "a person could fall in."

"Granny's goin' to make you a special treat," said Marie, trying to control her shaking arms as she lifted Paulie from the carriage and hugged him so hard he almost cried. "They're gonna try 'n take you away – but they can't – they can never have you. You and I are goin' to a special place; we'll see your mama."

Marie put Paulie in the high chair in the kitchen and began humming nursery rhymes while she prepared some nightshade tea. She drank two cups right away, then filled Paulie's bottle. A third of it remained in the teakettle. She tucked Paulie's bottle in her skirt pocket and lifted him from the high chair. "Up we go…right to bed. You and I are going to lie down on my bed and take a nap."

Hal and Trudy walked up to the gravesite and confirmed the marker. "Hello," said Hal, nodding to the gravediggers. "This is the coffin of Cynthia Luden?"

"Yup," said Homer, "popular lady, this one – you're the second folks to come by 'n pay their respects." He pointed to the flowers. "We musta spooked the other lady – she dropped these – she took off so fast… "

"That she did," said the other gravedigger, "and the

kid liked it…he was laughing his head off ridin' in the carriage."

"Marie!" said Trudy, grabbing Hal's arm. "Hurry!"

They almost knocked Carl down at the entrance gate of the cemetery. "Marie knows," said Trudy. "She's been here."

Hal turned and started running to Burt Street. "I've got to get Paulie," he shouted over his shoulder.

Trudy and Carl wasted no time getting to the car.

Paulie liked crawling around on Marie's bed. This was something new and he kept looking at her, wondering how long the fun would last. Marie gave him a hairbrush and a plastic hand mirror to play with while she pulled a small suitcase out from under the bed.

"You sit tight. Granny's goin' to put on a pretty dress before we have our tea." Marie opened the suitcase and removed a layer of tissue paper. Underneath it was her lace and satin wedding dress. Marie's mother had made it for her, using the handmade lace from her wedding gown. She held it up and looked in the mirror. "Yes," Marie said, looking at Paulie, "I'll put this on and then we can have our tea party." Marie took off her wool skirt, a hand-me-down from Margarite, and white cotton blouse, then with a solemn reverence she put on the wedding dress. After admiring herself in the mirror, she remembered bitterly that Jenette never had a chance to wear it. "We'll both see you soon, honey; maybe the Lord will let you put it on." Then she saw some remains of Paulie's breakfast on his sweater. "You'll have to have clean clothes too; we don't want your mama to think I've been neglecting you." Marie gave Paulie another trinket from the top of her dresser – an empty ring box. "Don't move; I'm going to get another shirt for you."

Marie stepped into the upstairs hallway and was about to open the dresser in which she kept Paulie's clothes. A banging on the front door distracted her. Standing at the top of the front stairs she could see Hal peering through the window in the front door.

Hal shook the door handle. "Marie! Open this door!"

Marie flew back into the bedroom and grabbed Paulie along with the baby bottle. Hiking the train of her wedding dress, she raced down the back stairs to the kitchen. Paulie, sensing her fear, started crying and squirming while Marie poured the remaining tea from the kettle into a glass jar.

Hal heard Paulie's screams. He kicked in the pane of glass in the door, and it broke into pieces on the foyer floor. Then he reached in and turned the handle. As he ran through the parlor toward the kitchen, Marie started out the back door. With Paulie in one arm and the jar of tea in her free hand, she couldn't hold up the hem of her wedding dress. The train of her gown caught on a nail in the back steps, Marie tripped and Paulie went flying. As she reached to pick him up, Marie saw Hal swooping down on them from the top of the back steps. During the moment he took to grab Paulie, Marie ran toward the garage.

Hal's only concern was Paulie. His face had scratches, and bits of dirt were stuck to his forehead. He saw the baby bottle on the driveway. "You can have something to drink in a minute," said Hal as he carried Paulie into the kitchen. "First let me clean up your face."

Trudy and Carl, followed by Police Chief Wilson Wood in his police car, parked in front of the "Burt Street Inn" sign and ran up to the front porch.

"What...?" said Trudy, looking at the shattered window glass, She ran through the parlor with Carl and Chief Wood at her heels. All three stopped abruptly when they saw Hal in the kitchen holding Paulie on the edge of the sink while gingerly washing his face.

"Marie dropped him in the driveway," said Hal, trying to appear calm. "I don't know where she is now." He pointed to the back yard. "I think she ran in that direction."

"Did she harm the boy?" asked Chief Wood, walking over to the back door and surveying the short driveway and garage.

"Not really," said Hal. "Paulie got these scratches when Marie dropped him – accidentally – I don't think she meant to. She tripped; when I grabbed him she kept going."

"All right, then," said the police chief, "if ya don't mind, I think I'll go out and look for Marie. We do have some questions for her."

"Good idea, I'll join you," said Trudy, seeing that Paulie was safely in Hal's arms.

"Me too," said Carl.

He stepped past Chief Wood, and pushed the screen door open. "After you…"

Wilson Wood took his time going down the steps, scanning the area. Trudy looked at Carl and threw her arms up in a helpless fashion. Carl mouthed the words *be nice*. Trudy obeyed and followed them outside.

"Guess she dropped this," said Chief Wood, holding up a baby bottle. "The little tyke might be thirsty."

Carl took the bottle and held it up to the light. "Not for this – looks like tea to me – nightshade tea."

Trudy grabbed the bottle. "Oh no – she gave *this* to Paulie… Carl – do something!"

Hearing this, Hal ran outside, holding Paulie over his shoulder. "Did she feed that stuff to Paulie?"

"We don't know," said Trudy, holding the bottle up, "but, it looks full, so probably not…"

"*Probably* isn't good enough! It wouldn't take much – he's just a kid," shouted Hal. "What are we gonna do?"

"We find out *what*, if anything, he's ingested," said Carl calmly. "Hal, I'll drive you and Paulie to the hospital. After a quick stomach pump, we'll have the answer." He turned to Wilson Wood. "Chief Wood, perhaps you wouldn't mind if Trudy helped in the search for Marie. We need to know how much of this stuff she gave to Paulie."

Carl and Hal raced to the car. Chief Wood told Trudy to look in the garage while he went to the side yard. "Sometimes people hide in the bushes…"

Trudy remained standing in the middle of the driveway, feeling hollow, and utterly helpless. My God, she thought, what have I done?… Paulie could be dying…and all because I didn't act quickly enough.

Trudy turned to watch Wilson scrambling around the corner of the house. What's he talking about – *look in the garage* – why would Marie be in the garage? Suddenly, in the still air, Trudy heard a noise – a *thump*. What's that…? She walked slowly across the driveway, toward the garage. The doors were open. One bay was empty because Walter, with Cynthia's urging, had removed Margarite's car two days after her death. The other bay was filled with gardening equipment, a lawn mower, and bags of peat moss. Trudy thought that the noise must have been a bag of peat falling down from the loft. She saw Margarite's old wooden wheelbarrow. Ohh… she thought, how Margarite loved that wheelbarrow. Trudy stepped into the garage, remembering the worn, smooth wooden handles.

Just as she moved closer, Marie jumped out from the darkness. She was holding sharp gardening shears and breathing heavily. Her face was pale and beads of sweat were on her forehead. The wedding dress was torn and dirty.

"Don't move," hissed Marie.

"How dare you!" Said Trudy, trying to step back.

"Ha – don't you "how dare me", said Marie. "You've ruined my life! You and your husband, and Hal – you all killed Jenette, and now…" Marie suddenly leaned over to catch her breath.

"Put down the shears," said Trudy, noticing the fruit jar nearby on the garage floor.

"Oh… no," rasped Marie, "I haven't finished yet." She poked the shears at Trudy's throat. "My Jenette was worth more than all three of you, and the others…they had to go – even Hal's girlfriend."

Chief Wood had his pistol drawn. He was trying to position himself for a clean shot at Marie.

" If only you had come to me, when you knew Jenette and Hal were in love."

Marie coughed as if she had been hit in the stomach. "How could I come to you? You always made it clear that Hal would marry into his own class." Marie spoke in a harsh whisper. "You know, I could never allow anymore Walkers." Suddenly Marie started shaking violently. She dropped the shears, and Trudy tried to catch her as she fell.

Chief Wood lowered his gun. "Step back, Trudy. I'm right behind you.

"She's dead?" asked Trudy.

Wilson took Marie's pulse. Then he nodded.

Trudy picked up the fruit jar.

"I think this is what killed her. Nightshade tea."

"Huh," said Chief Wood. "People sure do strange things." Wilson looked more closely at Marie. "What's she wearing?"

Trudy stood beside Wilson. "It looks like a wedding dress…" She put her hands to her face and took a deep breath. "This was to be her burial dress; she was going to kill Paulie, and then herself."

Wilson Wood cleared his throat. "Could you show me where the telephone's at. I'll have to get an ambulance over here."

"Yes, but first we have to find out about Paulie."

The telephone was ringing when Trudy entered the kitchen. It took her a couple of seconds to find the phone behind the teapots and jars on the kitchen counter. "Hello – Carl…is that you? Is Paulie?"

"Yes, Tru – he's fine – nothing but good old-fashion oatmeal in his tummy. He's a plucky little fella – in good health."

Trudy all but collapsed into a kitchen chair. "Oh, thank God – and Hal…how's he holding up?"

"Solid as a rock," said Carl. "We'll be along shortly. And – ah – Marie…?"

"Dead," said Trudy flatly, "in the garage – I'll fill you in when you get here. Wilson has to use the phone."

Carl and Hal drove in just as the ambulance was leaving with Marie. Chief Wood stayed behind to confirm that Paulie was all right.

"I see the youngsta' is in good health," said Wilson.

"He sure is," said Carl. "Dad might be a bit worse for wear – but that's normal." He gave Hal a pat on the back.

Trudy saw Wilson's puzzled expression and interceded before he could say anything. "We found a jar of the nightshade brew; looks as if Marie drank most of it."

Hal was quiet, and walked into the front parlor with Paulie in his arms. In the corner of the couch was the teddy bear of so long ago... Hal handed it to Paulie.

The other three remained in the kitchen in an awkward silence.

Carl cleared his throat. "Yes, Marie figured things out very quickly in the cemetery; she knew it was over."

"Um...Mrs. Walker, when you're ready..." said Wilson, "if you and your son, and you too, Doc," he said, looking at Carl, "can come to the police station and explain everything from the beginning – well...then – ah..." he glanced toward Hal in the parlor, "you folks can get on with things."

"We'd be happy to," said Trudy, having regained her composure. "I'd like to give this child some supper," she said, taking Paulie from Hal as they came back in the kitchen, "...and pack up his belongings so we can go directly from the station to my house in Brownsville."

"My sister's in her 'command mode' now," said Carl, smiling at Hal. "We just obey."

Again Wilson was confused, but seemed amenable. "Tha'd be fine; see ya shortly."

~~~~~~~~~

Much later that evening in Trudy's living room, Hal paced back and forth. "I'm the one," he said to Carl and Trudy, "I'm the one who ruined everything."

"Hal, stop it," said Trudy, barely keeping her voice below a shout.

Hal whirled around and faced his mother. "Don't you see – indirectly, I killed Dad. If I hadn't dumped Jenette…"

Carl stood up and pushed Hal toward a chair. "Okay, now it's my turn. Sit down, and listen." Carl went back to his chair, took a drink from his glass of scotch and proceeded. "You are not God – you were not put on earth to direct other people's actions – or thoughts. So get that out of your mind and focus on the present: you, your job, your son – in that order; all three are part of one package. And *that's* the package requiring your attention: from now on you can't do one without thinking of the other." Carl sat back in his chair and took a deep breath. "There – I've said my piece."

"Now it's *my* turn," said Trudy, noticing Hal's beleaguered expression. "Don't worry, I'll be quick." She cleared her throat. "Carl's right; but I have to explain the *how*-to part. Paulie will live with me for the foreseeable future…" Trudy put up her hand. "Don't worry, I've already got a nanny in mind, and then, in time…well…"

she smiled at Hal, "we'll see what's going on in your life."

Hal threw his arms up in mock surrender. "Okay – you two have me cornered. Now, let's eat – I'm starving."

"I second the motion," said Carl.

"Yes, indeed," said Trudy. "Eat and get to sleep. A certain little guy in this house is going to be waking us up pretty early in the morning."

EPILOGUE

That year everybody – Hal, Christy, Carl and Hen – joined Trudy and Paulie in Vermont for Christmas. The "nanny" Trudy hired to help her with Paulie turned out to be Louise, but she really got two for one. Lester let it be known that the boy shouldn't hang around women all day, so at every opportunity Lester had Paulie "help him with chores." On his first birthday, Paulie started walking; by Christmas, he was running to greet Lester when he came to the door.

On Christmas Eve, Hal proposed to Christy with the engagement ring Harold had given to Trudy. After tears, toasts, and phone calls to Christy's parents – who were in Colorado with Christy's brother and his young family – they made plans for a June wedding in Englewood.

After a honeymoon in Bermuda, Hal and Christy told Trudy of his plans to resurrect the paper mill, this time into a converter mill. He planned to buy rolls of paper from other mills and supply New England with tissue paper, paper towels (a growing market, he told Christy), and specialty gift paper. Hal explained to a skeptical Trudy that he'd learned enough at the bank to know how to apply for a construction loan.

In July, Hal and Christy moved into a house on Atkinson Street, smaller than the one Hal grew up in but, as Christy reminded him, a lot easier to take care of. The house at 23 Burt Street was sold at an auction to a young couple who wanted to try their hand at innkeeping.

Trudy, along with Lester and Louise, had a little trouble parting with Paulie, but once they saw all of the love and *energy* Hal and Christy could give him, they realized their roles of granny and honorary aunt and uncle weren't so bad.

The following spring Hal and Christy presented Paulie with a baby sister: little Trudy. In due time she proved to be just as curious and inquisitive as her grandmother in Brownsville.